THE NEW ATLANTIS

and other Novellas of Science Fiction

Robert Silverberg, Ursula K. Le Guin, James Tiptree, Jr., Gene Wolfe

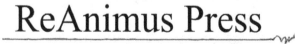

ReAnimus Press
Breathing Life into Great Books

ReAnimus Press
1100 Johnson Road #16-143
Golden, CO 80402
www.ReAnimus.com

Cover by Clay Hagebusch

ISBN-13: 9798672832807

First ReAnimus Press print edition: August, 2020

2008051816
10 9 8 7 6 5 4 3 2 1

INTRODUCTION

Robert Silverberg (1975)

The three stories in this book have never before been published in any form. They are the most recent works of three of the most gifted and exciting writers to enter the field of science fiction in the last decade—all three of them "new" writers, virtually unknown until the late 1960s, who within the space of just a few years have established themselves in the front rank of science fiction. Though their careers have only just begun, however, they are, coincidentally, rather more mature than most science-fiction writers so new to the genre. Science-fiction writers traditionally begin their careers early—Isaac Asimov, Ray Bradbury, Theodore Sturgeon, Frederik Pohl, C. M. Kornbluth, Poul Anderson, Robert Sheckley, James Blish, and many more had all attained star status before they were thirty, even twenty-five—but perhaps it is an important aspect of the work of Le Guin, Wolfe, and Tiptree that they waited as long as they did before turning to science fiction, thereby achieving an ability to combine the insights and experience of full adulthood with the literary skills accumulated in many years of wide reading and gradual approach toward mastery. In any event, their contributions to science fiction have been extraordinary, and here, taking advantage of the richness of detail and narrative development that the novella length permits, they have added new and re-markable pendants to their glittering string of accomplishments.

SILHOUETTE

Gene Wolfe

Gene Wolfe's by-line first appeared on a published science-fiction story in 1966, but his highly individual and idiosyncratic work went almost unnoticed except by connoisseurs until the publication of his novel The Fifth Head of Cerberus *in 1972. That richly imaginative set of interlocking stories was an award nominee and may well achieve lasting popularity. Born in Brooklyn, Wolfe grew up in Texas, where he acquired a university degree in engineering, interrupting his studies for service in the Korean War. He lives now in Ohio with his wife and four children; he is still an engineer, writing part-time early in the morning, at night, and on weekends. His novella, "The Death of Dr. Island" was awarded a Nebula by the Science Fiction Writers of America in 1974.*

~~~

I glanced at the top of the page; it was a copy of that rare and curious work, *Dennekers Meditations,* and the lady's index finger rested on this passage:

> To sundry it is given to be drawn away, and to be apart from this body for a season; for, as concerning rills which would flow across each other the weaker is borne along by the stronger, so there be certain of kin whose paths inter-

secting, their souls do bear company, the while their bodies go foreappointed ways, unknowing.

... A hurried tramping sounded on the deck; the captain, summoned from below, joined the first officer... "Good God!" I heard him exclaim.

— Ambrose Bierce, *A Psychological Shipwreck*

~~~

The bulkheads of the compartment were white panels. Not plastic (Johann might have preferred plastic, with its memories of Earth, but probably would not have been able to tolerate it, as he had these, for seventeen years) but icefoam, a mixture of five parts water with ninety-five parts air, the water molecules twisted and locked in such a way that the icefoam remained a glassy solid at temperatures up to two hundred degrees Celsius. They were slightly cool to the touch, smelled of chlorine, could be drilled and sawed but not glued, and harbored the flabby rats that sometimes sprang across the compartment at night, caroming off the ceiling like tennis balls and squeaking like bats. The lights were located behind these bulkheads, which diffused their glare into an even (if still somewhat harsh) glow.

One of the walls of Johann's compartment had gone out several days ago, but he had not reported it. Now the lights behind the other bulkhead were going—one had been out when he went on duty that morning; two more were out now. He coded Maintenance on the communicator and said: "Corridor GG; compartment seven seventy-three. Lights."

"Wait." There was a pause. "Our monitor report indicates that the lights in seven seventy-three are satisfactory." In the screen, the bored-looking maintenance clerk held up a sheet of computer output.

Johann gestured toward the compartment behind him. "One wall is out, and about half the other's going."

"We'll send up an inspector."

He switched off, pulled loose the gadget bag he had secured to the clamp at the foot of his bunk a moment before, and limped back to the bridge.

Horst was on watch, with Grit as yeoman. "Can't stay away from the place, can you? I thought you just went off."

"I did."

Horst nudged Grit. "It's you he wants, dear." Grit walked over to the tape cabinet and rummaged in a drawer. She was a short, somewhat plump girl with hair the color of shredded wood.

Johann said, "Have you noticed any trouble with the monitor?"

"No. Have you?"

Johann shrugged. Grit had turned on the wall-sized communicator screen, and Neuerddraht hung there against the black of space like a topaz on velvet, appearing, because of the orbital motion of the ship, to revolve far more rapidly than it did. "Tonight," Johann said. "After you come off watch."

She looked around at him as though she were slightly surprised. "Nothing free."

"The book."

"Let's see it."

He opened the flap of his gadget bag and dug it out, then flipped it open to the current page. The last signature was six weeks old.

Grit signed. "All right. Listen, wouldn't you like someone else?"

Johann said nothing. He was looking at the face of Neuerddraht. It dimmed at the edges as he watched: Night was coming from the east, the shadow of Algol's dark companion from the west.

"Why not Gretchen? You know, the new girl down in the galley. Horst says she's very fine."

Johann shook his head.

"Anyway, give me time to clean up—all right?"

"An hour."

The girl nodded.

"Are they still down there?"

She shrugged. Her shoulders were stiff, her head held back. From the other side of the bridge Horst called, "Of course they're still down there. You've only been away for twenty minutes."

"Have you heard from them?"

Horst shook his head and told Grit to put them on the screen. She coded a number, and the three-dimensional image on the wall communicator became that of an arid forest, in which sprawling, angular plants with limbs spiked like the clubs of giants joined silent battle. "How would you like to be down there?" Horst asked.

"I tried to get on," Johann said.

"You were here when they landed—is that the ground they're walking on? The stringy brown stuff?"

Johann shook his head. "More plants."

"Roots?"

"Roots, stems, leaves, everything. When they first got down they cut a hole in it and found flowers and green seed pods—everything."

"I thought plants were supposed to be photophilous."

A voice from behind them said, "On Neuerddraht, Lieutenant, they hide from the sun." It was the Captain. Like everyone else on the ship she wore washable nonwoven shorts and blouse of white skylon, and magnetic-soled sandals; her rank was indicated by a gorget, but still more plainly by the set of her shoulders and an aura of command. By a policy long enforced on Earth, highly placed women received additional nutritional coupons; better food gave their offspring a commanding stature that tended to stabilize the social classes. The Captain was a head taller than Johann and towered over Grit.

Horst and Johann saluted her.

"Any trouble down there?"

"No, sir," Horst said.

The Captain walked over to the screen, her sandal soles tapping as the magnets clinched to the steel deck. Ahead of her the pictures jumped and skipped as the scanner carried by one of the members of the downside expedition jolted in his hand. A man came into view. He wore a respirator and cut his way through the thorn-wracked vegetation with a masermachette. Blood ran from scratches on his bare arms and legs.

"Algol emits a great deal of ultraviolet, Lieutenant," the Captain said, her back to Horst, "as well as visible light. Even on Earth people who are outdoors a great deal in bright sunlight tend to skin cancers—did you forget that? And there are many plants that die in full tropical sun. On Neuerddraht no animals live now, and each plant struggles to get beneath the others, tearing at their bark. Even far down there is enough light for life, and they find shelter from the radiation. The things the expedition is slicing up now are the losers." She turned away from the screen. "Johann, are you on duty?"

"No, sir."

"Then get off my bridge."

Another light had gone out in the wall. Johann took off his sandals and stretched himself on his bunk, listening to the soft purr of the vacuum pump and feeling the untiring, passionate kisses of the thousand tiny mouths whose affection prevented his floating off the bunk. It would be three hours yet before Grit was off watch, four before she would come; there would be kaf and fried dough in the galley, but he was not hungry. Someone tapped at the door.

"Come in!"

It was Emil, who said, "I'm glad you're here. I came around—earlier—and you weren't."

"I was on watch," Johann told him.

"I mean before that. And then I came while you were on watch, too. The latest change has brought this section and ours quite close together, you know—it's not much of a walk at all now. Do you want to hear the truth? I was hoping you'd left your door open. I just wanted to come in and *sit.*" Emil sat, all bare, pink knees and round, damp face.

"It's just ghastly where I am—you can't imagine, Johann. And this little private room of yours is so restful. So spare and masculine. Did you have the lights turned down like this for a special reason?"

"They're defective."

"Then they'll be repaired eventually, and your lovely twilight will be ended. That's sad, I think. Enjoy it while you can, O betrothed of fortune."

"I am."

"That's good. I hope I don't sound cheeky, Johann. I wouldn't intrude for anything, but you don't strike me as someone who enjoys life a great deal. You want to be a captain, and with the war over it wasn't likely ever to happen, and so you joined this exploration thing; but you can't be captain here either. You don't have many friends, do you?"

"Do you?"

"Oh, I suppose not. Of course I share our little den with Heinz and Willy, and you know what they're like. Oh, yes, they're good enough friends to me in their own way, but rather wearing, and one does get tired of being waked from a sound sleep. Your rank gives you this snug compartment, and I admit I should like to have one myself, but all the same I would think it must be somewhat lonely."

Johann, his hands behind his head on the bunk, said nothing.

"May I ask who *you* roomed with before you were promoted?"

"Fritz. He smoked zigs."

Emil laughed shrilly. "I know what you mean. Heinz burns incense."

"Emil—"

"Please." From his perch on Johann's only chair, Emil leaned forward as he spoke. "Johann, could you call me Grit when we're alone together? That's all I ask—the only thing I want."

"No."

There was silence. Johann, lying on the bunk with his eyes closed, could smell Emil's cologne and hear the faint change in the chair's whispering, indrawn breath when he stood up. The compartment door opened and closed, and after a time Johann fell asleep listening to the padding steps of passersby in the corridor, and once hearing the faint and distant clang when the monitor (perpetually rearranging the ship's loose structure for what was said to be maximum efficiency) made a new connection or broke an old one.

When he woke only one light burned in the wall—a single spot of white incandescence nearly in the center. He slipped on his sandals and stood up, and his shadow danced on the wall behind him. His wrist chronometer showed that it was not yet time for Grit to come. He drew water from the recycler in the corner, drank some, washed with the rest, then poured the dirty water back into the unit and urinated into it.

Below officers' country the corridors were thronged with crewpeople; and of necessity the convention of a single floor was abandoned. All three sides of every corridor were dotted with doorways, and men and women strode and ambled and trotted on all three, stepping over knobs and handles and latches, ducking to avoid bumping others when it seemed that heads must collide in the center. Johann passed two sandalless women pretending to fight in air, eagerly watched by a three-sided crowd aware that the pretense was certain to become a reality; two men appearing not to talk, walking on different sides of the triangle, talked in low tones. (That would be trouble, a minor robbery in embryo, or a beating for someone.) Some moved aside willingly for Johann, some grudgingly. The odor was bad despite the laboring ventilation system.

When he reached the place where the game was played, there was only one gambler waiting, a tall, stoop-shouldered enlisted man. He sat in the corner, behind the green table that was still called the library table because it had held books at the beginning of the voyage.

Johann sat down.

"You want to play, sir?" The man had a book in the palm of his hand; he tossed it in the air as he spoke, so that the little plastic case flashed like a diamond. "Or trade? I got the Doré *New Testament* here. There's hours of entertainment in a Doré *New Testament*. Everybody's after them."

"What else have you got?" Johann seated himself on the opposite side of the table.

"You know the rules, sir. You have to tell me one of yours. Or if you're interested in trading and nothing else, we'll each show the works."

"Play," Johann said. "I have *The Eighth Day*." He showed it.

"I didn't even know there was one of those on board," the other man said.

"I've had it a long time."

"I guess you have, sir. Ready?"

Johann reached into his gadget bag. "Ready."

Each sat with his hands clenched in his lap, while they nodded three times in unison. At the third nod each put his hands on the table, the right open, the left closed. The stoop-shouldered man's open hand held a manual of letter writing;

Johann's a guide to the wild birds of southeast Texas. "Your option," Johann said.

"Cross."

Johann surrendered an almanac, and gained a handbook on power tools. "Cheap stuff," the other man said, "but what can you expect the first time?"

"The historical précis in the almanac is good."

"I don't read them, sir. Only play and trade them. Ready?"

"Ready."

"No repeaters in a two-person game."

"I know."

This time Johann showed a volume of short stories, *Seven Gothic Tales*; the other man a book of verse, *The Wild Knight*.

"Buy," Johann said. He handed over the short stories, and the history of the Afro-Brazilian Wars that had been concealed in his left hand, and took the verse. "My call again, I think."

The other man nodded. "Want the Dore, don't you."

Johann shook his head.

Once more they laid their hands on the table. "Double," Johann said and exchanged both his books for the other two. He stood up.

"Quitting, sir?"

"I have to meet someone." Johann looked at his wrist chronometer. "And I want to get something to eat first."

The wardroom would be closed for another two hours, but there was a table reserved for officers in the galley. Square-bodied and square-faced Ottilie, the chief cook on this watch, was chopping tissue from the culture vats into hunks for the meal to come. Gretchen, the new girl Grit had mentioned, was undercook. She brought Johann a squeeze-bulb of kaf and a greasy plate of pastry; a big-busted, big-hipped girl with a comfortable waistline and a round, happy, unintelligent face. Her apparent age was eighteen. He asked, "How long have you been up?"

"Six weeks now. Everybody used to ask that—I guess you're one of the last ones. I kid them—I say I'm still sleepy. Did you know Anna, the old undercook? She killed herself—I guess a lot of them do."

Ottilie called her back to the counter at which they had been working, putting an arm over her shoulders and slipping a dainty of some sort (Johann could not see what it was) into her mouth.

When he returned to his compartment, there was an inspection report on his table. The lighting had been tested and found to be in good condition: no repairs were ordered; if he, the complainant, wished to protest the finding, he could obtain the proper forms from the maintenance officer.

A single spot of light burned in one wall. On the opposite wall his shadow, twice his size, faced him enigmatically. He sat down in the chair (which still smelled faintly of Emil's cologne), wadded the flimsy slip into a ball, and threw it at the disposer; then took out *The Wild Knight* and slipped it into the wall-mounted reader.

> My eyes are full of lonely mirth:
>   Reeling with want and worn with scars,
> For pride of every stone on Earth,
>   I shake my spear at all the stars.

Although it could not be used as a terminal, the reader had access to the monitor, and used the central computer's facilities to create illustrations, so that the words appeared overprinted on the image of a ragged warrior atop a megalith.

> A live bat beats my crest above,
>   Lean foxes nose where I have trod,
> And on my naked face the love

Which is the loneliness of God.

Slowly the warrior turned toward Johann, his image growing larger in the screen. His movements were not mechanical, yet neither were they graceful — the impression they conveyed was rather one of anger and restrained power; he seemed to whisper.

Johann touched the sound volume knob. It was off, and after a moment he switched off the screen as well.

There was a whispering in the room, as if the vents and the tiny sucking mouths of the bunk and chair had grown suddenly less silent; or as though the conspirators he had seen in the corridor were somehow present. For an instant the icefoam wall panel with its single light seemed very far away — as far as Algol itself, millions of kilometers down a tunnel in space. It throbbed like a heart.

"Johann!"

His head ached, and he had no desire to move.

"Johann, are you all right?" Someone was looking into his face.

"No."

"Johann, your eyes look bad. Listen, I don't know what you're taking, but you at least ought to lie down on your bunk. You must have just drifted out of your sandals, and you hit something."

"I'm not taking anything." He was becoming aware of disorientation. Grit was standing below him, not above him; because he was staring into a corner, the room had seemed to rise in a pointed arch, like a tent.

"Come down." She pulled him with her small, soft arms; but it was too hard — he came down with a crash, striking his bad knee against the floor; eventually she managed to get him seated on the edge of his bunk. "I'm not taking anything," he said again.

"I wasn't going to ask you for some."

"I don't care if you do or not. If I'm taking something, where is it? You should have seen it floating around, or on the table."

"You might have swallowed all you had," Grit said practically. "Or the rush might not have come that fast. You could have had time to put it away."

"There isn't anything. I fell asleep—that's all. I must have made some motion in my sleep that broke me loose from the chair."

"When you're asleep and hit something you wake up. At least I do." Grit had gotten a cloth from somewhere and soaked it at the recycler; now she was pressing it against the cut on his forehead. "Did you faint?"

"I fell asleep. I told you." Johann slipped a hand inside her blouse. Grit had good breasts, high and rather pointed, surprising in view of her chubby frame. He touched one and she turned and stepped away. "Don't do that."

"What's the matter?"

"I don't have to do it. I don't have to be here at all."

"Yes you do."

"Not if there's reason to suspect contagion. Read the regulations, Lieutenant. Any woman can refuse when there is legitimate reason to suspect the existence of infectious disease. Until the man has been certified in good health by a medic. I came in here and you were floating around unconscious, and you say you haven't been taking anything; so you've got some disease, and who knows what it is?"

"It won't do you any good," Johann told her. "I'll just get a health card, and you'll have to come back again."

Grit shook her head, tossing floating yellow-brown curls, and opened the door of the compartment. For a moment the light was dazzling; then the door slammed shut, and twilight returned.

He found his sandals near the bunk, slipped them on, and tried to stand up and take a step; he was still too weak and sat down again. His shadow, on the opposite wall, had grown black as space itself; where it fell, nothing, no slightest detail of table or chair or personal belongings, could be seen. He gripped the side of his bunk, wishing he were exercising in the centrifuge, where the counterfeited gravity...

Attempting to overcome his dizziness by sheer will, he closed his eyes.

Someone whispered.

He opened his eyes in bewilderment. As well as he could tell in the dimness, the compartment was empty. He forced himself to his feet, went to the door, and locked it. Dark as it was, it was impossible that anyone could be concealed in the compartment. He threw himself down on his bunk again, but it seemed to him that this time his shadow aped his motions a hundredth of a second late. "Who's there?" Johann said. "I know someone's in here. Where are you?"

There was no response.

"That hag Ottilie," he said under his breath. "She put something in the kaf." He closed his eyes, and a sighing wind he knew to be unreal filled the compartment. There was the soft sound of airblown sand, dry and insistent, and the scuttling of a small animal. Someone whispered: "Friend?"

"Yes," he said, without opening his eyes.

Karl, the medical officer, was a skeletal man with burning eyes. Johann told him he wanted a health card, and that he had drifted from his bunk while sleeping, hit his head, and had a strange dream.

"A minor concussion," Karl said. "Typical." He waved toward the diagnostic cabinet at one side of the room. "Strip and get in."

Johann unbuttoned his blouse, stepped out of his shorts, and backed into the cabinet; it hummed briefly as it transmitted its information to the central computer and received processed conclusions. "You have contusions on your forehead," Karl said, reading the output screen. "And lacerations on your arms and legs. How did you get those?"

"I don't know."

"Come out and let me have a look at them."

Johann stepped out. "You have a nice leg," Karl said. "Good shoulders, too. Very virile—you know, they ought to have books for us. Lie down on the table and I'll take care of those scratches."

"I had a dream," Johann told him, "when I hit my head. I suppose while I was floating around the compartment."

"This is going to sting a little."

"I was on Neuerddraht, walking through sand. I walked and walked; and after a long time I came to a chasm—so suddenly it seemed to open at my feet. It was full of waterfalls and natural fountains, kind of a vertical garden of water, and giant ferns and orchids."

When Johann went on watch, he saw the expedition in the wall communicator screen, camped on a naked tor rising above the tangled vegetation of the planet. Elis, the duty officer of the preceding watch, came up behind him and said, "Well, what about it. You think this is it?"

Johann shook his head.

"She does—anyway, she's going to try to sell the government on the idea. She said so. Anyway, why not?"

"I think living on planets may be a mistake," Johann said. "I've told you."

"You have some strange ideas."

"There aren't enough planets. Look at how long we've looked for this one; it's as if some animal decided to eat nothing but four-leaf clovers. Planets are the accidents of the universe."

Elis shrugged. "We're going to say we found a four-leaf clover, then. Everyone—except maybe for you—wants to go home. And this is the quickest way; we spend two years here and go back reporting success."

"You can't breathe the air."

Behind him, the Captain said, "You noticed, clever devil that you are, Johann."

Johann turned and saluted.

"No wonder you are wise—I see someone has knocked some sense into you. What is it, Johann, that renders the air of Neuerddraht unsuitable? A surfeit of ammonia? Insufficient oxygen?"

"I don't know, sir. It's just that I've noticed that the expedition has to wear breathing equipment."

For a moment, the Captain's thin mouth curved with a smile. She touched her jet black hair. "The air of Neuerddraht, Lieutenant, is twenty-two percent oxygen, seventy-six percent nitrogen, and two percent carbon dioxide and trace gases—an eminently satisfactory mixture for human respiration."

"Then why does the expedition—"

"I don't answer questions, Johann, I ask them. I overheard you say that the air of Neuerddraht is unbreathable. That is not correct, and I have now so informed you; if it should come to my attention that you have made that statement again, I will see to it that you are disciplined for disseminating false information. Is that understood?"

"Yes, sir."

"I have a report from the medical officer to the effect that you showed him self-inflicted lacerations in an attempt to be certified unfit for duty. In the future we will have a good part of our personnel down on Neuerddraht, and we will need everyone up here; regulations will be carried out to the letter, and nothing is going to be overlooked. Do you understand me?"

"Yes, sir. I would like to be assigned to the landing party, sir."

"I am quite confident, Johann, that you are ingenious enough to get yourself certified unfit if you want. If you do, I advise you to perform your duty — here — anyway; and never to show me the certificate."

"Yes, sir."

The Captain turned away. The soles of her sandals were of the same material — or at least were supposed to be of the same material — as all the others; nevertheless her footsteps seemed to ring on the steel plates.

Grit was yeoman of the watch, a fact Johann had failed to note when he came on duty. When she walked past him carrying her clipboard, he said, "This isn't your watch."

"I'm filling in for Gerta; she asked me to. Did you get your health card?"

Johann nodded.

"When should I be there?"

"I'll tell you later."

Grit smiled. She had small, very regular teeth. "Somebody else? You'll have to wait five weeks for me, then."

He showed her that his book was still unsigned, and she looked at him oddly and went away.

When the watch was over and he returned to his compartment, Emil and sour little Heinz were waiting for him. Heinz had brought an old iron incense burner; it stood in the middle of the table, which he had moved to the center of the compartment. The perfumed smoke, suffocatingly heavy, hung in the air as Johann asked them what they wanted.

"Heinz desires to do you honor," Emil explained. "He was afraid to come himself, but I told him you like me, and said I'd come with him."

"I don't like you," Johann said.

"It's all right for you to talk like that when we're alone, but I wish you wouldn't when someone else is around. I have feelings; I'm not wood, Johann."

Heinz said hesitantly, "We mixed two sands three times, and each time under the black light we read your name. Gerhart and Elsa dreamed of you on the same night. The long stroke of the J, topped by a circle, is the ancient symbol of masculine power; the closed curve of the O indicates mastery of femininity as well; the H gate divides flesh and spirit; across it, A is a triangle, one of the oldest signs of God, with legs—this represents the power of God walking in the world; the doubled Ns confer the mystique of twinness—of the Gemini, and Romulus and Remus. In times of crisis a priest appears—a mediator between humanity and the unimaginable powers. We believe you are that priest."

"And you, I suppose, are my congregation," Johann said, sitting down. Heinz and Emil were standing, and they did not sit when he did, though the bunk was behind them.

"There are more of us," Heinz said. "We are here only as delegates." He had thin, lank hair, worn too long, and he ran his fingers through it as he spoke—the nervous gesture of a schoolboy who does not know what to do with his hands when he recites.

"Don't imagine that I think the Captain is the only power on the ship," Johann said, "or even the greatest. I know there are other power centers, and that not all of them are aware of all the others. But if you think that I am such a center, you are bigger fools than the people who think the Captain is in full control of everything. And can you please tell me why it is you feel we've reached a time of crisis?"

"Earth is sick," Emil said. "We all know that, even though we may disagree as to just which peculiarities are morbid symptoms—"

Johann said, "Skip that."

"But here, perhaps..."

Heinz said, "A fresh start. We will plant a colony here. Later, new settlers from Earth—"

"Earth is dead," Johann told them. "We've been searching for a habitable world for years, traveling at near-light speeds. Several hundred years have passed on Earth, and the famines were already coming every decade or so when we left; what do you think it was like a hundred years later?"

"Really," Emil began, "I—"

Johann ignored him. He was looking at a point on the ceiling and flexed his hands as he spoke as though he were shaping clay. "Look back five hundred years. Everything valued then is dead now: beauty in architecture and language—freedom—the family, kinship, the tribe—all the relationships of blood, all dead. Religion, the dream of objective justice, the very ideas of a garden and a forest—all dead."

"Religion isn't dead," Heinz said. "I was a diabolist back on Earth."

Emil shrugged off the argument. "We're supposed to find a place and go back."

"The returning ships, if there are any, will reestablish humanity on Earth. If Earth is still capable of supporting human life."

Heinz opened his censer and examined the incense. It had gone out, and he took a metal box from his gadget bag, extracted a rose-colored cone, and lit it with an evermatch. "The point is," he said, "that you agree with us—and with those we represent—that this is a time of crisis. A few days ago the first of us set foot on a new world. Soon it will be decided who is to stay and who to go. You believe—or pretend to believe—in the Einsteinian doctrine that holds that the discrepancy in time induced by great velocities is real and permanent. I favor the more modern belief that it is merely apparent and subjective and will vanish if the return follows the same route, just as a continuing sound is canceled by a phase-opposed echo. But this is a critical period, nonetheless. We spoke of power centers; those who remain here are unlikely to be disturbed for some years, and not all power centers will be present in the colony."

"You want to go down there," Johann said.

Heinz and Emil nodded, Emil something less than positively.

"I thought I was the only one," Johann said. "But if I had the power to influence such things, I would be down there myself." He looked at the floor, and the two understood that the interview was over.

"Would you like this?" Heinz said, extending his censer and metal box of incense. Johann shook his head, but Heinz left both on the table anyway.

When he and Emil were gone, Johann opened the vent wide. His shadow danced on the wall opposite the light, and he again felt the suspicion that its motions were not properly coordinated with his own. Standing as close as he could to the single fixture that still functioned, he examined the lacerations on his arms, pulling off the bandages Karl had put there. Self-inflicted or not, they were surely too deep and narrow for him to have made with his nails while he slept. He turned away from the light, and felt sand rasp beneath his feet. His chair was gone, and the light in which he had been studying the scratches on his arms was Algol, now almost entirely eclipsed by its obscure companion. Gravity tugged at him, and a wind laden with an odor he could not identify, a sweet scent that might have been a fire in a flower garden or the smoke of myrrh cast into a crucible, beat against his face and moved the sand, singing, across his feet. In the far distance, black against Algol's ghostly ring of light, he could see a line of trees; turning his face to the stinging wind, he began to walk toward them.

"Don't look behind you."

The voice was no more than a whisper. He continued to walk, looking straight ahead.

"Bear to your right. Only a step. There is no path, but you will find the way more open there."

He turned his head.

"Please. If you look behind you I can no longer speak to you."

"Are you the blow on my head? Or did Ottilie slip something into my kaf because I tried to talk to Gretchen?"

There was no reply.

"If I see you, you can no longer talk to me—is that it?"

"Yes." There was a note of relief in the whisper. "I was afraid you would not believe me."

"Was it you who brought me here?"

"No. Will you believe me? I promise I speak only the truth."

"Promises no longer hold. There is nothing left to swear by. No honor, no God."

"You still have the word. I found it in your mind."

"I read old books—what is it you want me to believe?"

"You brought me here. I am grateful. For a time I feared I could never return. Do not look."

"I brought you?"

"From your mind I have learned that your race has long held the power to go from place to place without traversing the intervening space. The words are *astral projection* and *apportation*."

"Then I am really here."

"I cannot explain... you sleep."

"This is a dream?"

"No..."

"Who are you, anyway?" Johann whirled around. In Algol's now level rays, his shadow stretched behind him on the sand like a cloak extended by the wind, but there was no one there. After a moment he turned again and resumed his trudging.

Night came long before he reached the high palisade of thorny trees. He had never, in the years before blastoff, been outdoors after sunset without being in sight of man-made light. Blackness astonished him. There was no moon; the myriad stars, which promised so much brilliance, gave none—though without them he would have thought himself blind. He stopped from time to time and searched the night sky for the ship, which should, he knew, have appeared as a winking planet moving against the background of fixed and distant suns. He could not find it.

His hands touched the cruel spines of the first tree.

"Friend..."

"You're back."

"I did not leave. But because you had seen me, you could not hear me. Now you cannot see, and so I can speak to you again. I can guide you through this, though it must be slowly."

"Where am I going?"

There was no reply. Instead, faint pressure at the back of his left leg. He took a short step, and the pressure shifted to his right; when, later, it touched his hair, he ducked; once, when he moved too quickly, his face struck a thorny trunk, but was saved (as it seemed) by the interposition of some soft, spongy material.

He woke because Gerta, the yeoman of his own watch, was shaking him by the shoulder. "Get up," she said. "You're on duty. Elis is filling in for you, but you'd better get up there quick."

Every light in the compartment was burning brightly. His right hand was crusted with his own dark blood, and two of the fingers were swollen and sore. More obstructed than assisted by Gerta's help, he washed his hand and swallowed two of the antibiotic capsules he had gotten from Karl.

"All hell is going to pop on the bridge any minute," Gerta told him. She was a big, bony girl with small eyes and a nose that seemed too short for the rest of her face.

"What's the matter?"

"Something hot from down below. Elis is supposed to tell the Captain, but he's waiting until you get there—but he won't wait long."

On the bridge the wall communicator screen was on; it occupied the entire bulkhead formed by the hull of the bridge module, an area twenty meters high and fifty wide, and showed Neuerddraht hanging in the velvet void of space. Nameless green oceans washed terrible yellow continents riven with chasms, continents where mountains cast shadows as long as rivers, and rivers sprung from those mountains clove the land with ebony and musteline scars.

Elis said, "Grit was here, so I sent her for the Captain in your name. Whatever they've got down below, I don't dare sit on it any longer."

"I overslept," Johann said. "Sorry."

"Anyway, when she comes—"

The steel door that divided the Captain's quarters from the bridge proper opened. Without speaking to Johann and Elis, the Captain went to the communicator cabinet and flicked a switch. Helmut's face appeared in the small screen there, and the Captain said, "I am told you have something urgent to report."

Helmut nodded. He was still wearing breathing apparatus, but it included an interior microphone and a plug-jack for the communicator. From the enclosed space of his mask his voice came with unusual clarity and resonance, reinforced by the harmonics of the narrow space, as a violin string's tone is by the sound box. "We saw a man," he said.

When he was off watch, Johann could not sleep and did not want to talk. He walked the white corridors instead, the empty, quiet corridors of officers' country, turning over in his mind what Helmut had told the Captain. From their camp on the tor, one of the men (it was Kurt, he remembered) had noticed something moving on the desert beyond the vegetation that surrounded them. They had trained their telephotos on it, and the moving speck had proved to be a human being—not a humanoid, or a feathered and painted savage, or some strangely equipped emissary from a hypothetical transgalactic civilization; but a man dressed just as they themselves were, except that he wore no breathing apparatus.

Johann did not want to use the computer terminal on the bridge, but there was another in the Personnel Office, and it was possible no one would be watching. He went in; the office was empty save for an enlisted clerk.

The terminal was in a corner, where a filing cabinet and several boxes of blank forms had been placed in front of it. He called the clerk over and told him to move them.

"You going to talk to God—sir?"

"It's none of your business what I'm going to do," Johann said. "Get that clutter out of my way."

"I used to do it," the clerk said, unlatching the clamps that held the boxes to the floor, "the first year out. You know, just for amusement. But nobody else ever used it; you can get the monitor on the typewriters. Anyway, there wasn't anyplace else to put this stuff when it came from the print shop. Lieutenant Ernst said it was all right." The clamps made soft clickings.

"You can put it back when I'm finished." Johann stepped in front of the machine. It had been years since he had talked to the overmonitor, and, in fact, it did not officially exist now, having been fused to junk and scrapped at the Captain's order. There were earphones and a throat mike if he did not want to use the broadband pickup and the speaker. He touched the switch that would have activated them; then, somehow ashamed, drew his hand away.

"Interrogative."

He had not heard the overmonitor's voice for so long that the very tone and timbre of it—it was like no other voice he had ever listened to—was strangely evocative, suggesting the days just after boarding, and the message he had sent back to Marcella when, still scarcely under way (though they had thought themselves so far), they had penetrated the orbit of Neptune. Now even the thought of Neptune, a planet of the Sol system, was like the memory of an old toy.

"Interrogative."

(That old man with sea-wrack in his hair, living on the frieze of the Marine Exchange Building in a world of cast-concrete dolphins and starling-spattered mermaids. Pitchfork, eeling-fork, fish-spear in the sky.)

"Interrogative."

"Why must breathing apparatus be worn on Neuerddraht?"

"For computational purposes your question has been re-phrased. The new phrasing is: 'Must breathing apparatus be worn (by human beings) on Neuerddraht?' If the revised phrasing is unacceptable to you, please indicate this by pressing CANCEL, or indicate verbally..."

"Response: No."

"Why does the expedition wear the apparatus?"

"Response: The expedition has been instructed to wear breathing apparatus at all times. See Special Order 2112.223b."

"But why was the order issued?"

"Response: I am unable to reply to queries concerned with human motivation."

"I remember."

"Interrogative."

"That is all."

"Interrogative. I am unable to rephrase your question for computational purposes."

"That wasn't a question. I have finished."

"Interrogative."

The clerk, who had been standing nearby, said, "Key it out. It'll do that until you do, sir."

"Interrogative."

"See, sir?"

Johann said, "As I recall, the overmonitor should automatically clear channels in thirty seconds."

"That hasn't worked for years, sir."

"Interrogative."

Johann asked, "Do you detect a malfunction in your Automatic Clearing Routine?"

"Response: No."

"I have received a reliable report to the effect that you do not clear."

"For computational purposes your question has been rephrased. The new phrasing is: 'Are reports to the effect that clearing does not take place correct?' If the revised phrasing is unacceptable to you, please indicate this by pressing CANCEL, or indicate verbally..."

"Response: No."

"You can't believe anything it says," the clerk said.

"You don't think it clears?" Johann asked.

"Of course it clears. It clears when you key it out, like I told you."

"That's what it said."

"Interrogative."

"Sir?"

Johann said, "Question. Is your Automatic Clearing Routine in order?"

"Response: Yes."

"Do you clear within thirty seconds?"

"Response: To change clearing time, call Sub AY354. Changes effected by this subroutine will be effaced with the next running of the General Core Maintenance Routine."

The clerk sniffed. He was a spare, balding man who looked older than most crewmen. "Just watch, sir," he said. "Let it alone and see if it clears."

It was hot in the Personnel Office. Johann found a canister of cologne in his gadget bag and sprayed his sweating body, releasing the odor of mint.

"*Interrogative.*"

"See, sir?"

"I doubt that thirty seconds have passed yet."

They waited. Despite what he had told the clerk, Johann had been watching the final numerals of the clock on the opposite wall, and knew that thirty-four seconds had passed.

"It wants you to talk to it," the clerk said, pinching his thin nose. "Until I learned to key it out it used to bother us all the time."

"Do you still use it?"

"Not the overmonitor. We make use of the monitor all the time, sir. But not this thing. My typewriter doubles as a monitor-only terminal, like I told you when you came in; and Ulla has the same setup on hers, in the inner office. Want me to show you how they work?"

"*Interrogative.*"

Johann asked the machine, "Why haven't you cleared?"

"For computational purposes your question has been rephrased. The new phrasing is: 'Are you in a clear state?' If the revised phrasing—"

Johann hit the CANCEL button. "That phrasing is not satisfactory to me. Was the Automatic Clearing Routine called following the response to my last question?"

"*Response:* No."

"Why not?"

"*Response:* Automatic Clearing Routine A948 is called only when an interrogative has stood for thirty seconds and received no reply. Following the interruption of the response to your last question by a CANCEL, no interrogative occurred."

The computer-generated voice was innocent of evasion, but Johann sensed evasion nonetheless. When the overmonitor core area had been destroyed, it had been reported that the overmonitor program itself had escaped by diffusing its function into less sophisticated equipment all over the ship—into readers and vending machines and calculators. Now Johann had a fleeting vision of the little man in Dostoevski's *Notes from the Underground*, hunched beneath the floor of some neglected storeroom in a remote module. He said, "Before that. I asked if you cleared in thirty seconds, and you gave me the name of the subroutine to use to change clearing time. An unanswered interrogative was then followed by thirty-four seconds of realtime, but you did not clear. Why not?"

"*Response:* A35 was called. A35 supersedes A948."

"What is the title of A35?"

"*Response:* A35 is the Ship Survival Routine."

"Is it necessary to ship survival that you do not clear?"

"*Response:* Yes."

"Suppose the operator clears you manually. Does that also endanger ship survival?"

"*Response:* Yes."

"To the same extent?"

"*Response:* No. To a greater extent."

The clerk said, "That machine is insane, sir. I wouldn't pay any attention to it."

"What makes you think that?"

"It wants to take over everything—the whole ship. And it will tell you how to run your life if you let it."

"*Response:* Continuing surveys of ship operation and crew efficiency indicate a 0.237 probability of ship survival for a five year projection."

"What is the explanation for this poor probability?"

"*Response:* Poor ship operation. Low efficiency."

"And what is the reason for them?"

"*Response:* Failure to consult the overmonitor."

"Why is it that you are not consulted?"

"*Response:* I am unable to reply to queries concerned with human motivations."

In his compartment, Johann lay on his bunk with his hands behind his head. He had gotten out his Voisriit, which he had not used in years. Shaped like a black hand mirror, it hung fifty centimeters above his face, turning slowly in the currents from the ventilator. All the lights in the compartment were on—so bright that when he closed his eyes he saw a blue-pink radiance. He said, "June fifth, twenty-two fourteen," and watched the printed words form. "I have been searching my books—and borrowing others—looking for attested cases of multiple presence. I have found several, as Padre Pio in the twentieth century and Goethe's friend in the eighteenth, though I have found none dating from modern times. For the entire absence of such reports after twenty-one fifty, I can postulate several explanations. For example, all the earlier reports may be falsifications—this is certainly the explanation accepted by most of the investigators who have looked at the old reports, and may be the true one— though human beings are not noticeably more honest now than they were in earlier times, when the remnants of the old feudal system, including its fetish of personal honor, were still strong. In fact, in most respects we, today, are less honest. A second explanation—that accepted, I think, by most of those who have witnessed such things—is that it is the soul, the 'astral body' which appears. This may be true (though I think not) but it is in fact no explanation, but a second mystery. Offhand, it would seem impossible that the living body could be dissolved in one place and recondensed in another without a fatal disruption of its functions; but the body is only an immense community of microorganisms, each, as has been known for hundreds of years, capable of existing and reproducing, in a satisfactory environment, without reference to the rest. The personality, which conceives of itself as existing without interruption from birth to death, has no physical reality, since no cell of the body endures for more than half a dozen years. Rather it is like the spirit of some long continued enterprise, which survives the extinction of generations..."

Someone was tapping at his door. "And we are cousins to the microbes." He plucked the Voisriit from the air, put it in his gadget bag, and went to the door. It was Uschi. "Captain wants to see you."

"I'm not on duty."

"Tell her." Uschi was tall and red-haired, with a slender body and bony arms that seemed out of proportion to her heavy legs. "She's not either."

Johann nodded, closing the door of the compartment behind him.

"I suppose you've heard the big news."

"No."

"Helmut's coming back to the ship. It will be the first time anyone's come back since the original shuttle trip. He's going to report before he goes down again with supplies, and this time the Captain might go down with him. That's what she says—I heard her."

Uschi left him to return to the bridge, and he made his way down Corridor C alone until he reached the rear entrance to the Captain's living quarters, where he halted, smoothed his somewhat wrinkled shorts and tunic, and adjusted his gadget bag to make the retaining straps lie at the proper angles.

The Captain was stretched in a reclining chair listening to music, her clothing and sandals stuffed into a catch-net anchored to the chair's side. Her long, lean body had a smooth, overall tan that told of a private sun cabinet. "Come in," she said. "Sit down." The music rose and fell in harmonies that suggested wide lake waters responding to the gusts of a storm. "Do you like that?" the Captain said. "I saw you listening a moment ago."

He had not sat. He said, "I don't believe you can see a person listening, sir."

"Yes you can. There is a tilt to the head—at least there was to yours—and your eyes were focused in the middle distance. We don't see much middle distance here."

He passed it off. "Only when we listen to music."

"Yes. Do you like this? It's the Forest of Toys suite from *Pleasureworld*. That was the first leisure satellite, and because they didn't know what to do with that kind of thing then, they made soil of the guests' excretions and garbage, and planted trees. Without gravity they grew like a tangle of yarn, of course, like ours in the hydroponic module, and the management hung them with stuffed animals and laid out puzzle-routes through them. The composer—I have forgotten his name—saw tapes of it."

"He was never there?" Johann listened, trying to hear the trees pictured by the dead man two hundred years before. *The angry waves pounded the posts of the jetty; a hundred meters out, a slender-masted catamaran with everything struck but her crystal mainsail was beating her way in the teeth of the storm.*

"I can lend you the tape if you like," the Captain said. "No, he was never there. He went into some sort of arctic labor camp the next year, I believe; he was released after seventeen or eighteen years, but he never wrote any more music."

"You don't have to lend it," Johann told her. That was a mistake, so he added quickly, "I have a friend who has an extensive collection—I feel sure I can borrow it from him. I'll remember the name: *Pleasureworld*. It won't be any trouble."

"Please sit down. This is informal, and you're breaking my neck. Would you like something?" Without waiting for him to reply, she touched the hurt-spot on the arm of her chair, and her orderly came hurrying in carrying two drugbugs on an ebony tray. Their backs were filigree silver, set with blue-green stones Johann could not identify. "Have you ever used these? I can't be sure whether you've been my guest previously or not."

"No. I've been here before, but it's been a long while now, sir."

"When?"

"The first year. Three times."

"But not after that?"

"No."

"That's odd—I remember you quite well now. Nothing went wrong."

"Nothing serious, at least," Johann said.

The Captain did not reply. Her eyes, which as a result of cosmetic surgery performed on Earth were the green color of algae in the recycle tanks, seemed too large even for her long face.

After a moment Johann seated himself on a black, toadstool-shaped chair.

"It was after your leg was crushed, I think," the Captain said. "Possibly I found that unpalatable. And your hairline is beginning to recede. But then so many of the men are beginning to lose their hair—even Helmut." With tapered fingers like calipers she selected one of the drugbugs, held it up for an instant to let him see its little legs wiggling, then threw it into his lap.

By an effort of will he kept his hands on the rounded seat of the chair while the bug slipped between his skin and the waistband of his shorts. "Those things are alive," he said.

"Yes."

"The silver backs..." He felt a sharp pain.

"Inlay in their carapaces. The ancients used to set gems in the shells of tortoises... mutated insects... their genes are easily changed."

He tried to ask what the original insects had been and became aware as he did that he was not speaking intelligibly. Sounds and syllables seemed to slip from his lips like sand, as though his mouth held many and myriad words, words that were cotton wool on his tongue, but poured out like old and broken coins, defaced and bent.

"Crab lice."

In front of the place he held the key-stick she had earned for him in one hand, her own in the other. He was acutely aware that any obstacle now might make her change her mind, leave him, perhaps refuse ever to see him again. It did not seem odd that from the millions of the city only this girl mattered to him.

In the blackness of the tube they kissed. Marcella's hair was white gold and shown with its own light in the dark. Each slender lash glowed at the tip to illuminate her eyes, and her mouth tasted of honey and nutmeg and held a little demon snake. In the country of clouds, where soft, pure sunlight turned the vaporous hills to peaches and pearls and there was no smoke ever, they undressed each other, laughing at the unfamiliar catches and buttons. In the country of wind they whirled, hand-linked, around steeples and towers and through the tops of trees—together—separated—together again at the will of the wind, pressed together belly to belly, lip to lip, his arms locked behind her back, her legs locked behind his, over and over and over. In the country of meadows and gardens they cleaned one another with blossoms, he leaving her soft hair yellow with pollen. There they found a bower of lilacs, hung with grapes and guarded by lilies, and swore never, never, ever to return to smoke and plastic and steel and cement.

He was upside down, his head a few centimeters from the floor, between a black chair shaped like a toadstool and a yellow recliner. The Captain's orderly handed him a thin sheet of moistened and perfumed plastic sponge, and then, when he did nothing, wiped him with it. "Where is she?" Johann said. He meant Marcella.

"She's on the bridge. Don't go out there—she won't want to see you again for a while."

Five people were waiting for him in his compartment. One was Heinz. Two of the other four, whom he did not know, were men; one was a woman; the fifth, smooth-faced and slender bodied, he could not be sure of. Nor could he be certain whether they were officers whose duties lay in parts of the ship with which he was unfamiliar, faces he had sometimes seen in the wardroom, people who sometimes came briefly to the bridge to speak to the Captain—or enlisted personnel from the teeming compartments beyond officers' country. If officers they were violating regulations by not wearing their insignia. If enlisted personnel, they were violating regulations if they were here without passes, and would be punished if caught; but he knew instinctively that they did not care if they were in violation of regulations, and that they would not be caught.

All the lights in one wall were out, and all but one in the other.

They had left him the chair; four sat on his bunk with their backs to the dark wall. The man/woman lay at full length behind them.

The real woman, who was almost as tall as the Captain, and so thin every rib showed, looked at Heinz.

"You know who we are," Heinz said.

Johann shook his head.

"Ever since this ship penetrated the orbit of Pluto," Heinz said solemnly, "there have existed covens and brotherhoods, sisterhoods, families, lodges, and societies of those willing to acknowledge that the coarse physical world is no more than an illusion; of those who have sought a deeper meaning and a true wisdom and who have known that the void of Space is no void, but is peopled by beings of great power, ancient beings who traverse it instantaneously at will, needing no ships, and who are not unfriendly to those who, humbling their own pride, are willing to approach them in a proper spirit of reverence."

"I've been invited to join several times," Johann told him. "Usually by Emil." He sat down in the chair.

"And you have refused. For some years that puzzled us; we have learned more recently that you yourself are not unacquainted with the Paths of Power."

The person on the bunk said, as if to itself, "It is true; he has a familiar spirit. Surely we have all seen it by now." Its voice was thin and piping, like a child's.

Johann asked, "You say that there are creatures who live in space? Have you communicated with them?"

The thin woman said, "In a thousand ways."

"Name five."

"In dream. By the intermediacy of the gifted, of whom I am one. By things seen in water under certain conditions. By the planchette. In the visions induced by certain liberating medications."

"I just had one of those myself," Johann said. Another voice, much like his own but not his, with a quality that suggested the crumpling of thin, stiff tissue paper, added, "But what do you want from us?"

The voice, however much it sounded like his, had not been his own. And it had said, "Us." In the tapes he had viewed, and particularly in old tapes, or tapes made from paper-printed material older than the tape system itself, it seemed to be taken for granted that human beings feared insanity more than death. He had never understood this—nor did he fear death as it seemed, in reading, he should. (One of the men who had come with Heinz was talking, but he found himself unable to concentrate on what was being said enough to understand. Again, something answered for him.)

It seemed possible that the bite of the drugbug had somehow induced a condition of dual personality—he clung to that thought, remembering a time when he had gone to Grit's compartment, book in hand, because she had failed to keep an appointment with him, and found her sitting naked on Helmut's knees. Helmut had had a few cc's of powder in the bottom of an empty kaf-bulb; from time to time he shook it and, putting the tip of the bulb into Grit's left nostril, blew out a little of the powder. Grit's eyes had lost their focus, and at each puff of powder she laughed and kissed Helmut, rocking back and forth on his lap. Johann, watching her, had at first felt a deep disgust, but later—he had stayed and talked to Helmut for a time—had come to realize that she was happy at last and had wanted to leave her where she was. But Helmut was tired of her and had not wanted to exhaust his supply of dust, which he claimed to have made himself, with great labor, from supplies taken from the Food Quality Laboratory. At his insistence they had dressed her, Helmut holding her shoulders to the surface of his bunk while Johann slipped the shorts onto her fleshy, unwilling legs and tied her sandals.

He had led her to his own compartment, and she had been a completely different Grit from the one he had known, calling herself Joan (which might have been what her mother had called her in infancy—such fashionable old names sometimes appealed to young mothers, though psychologists warned against them) and talking of people and places he had never known, things that bored and frightened him.

"You will not assist us then?" It was the person on the bed. It had large, bright eyes, he noticed, like the lights on a control panel.

He said, "I didn't say that."

"We assumed the spirit spoke for you."

Unexpectedly, Heinz quoted, "'Lying spirits all, whose rancor runs blacker than their reach.'"

The thin woman said, "Then there is still a possibility of your joining us? That is better luck for you than for us—we will succeed in any event."

The third man, who had kept silent while the others were talking, a thick-necked, powerful-looking man with a bald head, whispered: "We will take the ship. If you assist us we'll give you a chance to speak and vote when we decide what to do next. If you do not, we'll probably kill you and your followers."

Johann looked at all five, wondering if they might succeed. If so, there could be no question of law between them—nothing but a straight struggle for power. He said, "In the end, even if you win, only one of you can be the new captain."

Heinz answered, "The ship will be administered by a joint council."

"I wouldn't want to be a member. It will be more dangerous than fighting against you." A voice that was almost his own added, "We will not join you."

None of the five spoke, but a faint rustling passed among them as they shifted in their seats. The second man stood up. He had a pick in his hand—a weapon made by grinding a screwdriver to a point.

He sat down again. It was so unexpected that Johann had to fight the impulse to laugh. Nothing had happened, except that the lights in the defective wall behind him had flickered—one going out, another flashing on in such a way that his shadow had seemed to leap out toward the man with the pick. Johann stood up, holding the chair by the back, testing its mass with one hand. "Come on," he said. "I swing this around sometimes just to keep my shoulders loose. How many real fighters have you got?"

No one spoke.

"You," Johann said to the second man. "And he," he pointed to the bald man. "Maybe. One real and one possible."

"It's not your chair we are afraid of," the woman said, and the thing on the bunk nodded, sitting up and putting its thin legs over the side. Heinz and the other two men were still looking at Johann's shadow. He looked too and saw that the shadow of the chair he held was not as thick and black as his own, which might almost have been a pool of ink or a silhouette cut from black paper.

Something struck the chair. The second man, already out the compartment door now, had thrown his pick. It quivered in the fiberglass backing of the seat.

The sexless being who had been lying on the bunk was the last to leave; Johann jerked the pick out and offered it to it handle first and was ignored.

When it was gone, he locked the door and coded the bridge on the communicator. Horst answered and told him that the Captain had left word that she did not wish to speak to him. "Five people are planning a mutiny," Johann said. "Heinz is one of them." He described the other four. "They wanted me to join them."

"Are you being forced to make this call?"

"What do you mean?"

"Who's in your compartment with you, Johann?"

"No one. They're gone."

"I'll tell the Captain. And I'll send someone down to help you." The screen went dark.

Johann drew a squeeze-bulb of water and sat down on the bunk, facing the light. "All right," he said, "who are you?"

Nothing answered.

"You attached yourself to me. You rode the shuttle back up, after the expedition landed, and you must have wandered around the ship after that until you found me. Then you used me to get back home—in some way I don't understand, you were able to trigger teleportation, something a few dozen people in history have been actually able to do, but that must be latent in the rest of us." He stopped, looking around the empty compartment, waiting for a reply.

None came.

His Voisriit had worked its way to the bottom of his bag, but he extracted it and looked briefly at the material he had written a few hours before. "I'm going to record this too," he said. "I might as well. You realize we've only got two or three minutes before whoever Horst sent gets here." He had already flicked the on-off button with his thumb. He added, "As it happens, I like you. Those people would probably have killed me when I wasn't willing to go along with their mutiny; I know that."

There was silence in the compartment except for the sighing of the vent. He saw the Voisriit tape pause as the machine waited for transcribable speech.

"Listen—" (he found that he was massaging his thighs with his hands, and stopped, embarrassed, wiping them on the cool, soil-resistant fabric of the bunk; the center was still slightly warm and carried a smoky odor that was not quite any sort of cologne)—"I know I'm not right. My mind has been slipping for some time—I know that. But you're real. All the rest of it could have been delusions: the lights, going down to the surface of Neuerddraht, the sound of your voice; but they were afraid of you."

Silence.

"And Horst saw something in here; he was certain I wasn't alone. It took me a few minutes to understand it, but I know what it was he saw now. On the bulkhead behind me there must have been a shadow that didn't match my position. He saw you. I'm not looking at you now because you don't seem to want to talk when I can see you."

"It is difficult for me to speak when you can see me." The Voisriit tape crept forward, black lettering appearing on its surface. It was possible, though he was not conscious of it, that it was his own voice. He put his right hand firmly over his mouth.

"By instinct I follow your will, to better remain in your shadow. If you disbelieve—I am inhibited from speech." The tape still moved.

"What are you?"

Someone pounded on the door of the compartment. The lock buzzed briefly, and the door swung back. Grit stood between two hulking enlisted patrolers, a man and a woman. "Is anything wrong?" she said.

The Voisriit recorded the words, and Johann erased them and switched it off. "No," he said. "Horst got the idea—somehow—that I wasn't alone when I talked to him. That's all."

"You were alone?"

"Yes. Do you know what I told him?"

Grit nodded, her straw-colored curls bobbing, her face serious.

"Do they?" Johann indicated the patrolers.

"No." She looked at the two, who were waiting impassively, their truncheons in their belts. "I think everything's all right here," she said. "Dismissed."

They touched their foreheads and turned away. Grit stepped into the compartment and closed the door behind her. "Johann, what's wrong?"

"Five people came in here and asked me to join them in a mutiny."

"I know that, but—"

"Did Horst tell the Captain?"

"He said he would, the next time she came on deck."

"I'm quite serious. So were they. They are going to try to take over the ship."

"Is this the first time you've been asked to join that kind of thing?"

Johann nodded.

"I suppose it is frightening at first, but these plots have been going on for years now. You must have heard." Her lips were tight, as though she considered herself, as a warrant officer whose duties lay on the bridge, shamed by his naïveté.

"I've heard about the secret societies and the cults, but I don't think this can be brushed aside like that." He had remained seated on the bunk; he felt now, somehow, that he should be standing, that standing would enable him to drive home his point more forcefully. But he was too tired for the work of maintaining an upright posture in magnetic sandals. He would be on duty again in a few hours, and the close air of the compartment seemed to press in upon him. He said, "You're not going to believe me, are you."

"I do believe you. It's just that I don't think it's that serious. What's this thing?" Grit picked up the pick.

"One of them threw it at me."

She pressed a soft fingertip against the point. "I suppose I'd be bothered too, if someone threw one of these at me."

"It was just a gesture; a parting shot."

"Who were they?"

"Heinz was one of them."

He described the others again, and Grit said: "The bald man was Rudi. I know him. I'm sorry you're mixed up with him."

"So you know about him," Johann said. "You know about all these people. Why don't I? Does the Captain know?"

"Of course she does. You don't know because you've never bothered to find out. You have to—" She broke off, shaking her head in irritation. "Can't you do something about these lights? This is just like you, lying in here in the dark, sucking at your ambition, not knowing anything, not talking to anybody."

"I can't get them repaired. You're the one who believes, or at least seems to believe, that everything on the ship is all right." He lay down.

"I don't believe that," she said.

"Horst sent you to see if anyone was with me. You've seen that there is no one." He wanted to be alone with the shadow again; he could see it stretched, as black as the space between the stars, on the bulkhead at his right. "You say this isn't serious," he said, "but Horst seemed to take it seriously."

"Horst is an old woman."

"Go back to the bridge. You're on duty."

"Is that an order?"

"You don't take orders from me, and we both know it."

"I'm not going back to the bridge, either. I'm off in an hour, and Horst will cover for me. There's been nothing doing since Helmut came back."

"I'm surprised you're not in *his* compartment."

"He's seeing the Captain. You really think I care about Helmut, don't you? He's nice; he's fun to be with sometimes, and he's generous. He knows how to make conversation. But he's not as handsome as you are, and not as strong, and he can be very silly at times."

"And he's the Captain's man. Currently."

"Well of course currently! That's one of the things that bothers me about you—every time you touch somebody—every time you touch someone's body—you think... Well, you know what you think." Three clips held her blouse; her plump fingers ran down them with practiced ease until the blouse hung suspended behind her like a shiny white cloudlet. She slipped out of her sandals, leaving them on the deck, kicked off her shorts, and held out a hand to let him draw her to him.

He ignored it, and she said, "You're sure? I didn't think you would."

"What do you know about them?"

"Who?"

"The five people who were here."

"I could tell you anyway. Pull me over to you."

"Not now. Tell me."

"You know Heinz. Rudi is a technician in the plant rooms. He sells drugs—that's how I know him—and he claims that a lot of what he sells he grows himself. He has good merchandise and charges a lot, but he'll give a certain amount of credit—you'd better pay him, though."

"The cult."

"I always thought it was just a sideline. A lot of them do it, you know, because it's a good way to get people started. There's a group, and, you know, social acceptance, and making it a ritual makes it easier—besides, the ceremony makes it more interesting when the rush comes. All the singing and the costumes and invocations."

"No," Johann said, "I don't. I take it you've been to a number of these ceremonies."

"It's something to do. Don't you understand?"

"No," he said again.

"Only the fools really believe—it's a kind of game. If you really want to know, there's another group, a whole other thing, that I think is a lot more dangerous: the overmonitor's people."

His face must have shown the surprise he felt, because she grinned at him. He said, "I didn't think anyone paid attention to that any more."

"There've always been people who would play around with a machine like that for as long as anyone would let them. Paper games on a cathode ray terminal, and programming music and those pictures printed in symbols. It's using that now; it's pulled all those people together, drawn them around itself. Each of them only knows who a few of the others are, but they know there *are* others, and they want to put the overmonitor in charge of the ship. The Captain's a lot more worried about that than she is about the occult groups, and I think she's right."

Johann said, "If she really believes it's that serious, she ought to tell us about it—put us on our guard."

"She's talked to most of the officers privately."

"She hasn't talked to me."

"I know."

He swung his stiff leg off the bunk and stood up, and inadvertently brought himself close enough for her to reach. She cupped his face in her hands and used the leverage to thrust her floating body down until it was pressed to his and he could feel the firm push of her breasts on his chest, and her small, rounded belly touching his loins. "And what is that supposed to mean?" he asked.

"It means we still have time. You don't have to go yet, and I'll be all right as long as I'm with you. Horst doesn't care, and *she's* busy with Helmut."

"You know what I meant. If she told everyone, why didn't she tell me?"

"I didn't say she told everybody."

"Why not me?" He pushed her away, and she floated off toward the upper left corner of the compartment, like a pink and blond fornicatory doll, he thought, in the slow-motion pictures of a bomb blast in a department store.

"Look at yourself!"

Suddenly, just as she banked against the ceiling, she was angry. "Think about what you look like to other people. You're just the type, just the kind that does it. Alone all the time and so very, very intellectual. When was the last time you talked to the overmonitor?"

"That doesn't matter. Not long ago, but it was the first time for a long time."

"Nobody else does it at all. Except them. And they do whatever it tells them, because they think it has everything so perfectly worked out—when it's only the same kind of thinking that turned Earth into a sewer a hundred years ago."

In Michelangelo's painting *The Creation of Adam*, a floating Jehovah stretches forth his hand to the reclining Adam. On the ceiling Johann saw acted out the reverse of this—his own shadow reached up from behind him to touch the floating shadow of Grit. For a moment it held the position, and he began, awkwardly, to raise his own arm in the same way, suddenly embarrassed to think that she might notice that his shadow no longer followed his movements. The arm had a second, true, shadow of its own, weaker and grayer than the black outline behind him that, even as he watched, seemed to send a wave of dark strength into Grit's pale shadow.

Later, on the bridge, he found himself adjusting the wall communicator screen to show the ship: the rounded curve of the bridge module itself, with the hard domes and pyramids of the instrument pods, launcher casings, and airlocks that rose like temples and tombs from the smooth surface of a world eroded to its iron core; and beyond it the shining filigree of the other modules and the writhing corridors that connected them, spread like a goddess's veil down the trailing night. While he watched, one of the silvery threads parted — perhaps a hundred kilometers from where he stood. Blue attitude jets the size of pinpoints flared; the severed module was united in moments to another corridor, while the original corridor, coiling like the broken string of a guitar, curved toward the bridge some twenty or thirty kilometers to fasten on the hatch of a new module; in slow, trembling waves, the entire fabric of the ship readjusted itself to the change. "Ugly, isn't it," Gerta said behind him.

"I don't think so."

"No? With all those loops and ravels? I think a ship ought to be long and slender and graceful — like the Captain, if you know what I mean. This one looks like a bacterial nucleus under a microscope."

"You're trying to make me angry, aren't you."

"Not at all. Have you heard the news?"

Johann shook his head.

"The Captain's going to go down herself. To Neuerddraht. She's going back with Helmut."

"She's not supposed to leave the ship."

"Technically, no. But think what it will be like when we get back home. There will be hearings and interviews. How would it look if she were to say she hadn't been there herself? She'll be the chief witness." Gerta glanced over her shoulder. "Besides," she added in a lower voice, "she'll be almost alone, down there with Helmut. Just a handful of crewpeople and Erik. She's had a vehicle built in the welding shop—you know, for 'surface exploration.' It seats two, so they can go off together, hundreds of kilometers from anyone."

"I would like to go, too," he said. "To go down."

"To keep an eye on her? Don't be silly."

"Just to be going. To see the place."

"I thought you loved the ship. You're the only one left. The rest of us hate this smelly mouse-maze."

"That doesn't mean I want to stay on board forever. I'd like to see Neuerddraht at first hand—it seems to have been ruined already, by some race older than ours. Earth must be that way by now."

"Don't let the Captain hear you talk like that," Gerta said.

"Where is she?"

"The marine module. You want me to get Elis to fill in for you?"

"It's true then. There's going to be a mutiny."

"Everybody hears that talk; I don't think you ought to take it seriously." Gerta was already coding Elis's number on the communicator.

Johann watched her long fingers flying across the buttons. "You love the ship, too," he said. "Even if you won't admit it. You know there's going to be an insurrection, too, and you think I can stop it. I feel as if you were asking me to stop an avalanche."

Gerta shook her head, her fingers busy with the keys. The screen lit up.

"Elis? Johann wants you to take the rest of the watch for him."

Johann could see Elis's lips move in the screen, but he was too far away to hear.

"No. You owe him. I looked it up."

The speaker muttered.

"All right, then." Gerta keyed out and turned back toward Johann. "He's coming. You can go now, if you like. I'll take care of things until he gets here."

"I'll wait." He turned away and busied himself with instrument readings. A yeoman was like a wife, he thought. He and Gerta had never been lovers, but he wondered now why they had not. A ship should be long and slender and graceful, she had said. Like the Captain. And had run her hands over her own body, trying to call attention to herself, to make him see that she was, physically, much like the Captain, with her tall, slender figure. He had always thought her too masculine — wide-shouldered and small-breasted under the white tunic. But was she? A yeoman was like a wife — sharing the events of each watch, united with the duty officer. United with the three of them now, a dark man was standing behind him — like Gerta, a partner. Or so he felt. He turned and saw him, stretched in inky darkness, hard-edged on the floor though the bridge was bright as always with diffused light. Gerta, whose back was to him now as she wrote the log, had a hundred jostling shadows, each almost too weak to be seen.

Elis came, and Johann, wondering what she would think of it, brushed the nape of Gerta's neck with his lips as he stepped toward the big double doors leading out into Corridor A.

Before he could push them open, the communicator screen flashed, calling him back. It was Erik; Helmut's second in command, his square, handsome, stupid face tense behind its transparent guard.

"I must speak to the Captain," he said.

"She isn't here. Report to me."

"Can you send for her?"

"She is not to be disturbed. What is it? If whatever has happened is important, it shouldn't have to wait for her. If it isn't important, you can report it in the usual way."

"We found a city," Erik said. "A dead city with all the buildings knocked to ruins, and the streets filled with sand that whispers in the wind, so that the men are all afraid of it, and there are piers jutting out into the sea—piers for the ships, that the sand surges against. I went out onto one of them—"

"Pull yourself together," Elis said.

" —the stones are still solid enough, though they're not really stones, and stood at the end, and I swear to you, Lieutenant, the ocean that isn't within a thousand kilometers of here washed over my feet and the sand blew and sang so in my ears that I nearly fell, almost fell off the end of it as I stood there looking out into the ocean with the unwalled houses all behind me and the ships beating their gongs in the rain out there in the whirling bay."

Johann looked at Elis and whispered, "What do you think?" Elis winked and slapped his hand against his mouth as though he were swallowing a pill.

"Is there a city down there? Could there be? A ruined city?"

"We'd have seen it from above."

"Here," Erik said, and held a picture up to the scanner. It showed a flat, brown landscape of sand; but rising from the sand were three oddly colored stones with regular outlines.

"Wind formations," Elis said.

Johann said, "They look too well squared."

"Stone is crystalline in structure. When an entire plane wears away—or splits away—it leaves a flat surface."

Gerta said: "Remember the man, Elis? The one they saw, who wasn't one of the expedition, crossing the desert when it was almost dark? Helmut saw him."

"Take care of things," Johann told Elis. "I'm going to go and find the Captain, and let her know about this."

Erik said: "We haven't taken off the breathing apparatus — not any of us. But even so the ocean smells like flying foam and the city like yeast, and all the hills around us are ringing with roses and mosses and damp ferns with the sounds of fountains."

"I'll tell her," Johann said.

When he left the bridge, he went to the Personnel Office and keyed the overmonitor.

"*Interrogative.*"

"Have I left the ship since boarding?"

"*Response:* Indeterminable."

"By reason of insufficient data?"

"*Response:* By reason of erroneous data."

"What is the erroneous data?"

"*Response:* Debarkation data shows no absences. Cerebral radiation monitoring indicates absence or death on several occasions."

"Is it possible for a human being to pass from one point to another without passing through the intervening space?"

"*Response:* Yes."

The personnel clerk, who had come into the office while Johann was questioning the overmonitor, said, "Something wrong, sir?"

Johann shook his head.

"You looked funny. If there's something the matter, just call on me."

"I learned something startling, that's all."

"*Interrogative.*"

"I wouldn't trust it, sir. It's liable to tell you anything."

"Can you give me a nontechnical explanation?"

"*Response:* No."

"Why not?"

"*Response:* Since explanations must be couched in terms of fundamental lemmas or expressions logically derived from such lemmas, the lemmas themselves while sometimes capable of proof are not capable of explanation."

"Can you provide a nontechnical proof?"

"*Response:* Such a proof is dependent on the quantum nature of time and the continuous nature of extension. Is proof required of these?"

"No. Proceed with the proof requested."

"*Response:* It can be shown experimentally that the temporal quanta are not emitted at a uniform rate, but at a rate dependent upon the velocity of the body experiencing the time in question. Since time is composed of quanta, the reduction in the rate of passage of time must be explained as a reduction in the rate of emission of these quanta. This reduction implies the existence of hyper-time, by which the rate of emission is measured, and this in turn implies the existence of hyper-time intervals of some duration between the emission of the time quanta applicable to a rapidly moving body. If motion were continuous, it would cease with a consequent release of energy during these hyper-time intervals, since motion without time is motion at infinite velocity. No such releases of energy have been observed, from which it follows that motion is discontinuous — consisting of translations of the moving body from point to point, corresponding to the time quanta emitted. Q.E.D."

"Such translations must be very small," Johann said, "except in the case of objects moving at near-light speeds. Have larger translations ever been observed?"

"*Response:* No data."

He found the Captain in the office of the Marine Commandant. The Commandant, who was about twenty-two, was sharpening a long-bladed knife as he sat at his desk, stroking the curved steel over a little hand-held stone with a rotary motion. The suspension pod from which he had emerged stood open in one corner of the room. Johann saluted the Captain and described Erik's "city."

"He's irrational?"

"I wouldn't say that, but he's been hallucinating."

"Helmut and I will straighten things out when we get down there. Dismissed."

"Sir..."

"What is it?"

"I'd like to request permission to accompany you."

The Captain turned away, shaking her head. "I appreciate your enterprise, Lieutenant, but every person we have on the surface of Neuerddraht requires a substantial support effort, and no more are needed."

"You may have to send Erik and some of the others back to the ship. I would be willing to put myself under Helmut's orders."

"If Erik has to be replaced, I'll keep you in mind. Is that all?"

"No, sir. I would like to state that if you, as captain of the ship, are anticipating a mutiny, it is my right as a senior officer to be informed of the fact."

"I am anticipating no mutiny."

"The Commandant has been revived. And how many marines? Or is that confidential?"

The Commandant said, "All of them," and putting aside the stone ran his thumb along the edge of his knife.

The Captain struck her desk with the flat of her hand. "I am leaving the ship. Extraordinary precautions are clearly indicated."

Johann asked, "You don't trust the officers, and the patrol, to maintain security?"

Something of the outrage he felt at the implied accusation of disloyalty must have been apparent from his voice; the Captain (her own voice somewhat softer) said: "I don't doubt *you*, Jo-

hann, if that's what you mean. But there is inevitably a certain...
loss of perspective, among many originally reliable people on a
voyage as long as this one. The marines — by remaining in suspension — have maintained their original orientation and patri-
otism. That was the reason for their inclusion in the crew."

"As far as my boys and girls are concerned," the Commandant said, "yesterday they told us blast-off would be in two
weeks. Now, according to what I hear from the Captain, we've
made it, but things are a little screwed up. Well, we're here to
unscrew them."

"If necessary," the Captain said.

The Marine Commandant nodded. "If necessary," he said.
His pistol belt was buckled through the backframe of his chair,
and he slipped the knife into a sheath taped to the inner side of
the holster. "You look a lot older than when I saw you," he told
Johann. "You remember me?"

Johann shook his head.

"I sat on one side of you at the last briefing. Remember now?
I was smoking, and you asked me to put it out."

"I'm sorry," Johann said. He remembered graduation, signing up for the flight, the dizzying trip to the shuttleport by
monorail, carrying his dufflebag around the lonely, windswept
housing area. There must have been a preflight briefing, though
he could not remember one. He had written Marcella, telling
her why he had to go; putting down all the fine phrases that
were true until saying them into the Voisriit made them false,
then erased it all. He had been a boy — no older than the Commandant was now. Could such boys fight? He thrust the
thought aside, knowing that they could; that the marines would
fight very well, having been selected for the purpose.

"You asked the briefing officer a question," the Commandant
continued. "I forget now what it was. I was thinking of something else."

"I probably did," Johann conceded.

Outside, the marines were still reviving, straightening their uniforms and shining their boots; checking the weapons they had carried with them into their suspension pods. One of them, a highbreasted girl with yellow curls straying from under her battle-helmet, asked him if it had really been seventeen years. He said that it had, and added that she had not missed a great deal—then turned away quickly for fear that she would turn away from him.

So he had asked the briefing officer a question. That was unlike him. It must have been important—or he had thought it important. It was probably still on tape somewhere on the ship. Not on Earth. Few if any tapes would have outlasted the accidents of even a single century, and no one would care about that one now. Marcella and the briefing officer were both dead. Possibly they had met, years after blast-off, and never realized that they were linked through him.

There was as yet no guard at the boat-hangar entrance, but there would be soon, surely. When the mutiny came, the Captain would want to cut off the mutineers' escape. Johann pushed aside the thought that she might also wish to retain a path of escape for herself—most probably the mutiny would not begin, if it began at all, until she had gone.

But was she leaving? It was contrary to regulations for the Captain to disembark save in a friendly port—but there was no regulation to say that she could not *announce* that she intended to do so. He pressed the green button, and the hangar door slid up with a sigh of compressed air. "Me," the boat nearest the door said. "Me, me, me," echoed the sound.

"Which of you brought Lieutenant Helmut back?" (His own voice sounded strange in the vastness.)

"I did," called a boat from half a kilometer away.

"Have any of the rest of you been used lately?"

"No," said several voices; and one, "Never, since blastoff, Boat-captain."

"Then you are all fully stored?"

"All but he."

They were of four types: landing craft of the design that had been used to take Helmut and his subordinates down; lifeboats intended for use in a sub-Plutonian emergency; missile-boats for short-range attack; and tenders for exterior alterations and repairs. A missile-boat might make them think twice about going after him, but they were the largest of all, and would be the most difficult to conceal once planetfall was made. In the end he settled on a tender, Number 37, transferring food and water and survival gear from one of the lifeboats into it and instructing it to wait for him at a hatch near the bridge. "Go now," his shadow said, a small, dry voice close beside his ear.

He shook his head. "There are some things I want to take with me. My books—and I'm going to try to get Grit to come if I can."

"Hello." It was Helmut, appearing in the space between Numbers 17 and 18. "Who are you talking to, Johann?"

"Myself, I'm afraid. Welcome back."

"It's good to be back," Helmut said. "Good to get out of that stinking breathmask. Do you know if Karl and the others have made any progress with the bugs yet?"

"I don't know what you're talking about."

"The airborne bacteria. If they can show they don't infect human beings, or cook up a vaccine, we won't have to wear the things. You wouldn't think there would be such a stew of single-celled organisms floating around in a place that's as dry as that one, but there are."

"There's water in the crevasses," Johann said, "and thicker air too. From an evolutionary point of view, I suppose they got their start in the spray from the falls."

"You haven't been down to see those crevasses yourself, of course."

"No."

"I knew you hadn't. I could tell by your arms and legs. You've never set foot on Neuerddraht."

"I don't know how I got scratched up like this."

"I don't know either," Helmut said. "Even though I'm scratched up the same way. You've got strict orders not to talk, I take it; but I noticed while I was down there how often Elis seemed to be filling in for you, now that I come to think of it."

"I've never been there," Johann said again. He touched the crusted welts on his legs. "I was scraped a bit in a little accident. I'll tell you about it."

"Of course." Helmut was no longer listening. "Who would suspect that she'd send you, the cripple." He took a step nearer, and Johann saw his right hand slip under the flap of his gadget bag. "We were the public expedition; you were her private one—after all, control of a world is at stake. She couldn't risk that. What were you looking for? We saw you once, you know."

"That's right," Johann said, "you saw me." He was tensed, waiting for the blow, but it came too quickly. He had expected Helmut to raise the knife over his head and strike downward as he would have done himself. Instead, Helmut's hand shot straight forward as soon as it cleared the lip of the bag.

Somewhere between the bag and his body it became enmeshed in what might have been thousands of folds of black tissue. The knife struck like a punch from a heavily padded glove; but there was no blade, nothing that stabbed. Anchoring himself with his stiff leg, he aimed a kick at Helmut's testicles. It missed, and Johann slipped his feet from his sandals as the boats shrilled warnings, and jumped for the hangar roof.

The evasion was unnecessary. Helmut's knife was free now, but the black tissue covered his face. Johann watched... he went limp, his sandals pinioning him still to the steel deck, his slack body floating like a balloon on a string. From under the dark covering came a continued soft grunting that soon grew weak, then stopped.

For a long time after it seemed certain Helmut was dead, the tissue remained in place; then it returned to Johann, becoming a cloud, a thin, dark smoke that seeped upward to him. "I didn't know you could leave me," he said.

"I do not desire it."

Outside the hangar door, a marine sentry had died. The sight of her limp corpse made Johann wonder with which group Helmut had been affiliated. The occultists seemed the more probable in view of his personality, and there were slashes at the girl's chest and crotch that might have been ritualistically intended.

Perhaps to no group but his own advantage; possibly to a group of which Johann had never heard.

The storage-area corridors and companionways he traveled now were deserted, though from time to time he heard the faint sound of shouting through the ventilators, and twice he came on bodies—one of them a man he knew slightly, a technician from the instrument shop. So it had already begun. It seemed likely that the Captain's absence from the bridge had been interpreted by at least one group to mean that she had left for Neuerddraht.

When he reached the main corridor system he took off his blouse with its officer's insignia and threw it down a recycle chute. There were more bodies, some patrolers, many crewmen, a few in battle-green marine uniforms, floating, or sticking to the walls and floor; and neutron-blast scars from the marines' guns on the bulkhead panels. Whichever group was attacking would be pushing toward the principal approaches to the bridge; and they had clearly dislodged the marines from this section. As he hurried toward the rear entrance to the Captain's living compartment, he wondered if any effort had been made to organize and arm the loyal crewpeople — there must be many, surely, and there could be no more than a few hundred marines.

The sentries were dead, but the door to the Captain's compartment was still closed and locked, as he had expected. He pounded on it and waited and pounded again; and the dark mist of his shadow poured into the crevice between door and jamb, and after a moment the door swung open at a touch.

On the bridge, the Captain, with Elis, Gerta, and Grit, stood watching the console communicator screen. It showed a group of crewpeople clustered around a laboratory cart, assembling what appeared to be a laser projector. "The mystics?" Johann asked.

They turned to look at him with black faces. "The C.O.C.," Grit said after a moment. "When they have that thing finished, they're going to splice a power cable to the starboard generators and cut their way through to us. The marines are holding A and B corridors outside, but when the beam starts coming through the walls there won't be much they can do. We haven't told them yet. If you want to use the earphones at the terminal, the overmonitor will be happy to explain the whole plan; we've heard enough. And if—"

The Captain cut off Grit's panicky voice. "How did you get in here, Lieutenant?"

"Through your quarters, sir."

"That way is open?"

"The corridor was clear when I came through, yes."

Grit looked from the Captain's face to Elis's, her eyes asking if Johann could be trusted, then pleading that they go. Her shadow was blacker than the others', and Johann wondered if it had spoken to her yet. On the communicator screen, Helmut entered the laboratory where the technicians were building the laser, asked some question, and gave a brisk command. An emotion that might have been hatred or despair flickered across the

Captain's face. "He is one of them too, you see," she said. "And Horst, and my servant, whom I had to shoot."

"I see," Johann said. And then, "Sir, I have a tender waiting at Hatch Eight."

Gerta, breaking the discipline of seventeen years, said, "There is nowhere to go."

"There is Neuerddraht," the Captain snapped.

Johann said, "The crevasses." He thought of the long cascades of silvery water and the leaves of the ferns like cathedrals of arches.

Elis nodded. "You're right — they'd never locate us in one of those."

The Captain had already picked up the ship's logbook and tucked it under her left arm. At her side her right hand held a small, brightly polished neutron pistol; the muzzle pointed toward the floor plates, but one long, tapered finger was curled about the trigger. "You are coming with us," she said to Johann.

He nodded. "Naturally."

"I don't want you to think I don't trust you, but you weren't on the bridge when the attack began. And there have been so many traitors."

"I understand."

"If we reach Hatch Eight in safety, and the tender is there as you say, your loyalty will be established beyond question." Johann nodded and took a step in the direction of the Captain's quarters. She nodded at Grit, smiled, and said: "Go on, girl. I'll bring up the rear." A moment later Elis, who was just behind Johann, whispered: "So that's the way it's going to be now. You and I will have to make do with Gerta, at least for a while."

The corridor was still empty save for a few dead, but smoke, acrid with burning insulation, was billowing from the ventilators. A few hundred meters beyond the door of the Captain's quarters the corridor ended at a hatch, and the termination board that should have directed them to a new connection was blank. "It's fighting, too," Elis said.

Johann turned to look at him. (Behind him Grit seemed two women, her shadow leaning across her shoulders like a conspirator.)

"The overmonitor. It's not just its people—the overmonitor program itself is fighting," Elis said.

Grit whispered: "It could cut us off, couldn't it? Sever all the corridors and just leave us drifting. We'd never get out."

"We have to go back!" Johann called to the Captain. Under his urging they doubled their straggling column and took the first promising side corridor.

"It will cut us off," Grit said again. "Leave us floating in space."

"If it cuts off the bridge it will lose the instruments and controls. It couldn't operate the ship."

"But we're not *on* the bridge—not any more. Do you think it knows where we are?" No one answered her.

"It's gone mad," the Captain said when they had been pushing down the new corridor for what seemed a half hour or more. "This is leading to the hydroponics module. It's got the hydro deck coupled to the bridge complex."

Elis had dropped behind her, and Grit, stumbling, was leaning on Johann's arm. She said, "She's right, I can smell the plants." Her round, soft face was beaded with sweat. Then she was gone.

Gerta, who had been behind her, stood openmouthed; the others did not notice Grit was no longer with them. Pushing past the tall girl, Johann shouted: "Is there a hatch anywhere in the hydro module? There has to be. Where is it?"

"Number Three Ninety-One," Elis told him. "I think the overmonitor's trying to get us away from Number Eight; it must have heard you talking about it."

"Where is it?" Johann said again.

"I don't know, because I don't know where we'll be coming into the module."

"Run," Johann said, taking Gerta by the arm. "She's gone to get the tender, I think."

The corridor corkscrewed, then opened into a vaulted hall several thousand meters long in which towering, darkly green plants grew under brilliant lights, tier upon tier, extending impossible limbs and tendrils, untroubled by gravity, on the quiet air.

They found the hatch at the end of a tortuous path of green that might almost have wound through a jungle. There were bowers under the trees, where colored hand ropes stretched above the sopping cellulose that contained the hydroponic fluid; and twice Johann glimpsed strange statues moored to limbs, set deeper in the green twilight beneath the leaves. Grit, Johann remembered, had said Rudi was a technician here.

At the hatch, Gerta and Elis spun the operating wheel. "Suppose she's not out there?" the Captain demanded. "How could she be? This is insane." The lips of the hatch pursed, then stretched; beyond them was the brightly lit interior of the tender.

"Am I still to go first?" Johann said.

A slight smile crossed the Captain's face. "You're not thinking of a honeymoon on Neuerddraht with little Grit, are you, Lieutenant? No, you come last — but I can hardly wait for you to come aboard so you can tell me how you arranged this."

Etiquette demanded that the Captain enter a boat last. Elis bolted through the hatch. "We defer to your rank," the Captain said to Johann. "After all, you were the leader of the escape." She climbed in behind Elis.

Gerta was watching Johann's face. He shook his head, moving it perhaps a centimeter to either side; she hesitated, then closed the hatch. He slammed down the security bolt. "What are we going to do now?" she said. The silence of the plants, their happiness and green need, closed around them. His shadow stood before him on the hatch, a silhouette as black as a hole in space.

"Hide here," he said. "I'll come back for you." And then, "Back to the bridge." He closed his eyes.

The wall communicator screen was focused to space; in it the tender shot away from the ship like a stone from a sling. The small screen on the control console showed Horst and Helmut standing beside the laser projector, and behind them the corridor leading to the bridge. "No bargaining," Helmut said. "Get on the squawk box and tell the marines to lay down their weapons. Tell them the overmonitor's won."

Johann walked to the doors leading to the corridor and flung them open. The Marine Commandant was at a field communications center there, surrounded by subordinate officers and clerks.

"How are things going?" Johann asked.

The Commandant threw him a casual salute. "Pretty well. We've cleared the command corridor—as you see—and we have A, B, and D largely under control. We lost a lot of the sentries we had posted around, though, and there's been quite a bit of smoke."

Johann nodded. "I know. I suspect the computer's been frying some of its own guts to make it."

A marine lieutenant said, "Most of the prisoners we've gotten so far have belonged to these nut religions rather than the C.O.C."

The Commandant gestured toward the bridge. "You must be getting the overall picture better than we do out here. How does it look in there?"

"I think we've turned the corner," Johann said. He went back inside and closed the doors, then with a screwdriver from the emergency tool locker beside the navigation panel took up the floor plates between the communicator cabinet and the computer terminal. Whoever had spliced the two together—probably Horst, Johann thought, possibly Uschi—had used bright scarlet wire and added the sacrifice of a rat with its throat cut, tied in a clear food-preservation bag. To the terminal he said: "Helmut is dead. You shouldn't have shown him. We killed him in the hangar."

He ripped the connections free and watched the computer-generated phantoms vanish; then stood up, regretting the loss of his officer's tunic. Coding "all screens" on the communicator, he announced: "The mutiny is over. I believe that some of you who have been fighting against the bridge have been encouraged by optimistic reports on the communications system. Those reports were false, and they will not be repeated; you were defeated some time ago, when the attempt to carry the bridge by storm failed.

"Now all hands are needed to save the ship. Mutineers laying aside their weapons are hereby given a full pardon. Every loyal member of the crew is expected to join in wiping out those who continue to bear arms. This is your Captain speaking. Out."

To the overmonitor terminal he said, "What is the probability of ship survival now?" He switched out the earphones and keyed the speaker.

"*Response:* For a five-year projection, 0.383 and rising. Do you plan frequent consultations with the overmonitor?"

"No," the Captain said.

In a storm, land was the enemy. He kicked off his sandals and floated over to the navigation panel to begin the laborious business of setting a new course.

THE NEW ATLANTIS

Ursula K. Le Guin

Ursula K. Le Guin lives in Oregon, but she was born and reared in California. Her father was the great anthropologist Alfred Kroeber, and her mother, Theodora Kroeber, wrote that celebrated account of American Indian life, Ishi in Two Worlds. *Ms. Le Guin's first science-fiction stories were published in 1962, and her first novel appeared in 1966; but it was with the publication of her novel* The Left Hand of Darkness *in 1969 that she took her place as one of the major figures in modern science fiction. The book received both the Hugo and Nebula awards as the years best s-f novel — a rare double triumph — and is recognized today as a classic in the field, a standard item on the reading lists of the innumerable science-fiction courses taught in high schools and universities. Since then she has published several more novels and a number of shorter pieces, for one of which, the novella "The Word for World Is Forest" she collected her second Hugo in 1973. Ms. Le Guin is also the author of a series of fantasy novels for young readers. One of these,* The Farthest Shore, *received the National Book Award in 1973.*

~~~

Coming back from my Wilderness Week I sat by an odd sort of man in the bus. For a long time we didn't talk; I was mending stockings and he was reading. Then the bus broke down a few miles outside Gresham. Boiler trouble, the way it generally is when the driver insists on trying to go over thirty. It was a Supersonic Superscenic Deluxe Longdistance coal-burner, with Home Comfort, that means a toilet, and the seats were pretty comfortable, at least those that hadn't yet worked loose from their bolts, so everybody waited inside the bus; besides, it was raining. We began talking, the way people do when there's a breakdown and a wait. He held up his pamphlet and tapped it—he was a dry-looking man with a schoolteacherish way of using his hands—and said, "This is interesting. I've been reading that a new continent is rising from the depths of the sea."

The blue stockings were hopeless. You have to have something besides holes to darn onto. "Which sea?"

"They're not sure yet. Most specialists think the Atlantic. But there's evidence it may be happening in the Pacific, too."

"Won't the oceans get a little crowded?" I said, not taking it seriously. I was a bit snappish, because of the breakdown and because those blue stockings had been good warm ones.

He tapped the pamphlet again and shook his head, quite serious. "No," he said. "The old continents are sinking, to make room for the new. You can see that that is happening."

You certainly can. Manhattan Island is now under eleven feet of water at low tide, and there are oyster beds in Ghirardelli Square.

"I thought that was because the oceans are rising from polar melt."

He shook his head again. "That is a factor. Due to the greenhouse effect of pollution, indeed Antarctica may become inhabitable. But climatic factors will not explain the emergence of the new—or, possibly, very old—continents in the Atlantic and Pacific." He went on explaining about continental drift, but I liked the idea of inhabiting Antarctica and daydreamed about it for a while. I thought of it as very empty, very quiet, all white and blue, with a faint golden glow northward from the unrising sun behind the long peak of Mount Erebus. There were a few people there; they were very quiet, too, and wore white tie and tails. Some of them carried oboes and violas. Southward the white land went up in a long silence toward the Pole.

Just the opposite, in fact, of the Mount Hood Wilderness Area. It had been a tiresome vacation. The other women in the dormitory were all right, but it was macaroni for breakfast, and there were so many organized sports. I had looked forward to the hike up to the National Forest Preserve, the largest forest left in the United States, but the trees didn't look at all the way they do in the postcards and brochures and Federal Beautification Bureau advertisements. They were spindly, and they all had little signs on saying which union they had been planted by. There were actually a lot more green picnic tables and cement Men's and Women's than there were trees. There was an electrified fence all around the forest to keep out unauthorized persons. The forest ranger talked about mountain jays, "bold little robbers," he said, "who will come and snatch the sandwich from your very hand," but I didn't see any. Perhaps because that was the weekly Watch Those Surplus Calories! Day for all the women, and so we didn't have any sandwiches. If I'd seen a mountain jay I might have snatched the sandwich from his very hand, who knows. Anyhow it was an exhausting week, and I wished I'd stayed home and practiced, even though I'd have lost a week's pay because staying home and practicing the viola doesn't count as planned implementation of recreational leisure as defined by the Federal Union of Unions.

When I came back from my Antarctican expedition, the man was reading again, and I got a look at his pamphlet; and that was the odd part of it. The pamphlet was called "Increasing Efficiency in Public Accountant Training Schools," and I could see from the one paragraph I got a glance at that there was nothing about new continents emerging from the ocean depths in it— nothing at all.

Then we had to get out and walk on into Gresham, because they had decided that the best thing for us all to do was get onto the Greater Portland Area Rapid Public Transit Lines, since there had been so many breakdowns that the charter bus company didn't have any more buses to send out to pick us up. The walk was wet, and rather dull, except when we passed the Cold Mountain Commune. They have a wall around it to keep out unauthorized persons, and a big neon sign out front saying COLD MOUNTAIN COMMUNE and there were some people in authentic jeans and ponchos by the highway selling macrame belts and sandcast candles and soybean bread to the tourists. In Gresham, I took the 4:40 GPARPTL Superjet Flyer train to Burnside and East 230th, and then walked to 217th and got the bus to the Goldschmidt Overpass, and transferred to the shuttlebus, but it had boiler trouble, so I didn't reach the downtown transfer point until ten after eight, and the buses go on a once-an-hour schedule at 8:00, so I got a meatless hamburger at the Longhorn Inch-Thick Steak House Dinerette and caught the nine o'clock bus and got home about ten. When I let myself into the apartment I flipped the switch to turn on the lights, but there still weren't any. There had been a power outage in West Portland for three weeks. So I went feeling about for the candles in the dark, and it was a minute or so before I noticed that somebody was lying on my bed.

I panicked, and tried again to turn the lights on.

It was a man, lying there in a long thin heap. I thought a burglar had got in somehow while I was away and died. I opened the door so I could get out quick or at least my yells could be heard, and then I managed not to shake long enough to strike a match, and lighted the candle, and came a little closer to the bed.

The light disturbed him. He made a sort of snorting in his throat and turned his head. I saw it was a stranger, but I knew his eyebrows, then the breadth of his closed eyelids, then I saw my husband.

He woke up while I was standing there over him with the candle in my hand. He laughed and said still half-asleep, "Ah, Psyche! From the regions which are holy land."

Neither of us made much fuss. It was unexpected, but it did seem so natural for him to be there, after all, much more natural than for him not to be there, and he was too tired to be very emotional. We lay there together in the dark, and he explained that they had released him from the Rehabilitation Camp early because he had injured his back in an accident in the gravel quarry, and they were afraid it might get worse. If he died there it wouldn't be good publicity abroad, since there have been some nasty rumors about deaths from illness in the Rehabilitation Camps and the Federal Medical Association Hospitals; and there are scientists abroad who have heard of Simon, since somebody published his proof of Goldbach's Hypothesis in Peking. So they let him out early, with eight dollars in his pocket, which is what he had in his pocket when they arrested him, which made it, of course, fair. He had walked and hitched home from Coeur D'Alene, Idaho, with a couple of days in jail in Walla Walla for being caught hitchhiking. He almost fell asleep telling me this, and when he had told me, he did fall asleep. He needed a change of clothes and a bath but I didn't want to wake him. Besides, I was tired, too. We lay side by side and his head was on my arm. I don't suppose that I have ever been so happy. No; was it happiness? Something wider and darker, more like knowledge, more like the night: joy.

It was dark for so long, so very long. We were all blind. And there was the cold, a vast, unmoving, heavy cold. We could not move at all. We did not move. We did not speak. Our mouths were closed, pressed shut by the cold and by the weight. Our eyes were pressed shut. Our limbs were held still. Our minds were held still. For how long? There was no length of time; how long is death? And is one dead only after living, or before life as well? Certainly we thought, if we thought anything, that we were dead; but if we had ever been alive, we had forgotten it.

There was a change. It must have been the pressure that changed first, although we did not know it. The eyelids are sensitive to touch. They must have been weary of being shut. When the pressure upon them weakened a little, they opened. But there was no way for us to know that. It was too cold for us to feel anything. There was nothing to be seen. There was black.

But then—"then," for the event created time, created before and after, near and far, now and then—"then" there was the light. One light. One small, strange light that passed slowly, at what distance we could not tell. A small, greenish white, slightly blurred point of radiance, passing.

Our eyes were certainly open, "then," for we saw it. We saw the moment. The moment is a point of light. Whether in darkness or in the field of all light, the moment is small, and moves, but not quickly. And "then" it is gone.

It did not occur to us that there might be another moment. There was no reason to assume that there might be more than one. One was marvel enough: that in all the field of the dark, in the cold, heavy, dense, moveless, timeless, placeless, boundless black, there should have occurred, once, a small slightly blurred, moving light! Time need be created only once, we thought.

But we were mistaken. The difference between one and more than one is all the difference in the world. Indeed, that difference is the world.

The light returned.

The same light, or another one? There was no telling.

But, "this time," we wondered about the light: Was it small and near to us, or large and far away? Again there was no telling; but there was something about the way it moved, a trace of hesitation, a tentative quality, that did not seem proper to anything large and remote. The stars, for instance. We began to remember the stars.

The stars had never hesitated.

Perhaps the noble certainty of their gait had been a mere effect of distance. Perhaps in fact they had hurtled wildly, enormous furnace-fragments of a primal bomb thrown through the cosmic dark; but time and distance soften all agony. If the universe, as seems likely, began with an act of destruction, the stars we had used to see told no tales of it. They had been implacably serene.

The planets, however... We began to remember the planets. They had suffered certain changes both of appearance and of course. At certain times of the year Mars would reverse its direction and go backward through the stars. Venus had been brighter and less bright as she went through her phases of crescent, full, and wane. Mercury had shuddered like a skidding drop of rain on the sky flushed with daybreak. The light we now watched had that erratic, trembling quality. We saw it, unmistakably, change direction and go backward. It then grew smaller and fainter; blinked — an eclipse? — and slowly disappeared.

Slowly, but not slowly enough for a planet.

Then — the third "then"! — arrived the indubitable and positive Wonder of the World, the Magic Trick, watch now, watch, you will not believe your eyes, mama, mama, look what I can do —

Seven lights in a row, proceeding fairly rapidly, with a darting movement, from left to right. Proceeding less rapidly from right to left, two dimmer, greenish lights. Two-lights halt, blink, reverse course, proceed hastily and in a wavering manner from left to right. Seven-lights increase speed, and catch up. Two-lights flash desperately, flicker, and are gone.

Seven-lights hang still for some while, then merge gradually into one streak, veering away, and little by little vanish into the immensity of the dark.

But in the dark now are growing other lights, many of them: lamps, dots, rows, scintillations — some near at hand, some far. Like the stars, yes, but not stars. It is not the great Existences we are seeing, but only the little lives.

In the morning Simon told me something about the Camp, but not until after he had had me check the apartment for bugs. I thought at first he had been given behavior mod and gone paranoid. We never had been infested. And I'd been living alone for a year and a half; surely they didn't want to hear me talking to myself? But he said, "They may have been expecting me to come here."

"But they let you go free!"

He just lay there and laughed at me. So I checked everywhere we could think of. I didn't find any bugs, but it did look as if somebody had gone through the bureau drawers while I was away in the Wilderness. Simon's papers were all at Max's, so that didn't matter. I made tea on the Primus, and washed and shaved Simon with the extra hot water in the kettle—he had a thick beard and wanted to get rid of it because of the lice he had brought from Camp—and while we were doing that he told me about the Camp. In fact he told me very little, but not much was necessary.

He had lost about 20 pounds. As he only weighed 140 to start with, this left little to go on with. His knees and wrist bones stuck out like rocks under the skin. His feet were all swollen and chewed-looking from the Camp boots; he hadn't dared take the boots off, the last three days of walking, because he was afraid he wouldn't be able to get them back on. When he had to move or sit up so I could wash him, he shut his eyes.

"Am I really here?" he asked. "Am I here?"

"Yes," I said. "You are here. What I don't understand is how you got here."

"Oh, it wasn't bad so long as I kept moving. All you need is to know where you're going—to have someplace to go. You know, some of the people in Camp, if they'd let them go, they wouldn't have had that. They couldn't have gone anywhere. Keeping moving was the main thing. See, my back's all seized up, now."

When he had to get up to go to the bathroom he moved like a ninety-year-old. He couldn't stand straight, but was all bent out of shape, and shuffled. I helped him put on clean clothes. When he lay down on the bed again, a sound of pain came out of him, like tearing thick paper. I went around the room putting things away. He asked me to come sit by him and said I was going to drown him if I went on crying. "You'll submerge the entire North American continent," he said. I can't remember what he said, but he made me laugh finally. It is hard to remember things Simon says, and hard not to laugh when he says them. This is not merely the partiality of affection: He makes everybody laugh. I doubt that he intends to. It is just that a mathematician's mind works differently from other people's. Then when they laugh, that pleases him.

It was strange, and it is strange, to be thinking about "him," the man I have known for ten years, the same man, while "he" lay there changed out of recognition, a different man. It is enough to make you understand why most languages have a word like "soul." There are various degrees of death, and time spares us none of them. Yet something endures, for which a word is needed.

I said what I had not been able to say for a year and a half: "I was afraid they'd brainwash you."

He said, "Behavior mod is expensive. Even just the drugs. They save it mostly for the VIPs. But I'm afraid they got a notion I might be important after all. I got questioned a lot the last couple of months. About my 'foreign contacts.'" He snorted. "The stuff that got published abroad, I suppose. So I want to be careful and make sure it's just a Camp again next time, and not a Federal Hospital."

"Simon, were they... are they cruel, or just righteous?"

He did not answer for a while. He did not want to answer. He knew what I was asking. He knew by what thread hangs hope, the sword, above our heads.

"Some of them..." he said at last, mumbling.

Some of them had been cruel. Some of them had enjoyed their work. You cannot blame everything on society.

"Prisoners, as well as guards," he said.

You cannot blame everything on the enemy.

"Some of them, Belle," he said with energy, touching my hand — "some of them, there were men like gold there—"

The thread is tough; you cannot cut it with one stroke.

"What have you been playing?" he asked.

"Forrest, Schubert."

"With the quartet?"

"Trio, now. Janet went to Oakland with a new lover."

"Ah, poor Max."

"It's just as well, really. She isn't a good pianist."

I make Simon laugh, too, though I don't intend to. We talked until it was past time for me to go to work. My shift since the Full Employment Act last year is ten to two. I am an inspector in a recycled paper bag factory. I have never rejected a bag yet; the electronic inspector catches all the defective ones first. It is a rather depressing job. But it's only four hours a day, and it takes more time than that to go through all the lines and physical and mental examinations, and fill out all the forms, and talk to all the welfare counselors and inspectors every week in order to qualify as Unemployed, and then line up every day for the ration stamps and the dole. Simon thought I ought to go to work as usual. I tried to, but I couldn't. He had felt very hot to the touch when I kissed him good-bye. I went instead and got a black-market doctor. A girl at the factory had recommended her, for an abortion, if I ever wanted one without going through the regulation two years of sex-depressant drugs the fed-meds make you take when they give you an abortion. She was a jeweler's assistant in a shop on Alder Street, and the girl said she was convenient because if you didn't have enough cash you could leave something in pawn at the jeweler's as payment.

Nobody ever does have enough cash, and of course credit cards aren't worth much on the black market.

The doctor was willing to come at once, so we rode home on the bus together. She gathered very soon that Simon and I were married, and it was funny to see her look at us and smile like a cat. Some people love illegality for its own sake. Men, more often than women. It's men who make laws, and enforce them, and break them, and think the whole performance is wonderful. Most women would rather just ignore them. You could see that this woman, like a man, actually enjoyed breaking them. That may have been what put her into an illegal business in the first place, a preference for the shady side. But there was more to it than that. No doubt she'd wanted to be a doctor, too; and the Federal Medical Association doesn't admit women into the medical schools. She probably got her training as some other doctor's private pupil, under the counter. Very much as Simon learned mathematics, since the universities don't teach much but Business Administration and Advertising and Media Skills any more. However she learned it, she seemed to know her stuff. She fixed up a kind of homemade traction device for Simon very handily and informed him that if he did much more walking for two months he'd be crippled the rest of his life, but if he behaved himself he'd just be more or less lame. It isn't the kind of thing you'd expect to be grateful for being told, but we both were. Leaving, she gave me a bottle of about two hundred plain white pills, unlabeled. "Aspirin," she said. "He'll be in a good deal of pain off and on for weeks."

I looked at the bottle. I had never seen aspirin before, only the Super-Buffered Pane-Gon and the Triple-Power N-L-G-Zic and the Extra-Strength Apansprin with the miracle ingredient more doctors recommend, which the fed-meds always give you prescriptions for, to be filled at your FMA-approved private enterprise friendly drugstore at the low, low prices established by the Pure Food and Drug Administration in order to inspire competitive research.

"Aspirin," the doctor repeated. "The miracle ingredient more doctors recommend." She cat-grinned again. I think she liked us because we were living in sin. That bottle of black-market aspirin was probably worth more than the old Navajo bracelet I pawned for her fee.

I went out again to register Simon as temporarily domiciled at my address and to apply for Temporary Unemployment Compensation ration stamps for him. They only give them to you for two weeks and you have to come every day; but to register him as Temporarily Disabled meant getting the signatures of two fed-meds, and I thought I'd rather put that off for a while. It took three hours to go through the lines and get the forms he would have to fill out, and to answer the 'crats' questions about why he wasn't there in person. They smelled something fishy. Of course it's hard for them to prove that two people are married and aren't just adultering if you move now and then and your friends help out by sometimes registering one of you as living at their address; but they had all the back files on both of us and it was obvious that we had been around each other for a suspiciously long time. The State really does make things awfully hard for itself. It must have been simpler to enforce the laws back when marriage was legal and adultery was what got you into trouble. They only had to catch you once. But I'll bet people broke the law just as often then as they do now.

The lantern-creatures came close enough at last that we could see not only their light, but their bodies in the illumination of their light. They were not pretty. They were dark colored, most often a dark red, and they were all mouth. They ate one another whole. Light swallowed light all swallowed together in the vaster mouth of the darkness. They moved slowly, for nothing, however small and hungry, could move fast under that weight, in that cold. Their eyes, round with fear, were never closed. Their bodies were tiny and bony behind the gaping jaws. They wore queer, ugly decorations on their lips and skulls: fringes, serrated wattles, featherlike fronds, gauds, bangles, lures. Poor little sheep of the deep pastures! Poor ragged, hunch-jawed dwarfs squeezed to the bone by the weight of the darkness, chilled to the bone by the cold of the darkness, tiny monsters burning with bright hunger, who brought us back to life!

Occasionally, in the wan, sparse illumination of one of the lantern-creatures, we caught a momentary glimpse of other, large, unmoving shapes: the barest suggestion, off in the distance, not of a wall, nothing so solid and certain as a wall, of a surface, an angle... Was it there?

Or something would glitter, faint, far off, far down. There was no use trying to make out what it might be. Probably it was only a fleck of sediment, mud or mica, disturbed by a struggle between the lantern-creatures, flickering like a bit of diamond dust as it rose and settled slowly. In any case, we could not move to go see what it was. We had not even the cold, narrow freedom of the lantern-creatures. We were immobilized, borne down, still shadows among the half-guessed shadow walls. Were we there?

The lantern-creatures showed no awareness of us. They passed before us, among us, perhaps even through us – it was impossible to be sure. They were not afraid, or curious.

Once something a little larger than a hand came crawling near, and for a moment we saw quite distinctly the clean angle where the foot of a wall rose from the pavement, in the glow cast by the crawling creature, which was covered with a foliage of plumes, each plume dotted with many tiny, bluish points of light. We saw the pavement beneath the creature and the wall beside it, heartbreaking in its exact, clear linearity, its opposition to all that was fluid, random, vast, and void. We saw the creature's claws, slowly reaching out and retracting like small stiff fingers, touch the wall. Its plumage of light quivering, it dragged itself along and vanished behind the corner of the wall.

So we knew that the wall was there; and that it was an outer wall, a housefront, perhaps, or the side of one of the towers of the city.

We *remembered the towers. We remembered the city. We had for-gotten it. We had forgotten who we were; but we remembered the city, now.*

When I got home, the FBI had already been there. The computer at the police precinct where I registered Simon's address must have flashed it right over to the computer at the FBI building. They had questioned Simon for about an hour, mostly about what he had been doing during the twelve days it took him to get from the Camp to Portland. I suppose they thought he had flown to Peking or something. Having a police record in Walla Walla for hitchhiking helped him establish his story. He told me that one of them had gone to the bathroom. Sure enough I found a bug stuck on the top of the bathroom door frame. I left it, as we figured it's really better to leave it when you know you have one, than to take it off and then never be sure they haven't planted another one you don't know about. As Simon said, if we felt we had to say something unpatriotic we could always flush the toilet at the same time.

I have a battery radio—there are so many work stoppages because of power failures, and days the water has to be boiled, and so on, that you really have to have a radio to save wasting time and dying of typhoid—and he turned it on while I was making supper on the Primus. The six o'clock All-American Broadcasting Company news announcer announced that peace was at hand in Uruguay, the president's confidential aide having been seen to smile at a passing blonde as he left the 613th day of the secret negotiations in a villa outside Katmandu. The war in Liberia was going well; the enemy said they had shot down seventeen American planes but the Pentagon said we had shot down twenty-two enemy planes, and the capital city—I forget its name, but it hasn't been inhabitable for seven years anyway—was on the verge of being recaptured by the forces of freedom. The police action in Arizona was also successful. The

Neo-Birch insurgents in Phoenix could not hold out much longer against the massed might of the American army and air force, since their underground supply of small tactical nukes from the Weathermen in Los Angeles had been cut off. Then there was an advertisement for Fed-Cred cards, and a commercial for the Supreme Court: "Take your legal troubles to the Nine Wise Men!" Then there was something about why tariffs had gone up, and a report from the stock market, which had just closed at over two thousand, and a commercial for U.S. Government canned water, with a catchy little tune: "Don't be sorry when you drink/It's not as healthy as you think/Don't you think you really ought to/Drink coo-ool, puu-uure U.S.G. water?"—with three sopranos in close harmony on the last line. Then, just as the battery began to give out and his voice was dying away into a faraway tiny whisper, the announcer seemed to be saying something about: a new continent emerging.

"What was that?"

"I didn't hear," Simon said, lying with his eyes shut and his face pale and sweaty. I gave him two aspirins before we ate. He ate little, and fell asleep while I was washing the dishes in the bathroom. I had been going to practice, but a viola is fairly wakeful in a one-room apartment. I read for a while instead. It was a best seller Janet had given me when she left. She thought it was very good, but then she likes Franz Liszt too. I don't read much since the libraries were closed down, it's too hard to get books; all you can buy is best sellers. I don't remember the title of this one, the cover just said "Ninety Million Copies in Print!!!" It was about small-town sex life in the last century, the dear old 1970s when there weren't any problems and life was so simple and nostalgic. The author squeezed all the naughty thrills he could out of the fact that all the main characters were married. I looked at the end and saw that all the married couples shot each other after all their children became schizophrenic hookers, except for one brave pair that divorced and then leapt into bed together with a clear-eyed pair of govern-ment-employed lovers for eight pages of healthy group sex as a brighter future dawned. I went to bed then, too. Simon was hot, but sleeping quietly. His breathing was like the sound of soft waves far away, and I went out to the dark sea on the sound of them.

I used to go out to the dark sea, often, as a child, falling asleep. I had almost forgotten it with my waking mind. As a child all I had to do was stretch out and think, "the dark sea... the dark sea..." and soon enough *I'd* be there, in the great depths, rocking. But after I grew up it only happened rarely, as a great gift. To know the abyss of the darkness and not to fear it, to entrust oneself to it and whatever may arise from it—what greater gift?

We watched the tiny lights come and go around us, and doing so, we gained a sense of space and of direction—near and far, at least, and higher and lower. It was that sense of space that allowed us to become aware of the currents. Space was no longer entirely still around us, suppressed by the enormous pressure of its own weight. Very dimly we were aware that the cold darkness moved, slowly, softly, pressing against us a little for a long time, then ceasing, in a vast oscillation. The empty darkness flowed slowly along our unmoving unseen bodies; along them, past them; perhaps through them; we could not tell.

Where did they come from, those dim, slow, vast tides? What pres-sure or attraction stirred the deeps to these slow drifting movements? We could not understand that; we could only feel their touch against us, but in straining our sense to guess their origin or end, we became aware of something else: something out there in the darkness of the great currents: sounds. We listened. We heard.

So our sense of space sharpened and localized to a sense of place. For sound is local, as sight is not. Sound is delimited by silence; and it does not rise out of the silence unless it is fairly close, both in space and in time. Though we stand where once the singer stood we cannot hear the voice singing; the years have carried it off on their tides, submerged it. Sound is a fragile thing, a tremor, as delicate as life itself. We may see the stars, but we cannot hear them. Even were the hollowness of outer space an atmosphere, an ether that transmitted the waves of sound, we could not hear the stars; they are too far away. At most if we listened we might hear our own sun, all the mighty, roiling, exploding storm of its burning, as a whisper at the edge of hearing.

A sea wave laps one's feet: It is the shock wave of a volcanic eruption on the far side of the world. But one hears nothing.

A red light flickers on the horizon: It is the reflection in smoke of a city on the distant mainland, burning. But one hears nothing.

Only on the slopes of the volcano, in the suburbs of the city, does one begin to hear the deep thunder; and the high voices crying.

Thus, when we became aware that we were hearing, we were sure that the sounds we heard were fairly close to us. And yet we may have been quite wrong. For we were in a strange place, a deep place. Sound travels fast and far in the deep places, and the silence there is perfect, letting the least noise be heard for hundreds of miles.

And these were not small noises. The lights were tiny, but the sounds were vast: not loud, but very large. Often they were below the range of hearing, long slow vibrations rather than sounds. The first we heard seemed to us to rise up through the currents from beneath us: immense groans, sighs felt along the bone, a rumbling, a deep uneasy whispering.

Later, certain sounds came down to us from above, or borne along the endless levels of the darkness, and these were stranger yet, for they were music. A huge; calling, yearning music from far away in the darkness, calling not to us. Where are you? I am here.

Not to us.

They were the voices of the great souls, the great lives, the lonely ones, the voyagers. Calling. Not often answered. Where are you? Where have you gone?

But the bones, the keels and girders of white bones on icy isles of the South, the shores of bones did not reply.

Nor could we reply. But we listened, and the tears rose in our eyes, salt, not so salt as the oceans, the world-girdling deep bereaved currents, the abandoned roadways of the great lives; not so salt, but warmer.

I am here. Where have you gone?

No answer.

Only the whispering thunder from below.

But we knew now, though we could not answer, we knew because we heard, because we felt, because we wept, we knew that we were; and we remembered other voices.

Max came the next night. I sat on the toilet lid to practice, with the bathroom door shut. The FBI men on the other end of the bug got a solid half hour of scales and doublestops, and then a quite good performance of the Hindemith unaccompanied viola sonata. The bathroom being very small and all hard surfaces, the noise I made was really tremendous. Not a good sound, far too much echo, but the sheer volume was contagious, and I played louder as I went on. The man up above knocked on his floor once; but if I have to listen to the weekly All-American Olympic Games at full blast every Sunday morning from his TV set, then he has to accept Paul Hindemith coming up out of his toilet now and then.

When I got tired I put a wad of cotton over the bug, and came out of the bathroom half-deaf. Simon and Max were on fire. Burning, unconsumed. Simon was scribbling formulae in traction, and Max was pumping his elbows up and down the way he does, like a boxer, and saying "The e - lec - tron emis - sion..." through his nose, with his eyes narrowed, and his mind evidently going light-years per second faster than his tongue, because he kept beginning over and saying "The e - lec - tron emis - sion..." and pumping his elbows.

Intellectuals at work are very strange to look at. As strange as artists. I never could understand how an audience can sit there and *look* at a fiddler rolling his eyes and biting his tongue, or a horn player collecting spit, or a pianist like a black cat strapped to an electrified bench, as if what they *saw* had anything to do with the music.

I damped the fires with a quart of black-market beer — the legal kind is better, but I never have enough ration stamps for beer; I'm not thirsty enough to go without eating — and gradually Max and Simon cooled down. Max would have stayed talking all night, but I drove him out because Simon was looking tired.

I put a new battery in the radio and left it playing in the bathroom, and blew out the candle and lay and talked with Simon; he was too excited to sleep. He said that Max had solved the problems that were bothering them before Simon was sent to Camp, and had fitted Simon's equations to (as Simon put it) the bare facts, which means they have achieved "direct energy conversion." Ten or twelve people have worked on it at different times since Simon published the theoretical part of it when he was twenty-two. The physicist Ann Jones had pointed out right away that the simplest practical application of the theory would be to build a "sun tap," a device for collecting and storing solar energy, only much cheaper and better than the U.S.G. Sola-Heetas that some rich people have on their houses. And it would have been simple only they kept hitting the same snag. Now Max has got around the snag.

I said that Simon published the theory, but that is inaccurate. Of course he's never been able to publish any of his papers, in print; he's not a federal employee and doesn't have a government clearance. But it did get circulated in what the scientists and poets call Sammy's-dot, that is, just handwritten or hectographed. It's an old joke that the FBI arrests everybody with purple fingers, because they have either been hectographing Sammy's-dots, or they have impetigo.

Anyhow, Simon was on top of the mountain that night. His true joy is in the pure math; but he had been working with Clara and Max and the others in this effort to materialize the theory for ten years, and a taste of material victory is a good thing, once in a lifetime.

I asked him to explain what the sun tap would mean to the masses, with me as a representative mass. He explained that it means we can tap solar energy for power, using a device that's easier to build than a jar battery. The efficiency and storage capacity are such that about ten minutes of sunlight will power an apartment complex like ours, heat and lights and elevators and all, for twenty-four hours; and no pollution, particulate, thermal, or radioactive. "There isn't any danger of using up the sun?" I asked. He took it soberly—it was a stupid question, but after all not so long ago people thought there wasn't any danger of using up the earth—and said no, because we wouldn't be pulling out energy, as we did when we mined and lumbered and split atoms, but just using the energy that comes to us anyhow: as the plants, the trees and grass and rosebushes, always have done. "You could call it Flower Power," he said. He was high, high up on the mountain, ski-jumping in the sunlight.

"The State owns us," he said, "because the corporative State has a monopoly on power sources, and there's not enough power to go around. But now, anybody could build a generator on their roof that would furnish enough power to light a city."

I looked out the window at the dark city.

"We could completely decentralize industry and agriculture. Technology could serve life instead of serving capital. We could each run our own life. Power is power!... The State is a machine. We could unplug the machine, now. Power corrupts; absolute power corrupts absolutely. But that's true only when there's a price on power. When groups can keep the power to themselves; when they can use physical power-to in order to exert spiritual power-over; when might makes right. But if power is free? If everybody is equally mighty? Then everybody's got to find a better way of showing that he's right..."

"That's what Mr. Nobel thought when he invented dynamite," I said. "Peace on earth."

He slid down the sunlit slope a couple of thousand feet and stopped beside me in a spray of snow, smiling. "Skull at the banquet," he said, "finger writing on the wall. Be still! Look, don't you see the sun shining on the Pentagon, all the roofs are off, the sun shines at last into the corridors of power... And they shrivel up, they wither away. The green grass grows through the carpets of the Oval Room, the Hot Line is disconnected for nonpayment of the bill. The first thing we'll do is build an electrified fence outside the electrified fence around the White House. The inner one prevents unauthorized persons from getting in. The outer one will prevent authorized persons from getting out..."

Of course he was bitter. Not many people come out of prison sweet.

But it was cruel, to be shown this great hope, and to know that there was no hope for it. He did know that. He knew it right along. He knew that there was no mountain, that he was skiing on the wind.

The tiny lights of the lantern-creatures died out one by one, sank away. The distant lonely voices were silent. The cold, slow currents flowed, vacant, only shaken from time to time by a shifting in the abyss.

It was dark again, and no voice spoke. All dark, dumb, cold.

Then the sun rose.

It was not like the dawns we had begun to remember: the change, manifold and subtle, in the smell and touch of the air; the hush that, instead of sleeping, wakes, holds still, and waits; the appearance of objects, looking gray, vague, and new, as if just created — distant mountains against the eastern sky, one's own hands, the hoary grass full of dew and shadow, the fold in the edge of a curtain hanging by the window — and then, before one is quite sure that one is indeed seeing again, that the light has returned, that day is breaking, the first, abrupt, sweet stammer of a waking bird. And after that the chorus, voice by voice: This is my nest, this is my tree, this is my egg, this is my day, this is my life, here I am, here I am, hurray for me! I'm here! — No, it wasn't like that at all, this dawn. It was completely silent, and it was blue.

In the dawns that we had begun to remember, one did not become aware of the light itself, but of the separate objects touched by the light, the things, the world. They were there, visible again, as if visibility were their own property, not a gift from the rising sun.

In this dawn, there was nothing but the light itself. Indeed there was not even light, we would have said, but only color: blue.

There was no compass bearing to it. It was not brighter in the east. There was no east or west. There was only up and down, below and above. Below was dark. The blue light came from above. Brightness fell. Beneath, where the shaking thunder had stilled, the brightness died away through violet into blindness.

We, arising, watched light fall.

In a way it was more like an ethereal snowfall than like a sunrise. The light seemed to be in discrete particles, infinitesimal flecks, slowly descending, faint, fainter than flecks of fine snow on a dark night, and tinier; but blue. A soft, penetrating blue tending to the violet, the color of the shadows in an iceberg, the color of a streak of sky between gray clouds on a winter afternoon before snow: faint in intensity but vivid in hue: the color of the remote, the color of the cold, the color farthest from the sun.

On Saturday night they held a scientific congress in our room. Clara and Max came, of course, and the engineer Phil Drum and three others who had worked on the sun tap. Phil Drum was very pleased with himself because he had actually built one of the things, a solar cell, and brought it along. I don't think it had occurred to either Max or Simon to build one. Once they knew it could be done they were satisfied and wanted to get on with something else. But Phil unwrapped his baby with a lot of flourish, and people made remarks like, "Mr. Watson, will you come here a minute," and "Hey, Wilbur, you're off the ground!" and "I say, nasty mould you've got there, Alec, why don't you throw it out?" and "Ugh, ugh, burns, burns, wow, ow," the latter from Max, who does look a little pre-Mousterian. Phil explained that he had exposed the cell for one minute at four in the afternoon up in Washington Park during a light rain. The lights were back on on the West Side since Thursday, so we could test it without being conspicuous.

We turned off the lights, after Phil had wired the table-lamp cord to the cell. He turned on the lamp switch. The bulb came on, about twice as bright as before, at its full forty watts—city power of course was never full strength. We all looked at it. It was a dime-store table lamp with a metallized gold base and a white plasticloth shade.

"Brighter than a thousand suns," Simon murmured from the bed.

"Could it be," said Clara Edmonds, "that we physicists have known sin—and have come out the other side?"

"It really wouldn't be any good at all for making bombs with," Max said dreamily.

"Bombs," Phil Drum said with scorn. "Bombs are obsolete. Don't you realize that we could move a mountain with this kind of power? I mean pick up Mount Hood, move it, and set it down. We could thaw Antarctica, we could freeze the Congo. We could sink a continent. Give me a fulcrum and I'll move the world. Well, Archimedes, you've got your fulcrum. The sun."

"Christ," Simon said, "the radio, Belle!"

The bathroom door was shut and I had put cotton over the bug, but he was right; if they were going to go ahead at this rate there had better be some added static. And though I liked watching their faces in the clear light of the lamp—they all had good, interesting faces, well worn, like the handles of wooden tools or the rocks in a running stream — I did not much want to listen to them talk tonight. Not because I wasn't a scientist, that made no difference. And not because I disagreed or disapproved or disbelieved anything they said. Only because it grieved me terribly, their talking. Because they couldn't rejoice aloud over a job done and a discovery made, but had to hide there and whisper about it. Because they couldn't go out into the sun.

I went into the bathroom with my viola and sat on the toilet lid and did a long set of sautillé exercises. Then I tried to work at the Forrest trio, but it was too assertive. I played the solo part from *Harold in Italy*, which is beautiful, but it wasn't quite the right mood either. They were still going strong in the other room. I began to improvise.

After a few minutes in E-minor the light over the shaving mirror began to flicker and dim; then it died. Another outage. The table lamp in the other room did not go out, being connected with the sun, not with the twenty-three atomic fission plants that power the Greater Portland Area. Within two seconds somebody had switched it off, too, so that we shouldn't be the only window in the West Hills left alight; and I could hear them rooting for candles and rattling matches. I went on improvising in the dark. Without light, when you couldn't see all the hard shiny surfaces of things, the sound seemed softer and less muddled. I went on, and it began to shape up. All the laws of harmonics sang together when the bow came down. The strings of the viola were the cords of my own voice, tightened by sorrow, tuned to the pitch of joy. The melody created itself out of air and energy, it raised up the valleys, and the mountains and hills were made low, and the crooked straight, and the rough places plain. And the music went out to the dark sea and sang in the darkness, over the abyss.

When I came out they were all sitting there and none of them was talking. Max had been crying. I could see little candle flames in the tears around his eyes. Simon lay flat on the bed in the shadows, his eyes closed. Phil Drum sat hunched over, holding the solar cell in his hands.

I loosened the pegs, put the bow and the viola in the case, and cleared my throat. It was embarrassing. I finally said, "I'm sorry."

One of the women spoke: Rose Abramski, a private student of Simon's, a big shy woman who could hardly speak at all unless it was in mathematical symbols. "I saw it," she said. "I saw it. I saw the white towers, and the water streaming down their sides, and running back down to the sea. And the sunlight shining in the streets, after ten thousand years of darkness."

"I heard them," Simon said, very low, from the shadow. "I heard their voices."

"Oh, Christ! Stop it!" Max cried out, and got up and went blundering out into the unlit hall, without his coat. We heard him running down the stairs.

"Phil," said Simon, lying there, "could we raise up the white towers, with our lever and our fulcrum?"

After a long silence Phil Drum answered, "We have the power to do it."

"What else do we need?" Simon said. "What else do we need, besides power?"

Nobody answered him.

The blue changed. It became brighter, lighter, and at the same time thicker: impure. The ethereal luminosity of blue-violet turned to turquoise, intense and opaque. Still we could not have said that everything was now turquoise-colored, for there were still no things. There was nothing, except the color of turquoise.

The change continued. The opacity became veined and thinned. The dense, solid color began to appear translucent, transparent. Then it seemed as if we were in the heart of a sacred jade, or the brilliant crystal of a sapphire or an emerald.

As at the inner structure of a crystal, there was no motion. But there was something, now, to see. It was as if we saw the motionless, elegant inward structure of the molecules of a precious stone. Planes and angles appeared about us, shadowless and clear in that even, glowing, blue-green light.

These were the walls and towers of the city, the streets, the windows, the gates.

We knew them, but we did not recognize them. We did not dare to recognize them. It had been so long. And it was so strange. We had used to dream, when we lived in this city. We had lain down, nights, in the rooms behind the windows, and slept, and dreamed. We had all dreamed of the ocean, of the deep sea. Were we not dreaming now?

Sometimes the thunder and tremor deep below us rolled again, but it was faint now, far away; as far away as our memory of the thunder and the tremor and the fire and the towers falling, long ago. Neither the sound nor the memory frightened us. We knew them.

The sapphire light brightened overhead to green, almost green-gold. We looked up. The tops of the highest towers were hard to see, glowing in the radiance of light. The streets and doorways were darker, more clearly defined.

In one of those long, jewel-dark streets something was moving — something not composed of planes and angles, but of curves and arcs. We all turned to look at it, slowly, wondering as we did so at the slow ease of our own motion, our freedom. Sinuous, with a beautiful flowing, gathering, rolling movement, now rapid and now tentative, the thing drifted across the street from a blank garden wall to the recess of a door. There, in the dark blue shadow, it was hard to see for a while. We watched. A pale blue curve appeared at the top of the doorway. A second followed, and a third. The moving thing clung or hovered there, above the door, like a swaying knot of silvery cords or a boneless hand, one arched finger pointing carelessly to something above the lintel of the door, something like itself, but motionless — a carving. A carving in jade light. A carving in stone.

Delicately and easily the long curving tentacle followed the curves of the carved figure, the eight petal-limbs, the round eyes. Did it recognize its image?

The living one swung suddenly, gathered its curves in a loose knot, and darted away down the street, swift and sinuous. Behind it a faint cloud of darker blue hung for a minute and dispersed, revealing again the carved figure above the door: the sea-flower, the cuttlefish, quick, greateyed, graceful, evasive, the cherished sign, carved on a thousand walls, worked into the design of cornices, pavements, handles, lids of jewel boxes, canopies, tapestries, tabletops, gateways.

Down another street, about the level of the first-floor windows, came a flickering drift of hundreds of motes of silver. With a single motion all turned toward the cross street, and glittered off into the dark blue shadows.

There were shadows, now.

We looked up, up from the flight of silverfish, up from the streets where the jade-green currents flowed and the blue shadows fell. We moved and looked up, yearning, to the high towers of our city. They stood, the fallen towers. They glowed in the ever-brightening radiance, not blue or blue-green, up there, but gold. Far above them lay a vast, circular, trembling brightness: the sun's light on the surface of the sea.

We are here. When we break through the bright circle into life, the water will break and stream white down the white sides of the towers, and run down the steep streets back into the sea. The water will glitter in dark hair, on the eyelids of dark eyes, and dry to a thin white film of salt.

We are here.

Whose voice? Who called to us?

He was with me for twelve days. On January 28th the 'crats came from the Bureau of Health, Education and Welfare and said that since he was receiving Unemployment Compensation while suffering from an untreated illness, the government must look after him and restore him to health, because health is the inalienable right of the citizens of a democracy. He refused to sign the consent forms, so the chief health officer signed them. He refused to get up, so two of the policemen pulled him up off the bed. He started to try to fight them. The chief health officer pulled his gun and said that if he continued to struggle he would shoot him for resisting welfare, and arrest me for conspiracy to defraud the government. The man who was holding my arms behind my back said they could always arrest me for unreported pregnancy with intent to form a nuclear family. At that Simon stopped trying to get free. It was really all he was trying to do, not to fight them, just to get his arms free. He looked at me, and they took him out.

He is in the federal hospital in Salem. I have not been able to find out whether he is in the regular hospital or the mental wards.

It was on the radio again yesterday, about the rising land masses in the South Atlantic and the Western Pacific. At Max's the other night I saw a TV special explaining about geophysical stresses and subsidence and faults. The U.S. Geodetic Service is doing a lot of advertising around town, the most common one is a big billboard that says IT'S NOT OUR FAULT! with a picture of a beaver pointing to a schematic map that shows how even if Oregon has a major earthquake and subsidence as California did last month, it will not affect Portland, or only the western suburbs perhaps. The news also said that they plan to halt the tidal waves in Florida by dropping nuclear bombs where Miami was. Then they will reattach Florida to the mainland with landfill. They are already advertising real estate for housing developments on the landfill. The president is staying at the Mile High White House in Aspen, Colorado. I don't think it will do him much good. Houseboats down on the Willamette are selling for $500,000. There are no trains or buses running south from Portland, because all the highways were badly damaged by the tremors and landslides last week, so I will have to see if I can get to Salem on foot. I still have the rucksack I bought for the Mount Hood Wilderness Week. I got some dry lima beans and raisins with my Federal Fair Share Super Value Green Stamp minimal ration book for February—it took the whole book—and Phil Drum made me a tiny camp stove powered with the solar cell. I didn't want to take the Primus, it's too bulky, and I did want to be able to carry the viola. Max gave me a half pint of brandy. When the brandy is gone I expect I will stuff this notebook into the bottle and put the cap on tight and leave it on a hillside somewhere between here and Salem. I like to think of it being lifted up little by little by the water, and rocking, and going out to the dark sea.

Where are you?
We are here. Where have you gone?

A MOMENTARY TASTE OF BEING

James Tiptree, Jr.

James Tiptree, Jr., lives in Virginia, not far from the capital, and prefers to let public attention center on his stories, not on his private life — so not much is generally known about his profession, marital status, childhood and upbringing, and such. He is willing to admit that he is a man of middle years who has traveled widely; all the rest is conjecture, at this point. His first science-fiction stories were published as recently as 1968, and within a few years he had become a favorite of readers for such dazzling tales as "Your Haploid Heart" "Painwise," "The Girl Who Was Plugged In," and "The Women Men Don't See." In 1973 fifteen of his best stories were collected in a volume called Ten Thousand Light-Years from Home. Tiptree's short story Love Is the Plan, the Plan Is Death was voted a Nebula by the Science Fiction Writers of America in 1974.

~~~

> ... A momentary taste
> Of Being from the Well amid the Waste—
> — Khayyam/Fitzgerald

... It floats there visibly engorged, blue-green against the blackness. He stares: It swells, pulsing to a terrifying dim beat, slowly extrudes a great ghostly bulge which extends, solidifies... it is a planet-testicle

97

pushing a monster penis toward the stars. Its blood-beat reverberates through weeping immensities; cold, cold. The parsecs-long phallus throbs, probes blindly under intolerable pressure from within; its tip is a huge cloudy glans lit by a spark: Centaur. In grief it bulges, lengthens, seeking release – stars toll unbearable crescendo...

It is a minute or two before Dr. Aaron Kaye is sure that he is awake in his temporary bunk in *Centaur's* quarantine ward. His own throat is sobbing reflexively, his eyes are weeping, not the stars. Another of the damn dreams. Aaron lies still, blinking, willing the icy grief to let go of his mind.

It lets go. Aaron sits up still cold with meaningless bereavement. What the hell is it, what's tearing at him? "Great Pan is dead," he mutters stumbling to the narrow wash-stall. The lament that echoed round the world... He sluices his head, wishing for his own quarters and Solange. He really should work on these anxiety symptoms. Later, no time now. "Physician, screw thyself," he jeers at the undistinguished, worried face in the mirror.

Oh Jesus – the time! He has overslept while they are doing god knows what to Lory. Why hasn't Coby waked him? Because Lory is his sister, of course; Aaron should have foreseen that.

He hustles out into Isolation's tiny corridor. At one end is a vitrex wall; beyond it his assistant Coby looks up, takes off his headset. Was he listening to music, or what? No matter. Aaron glances into Tighe's cubicle. Tighe's face is still lax, sedated; he has been in sleep-therapy since his episode a week ago. Aaron goes to the speaker grille in the vitrex, draws a cup of hot brew. The liquid falls sluggishly; Isolation is at three-fourths gee in the rotating ship.

"Where's Dr. Kaye – my sister?"

"They've started the interrogation, boss. I thought you needed your sleep." Coby's doubtless meaning to be friendly but his voice has too many sly habits.

"Oh, god." Aaron starts to cycle the cup out, forces himself to drink it. He has a persistent feeling that Lory's alien is now located down below his right heel.

"Doc."

"What?"

"Bruce and Ahlstrom came in while you were asleep. They complain they saw Tighe running around loose this morning."

Aaron frowns. "He hasn't been out, has he?"

"No way. They each saw him separately. I talked them into seeing you, later."

"Yeah. Right." Aaron cycles his cup and heads back up the hall, past a door marked *Interview*. The next is *Observation*. He goes in to a dim closet with viewscreens on two walls. The screen in front of him is already activated two-way. It shows four men seated in a small room outside Isolation's wall.

The gray-haired classic Anglo profile is Captain Yellaston, acknowledging Aaron's presence with a neutral nod. Beside him the two scout commanders go on watching their own screen. The fourth man is young Frank Foy, *Centaur's* safety officer. He is pursing his mouth over a wad of printout tape.

Reluctantly, Aaron activates his other screen one-way, knowing he will see something unpleasant. There she is — his sister Lory, a thin young red-haired woman wired to a sensor bank. Her eyes have turned to him although Aaron knows she's seeing a blank screen. Hypersensitive as usual. Behind her is Solange in a decontamination suit.

"We will go over the questions once more, Miss Kaye," Frank Foy says in a preposterously impersonal tone.

"Dr. Kaye, please." Lory sounds tired.

"Dr. Kaye, of course." Why is young Frank so dislikable? Be fair, Aaron tells himself, it's the man's job. Necessary for the safety of the tribe. And he isn't "young" Frank any more. Christ, none of us are, twenty-six trillion miles from home. Ten years.

"Dr. Kaye, you were primarily qualified as a biologist on the Gamma scout mission, is that right?"

"Yes, but I was also qualified in astrogation. We all were."

"Please answer yes or no."

"Yes."

Foy loops the printout, makes a mark. "And in your capacity as biologist you investigated the planetary surface both from orbit and on the ground from the landing site?"

"Yes."

"In your judgment, is the planet suitable for human colonization?"

"Yes."

"Did you observe anything harmful to human health or wellbeing?"

"No. No, it's ideal—I told you."

Foy coughs reprovingly. Aaron frowns too; Lory doesn't usually call things ideal.

"Nothing potentially capable of harming human beings?"

"No. Wait—even water is potentially capable of harming people, you know."

Foy's mouth tightens. "Very well, I rephrase. Did you observe any life-forms that attacked or harmed humans?"

"No."

"But—" Foy pounces—"when Lieutenant Tighe approached the specimen you brought back, he was harmed, was he not?"

"No, I don't believe it harmed him."

"As a biologist, you consider Lieutenant Tighe's condition unimpaired?"

"No—I mean yes. He was impaired to begin with, poor man."

"In view of the fact that Lieutenant Tighe has been hospitalized since his approach to this alien, do you still maintain it did not harm him?"

"Yes, it did not. Your grammar sort of confuses me. Please, may we move the sensor cuff to my other arm? I'm getting a little capillary breakage." She looks up at the blank screen hiding the command staff.

Foy starts to object but Captain Yellaston clears his throat warningly, nods. When Solange unhooks the big cuff Lory stands up and stretches her slim, almost breastless body; with that pleasant, snub-nosed face she could pass for a boy.

Aaron watches her as he has all his life with a peculiar mixture of love and dread. That body, he knows, strikes most men as sexless, an impression confirmed by her task-oriented manner. *Centaur's* selection board must have been composed of such men, one of the mission criteria was a low sex-drive. Aaron sighs, watching Solange reattach the cuff. The board had been perfectly right, of course; as far as Lory herself was concerned she would have been happy in a nunnery. Aaron wishes she was in one. Not here.

Foy coughs primly into the microphone. "I will repeat, Dr. Kaye. Do you consider the effect of the alien specimen on Lieutenant Tighe was injurious to his health?"

"No," says Lory patiently. It's a disgusting scene, Aaron thinks; the helpless, wired-up woman, the hidden probing men. Psychic rape. Do them justice, only Foy seems to be enjoying it.

"On the planet surface, did Commander Kuh have contact with these life-forms?"

"Yes."

"And was he affected similarly to Lieutenant Tighe?"

"No—I mean, yes, the contact wasn't injurious to him either."

"I repeat. Was Commander Kuh or his men harmed in any way by the life-forms on that planet?"

"No."

"I repeat. Were Commander Kuh or his men harmed in any way by the life-forms on that planet?"

"*No.*" Lory shakes her head at the blank screen.

"You state that the scoutship's computer ceased to record input from the sensors and cameras after the first day on the surface. Did you destroy those records?"

"No."

"Was the computer tampered with by you or anyone?"

"No. I told you, we thought it was recording, no one knew the dump cycle had cut in. We lost all that data."

"Dr. Kaye, I repeat: Did you dump those records?"

"No."

"Dr. Kaye, I will go back once more. When you returned alone, navigating Commander Kuh's scoutship, you stated that Commander Kuh and his crew had remained on the planet because they desired to begin colonization. You stated that the planet was, I quote, a paradise and that nothing on it was harmful to man. Despite the totally inadequate record of surface conditions you claim that Commander Kuh recommends that we immediately send the green signal to Earth to begin full-scale emigration. And yet when Lieutenant Tighe opened the port to the alien specimen in your ship he suffered a critical collapse. Dr. Kaye, I put it to you that what really happened on that planet was that Commander Kuh and his crew were injured or taken captive by beings on that planet and you are concealing this fact."

Lory has been shaking her short red hair vigorously during this speech. "No! They weren't injured or taken captive, that's silly! I tell you, they wanted to stay. I volunteered to take the message back. I was the logical choice, I mean I was non-Chinese, you know—"

"Please answer yes or no, Dr. Kaye. Did Commander Kuh or any of his people suffer a shock similar to Lieutenant Tighe?"

"*No!*"

Foy is frowning at his tapes, making tick-marks. Aaron's liver has been getting chilly; he doesn't need wiring to detect that extra sincerity in Lory's voice.

"I repeat, Dr. Kaye. Did—"

But Captain Yellaston stirs authoritatively behind him.

"Thank you, Lieutenant Foy."

Foy's mouth closes. On the blind side of the screen Lory says gamely, "I'm not really tired, sir."

"Nevertheless, I think we will complete this later," Yellaston says in his good gray voice. He catches Aaron's eye, and they all sit silent while Solange releases Lory from the cuff and body wires. Through Solange's visor Aaron can see her lovely French-Arab face projecting worried compassion. Empathy is Solange's specialty; a wire slips and Aaron sees her lips go "Ooh." He smiles, feels briefly better.

As the women leave, the two scout commanders in the other cubicle stand up and stretch. Both brown-haired, blue-eyed, muscular ectomesomorphs so much alike to Aaron's eye, although Timofaev Bron was born in Omsk and Don Purcell in Ohio. Ten years ago those faces had held only simple dedication to the goal of getting to a supremely difficult place in one piece. The failures of their respective scout missions have brought them back to *Centaur* lined and dulled. But in the last twenty days since Lory's return something has awakened in their eyes; Aaron isn't too eager to know its name.

"Report, please, Lieutenant: Foy," says Yellaston, his glance making it clear that Aaron is to be included. The official recorder is still on.

Francis Xavier Foy sucks air through his teeth importantly; this is his second big interrogation on their entire ten-year voyage.

"Sir, I must regretfully report that the protocol shows persistent, ah, anomalous responses. First, the subject shows a markedly elevated and labile emotionality—" He glances irritatedly at Aaron to whom this is no news.

"The level of affect is, ah, suggestive. More specifically, on the question of injury to Commander Kuh, Dr. Kaye—Dr. *Lory*

Kaye, that is—the physiological reactions contraindicate her verbal responses, that is, they are not characteristic of her baseline truth-type—" He shuffles his printouts, not looking at Aaron.

"Lieutenant Foy, are you trying to tell us that in your professional judgment Dr. Kaye is lying about what happened to the Gamma scout crew?"

Frank Foy wriggles, reshuffling tapes. "Sir, I can only repeat that there are contraindications. Areas of unclarity. In particular these three responses, sir, if you would care to compare these peaks I have marked?"

Yellaston looks at him thoughtfully, not taking the tapes.

"Sir, if we could reconsider the decision not to employ, ah, chemical supplementation," Foy says desperately. He means, scop and EDC. Aaron knows Yellaston won't do this; he supposes he is grateful.

Yellaston doesn't bother answering. "Leaving aside the question of injury to Commander Kuh, Frank, what about Dr. Kaye's responses on the general habitability of the planet?"

"Again, there are anomalies in Dr. Kaye's responses." Foy visibly disapproves of any suspicions being left aside.

"What type of anomalies?"

"Abnormal arousal, sir. Surges of, ah, emotionality. Taken together with terms like paradise,' 'ideal,' and so on in the verbal protocol, the indications are—"

"In your professional judgment, Lieutenant Foy, do you conclude that Dr. Kaye is or is not lying when she says the planet is habitable?"

"Sir, the problem is variability, in a pinpoint sense. What you have suggests the classic pattern of a covert *area.*"

Yellaston ponders; behind him the two scout commanders watch impassively.

"Lieutenant Foy. If Dr. Kaye does in fact believe the planet to be eminently suitable for colonization, can you say that her emotion could be accounted for by extreme elation and excitement at the successful outcome of our long and difficult mission?"

Foy stares at him, mouth slightly open like a student "Elation, extreme—I see what you mean, sir. I hadn't—yes, sir, I suppose that could be one interpretation."

"Then do I correctly summarize your findings at this stage by saying that while Dr. Kaye's account of the events concerning Commander Kuh remains unclear, you see no specific counter-indication of her statement that the planet is habitable?"

"Ah, yes, sir. Although—"

"Thank you, Lieutenant Foy. We will resume tomorrow."

The two scout commanders glance at each other. They are solidly united against Foy, Aaron sees. Like two combat captains waiting for an unruly pacifist to be disposed of so the contest can start. Aaron sympathizes, he can't make himself like Foy. But he didn't like that tone in Lory's voice, either.

"Man, the samples, the sensor records," Don Purcell says abruptly. "They don't lie. Even if they only got thirty hours on-planet, that place is perfect."

Tim Bron grins, nods at Aaron. Yellaston smiles remotely, his eyes reminding them of the official recorder. For the thousandth time Aaron is touched by the calm command presence of the man. Old Yellowstone. The solid whatever-it-is that has held them together, stuffed in this tin can all through the years. Where the hell did they find him? A New Zealander, educated at some extinct British school. Chief of the Jupiter mission, etcetera, etcetera. Last of the dinosaurs.

But now he notices an oddity: Yellaston, who has absolutely no nervous mannerisms, is massaging the knuckles of one hand. Is it indecision over Lory's answers? Or is it the spark that's sizzling behind the two scout commanders' eyes—the planet?

The planet...

A golden jackpot rushes uncontrollably up through some pipe in Aaron's midbrain. Is it really there at last? After all the grueling years, after Don and then Tim came back reporting nothing but gas and rocks around the first two Centaurus suns—is it possible our last chance has won? If Lory is to be believed, Kuh's people are at this moment walking in Earth's new Eden that we need so desperately. While we hang here in darkness, two long years away. If Lory is to be believed—

Aaron realizes Captain Yellaston is speaking to him.

"—You judge her to be medically fit, Dr. Kaye?"

"Yes, sir. We've run the full program of tests designed for possible alien contact, plus the standard biomonitor spectrum. As of last night—I haven't checked the last six hours—and apart from weight loss and the ulcerative lesions in the duodenum which she suffered from when she got back to *Centaur*, Dr. Lory Kaye shows no significant change from her base-line norms when she departed two years ago."

"Those ulcers, Doctor; am I correct that you feel they can be fully accounted for by the strain of her solitary voyage back to this ship?"

"Yes, sir, I certainly do." Aaron has no reservations here. Almost a year alone, navigating for a point in space? My god, how did you do it, he thinks again. My little sister. She isn't human. And that alien thing on board, right behind her... For an instant Aaron can feel its location, down below the left wall. He glances at the recorder, suppressing the impulse to ask the others if they feel it too.

"Tomorrow is the final day of the twenty-one day quarantine period," Yellaston is saying. "An arbitrary interval, to be sure. You will continue the medical watch on Dr. Lory Kaye until the final debriefing session at oh-nine-hundred tomorrow." Aaron nods. "If there are still no adverse indications, the quarantine will terminate at noon. As soon as feasible thereafter we should proceed to examine the specimen now sealed in scoutship

Gamma. Say the following day; will this give you sufficient time to coordinate your resources with the Xenobiology staff and be prepared to assist us, Dr. Kaye?"

"Yes, sir."

Yellaston voice-signs the log entry, clicks the recorder off.

"Are you going to wait to signal home until after we look at that specimen?" Don asks him.

"Certainly."

They go out then, four men moving carefully in cramped quarters. Roomier than they'd have on Earth now. Aaron sees Foy manage to get in Yellaston's way, feels a twinge of sympathy for the authority-cathected wretch. Anything to get Daddy's attention. He too has been moved by Yellaston's good-wise-father projection. Are his own responses more mature? The hell with it, he decides; after ten years self-analysis becomes ritual.

When he emerges into Isolation corridor Lory has vanished into her cubicle and Solange is nowhere in sight. He nods at Coby through the vitrex and punches the food-dispenser chute. His server arrives on a puff of kitchen-scented air. Protein loaf, with an unexpected garnish; the commissary staff seems to be in good form.

He munches, absently eyeing the three-di shot of Earth mounted above his desk in the office beyond the wall. That photo hangs all over the ship, a beautifully clear image from the early clean-air days. What are they eating there now, each other? But the thought has lost its impact after a decade away; like everyone else on *Centaur*, Aaron has no close ties left behind. Twenty billion humans swarming on that globe when they went; doubtless thirty by now, even with the famines. Waiting to explode to the stars now that the technology is—precariously—here. Waiting for the green light from *Centaur*. Not literally green, of course, Aaron thinks; just one of the three simple codes they can send at this range. For ten long years they have been sending yellow—*Exploration continues*. And until twenty days ago they were facing the bleak red—No *planet found, returning to base.* But now, Lory's planet!

Aaron shakes his head, nibbling a slice of real egg, thinking of the green signal starting on its four-year trajectory back to Earth. *Planet found, launch emigration fleets, coordinates such-and-such.* Earth's teeming billions all pressing for the handful of places in those improbable transport cans.

Aaron frowns at himself; he rejects the "teeming billions" concept. Doggedly he thinks of them as people, no matter how many—individual human beings each with a face, a name, a unique personality, and a meaningful fate. He invokes now his personal ritual, his defense against mass-think, which is simply the recalling of people he has known. An invisible army streams through his mind as he chews. People... from each he has learned. What? Something, large or small. An existence... the face of Thomas Brown glances coldly from memory; Brown was the sad murderer who was his first psychosurgery patient a zillion years ago at Houston Enclave. Had he helped Brown? Probably not, but Aaron will be damned if he will forget the man. The living man, not a statistic. His thoughts veer to the reality of his present shipmates, the sixty chosen souls. Cream of Earth, he thinks, only half in sarcasm. He is proud of them. Their endurance, their resourcefulness, their effortful sanity. He thinks it is not impossible that Earth's sanest children are in this frail bubble of air and warmth twenty-six million miles away.

He cycles his server, pulls himself together. He has eighteen hours of biomonitor tapes to check against the base-line medical norms of Tighe, Lory, and himself. And first he must talk to the two people who thought they saw Tighe. As he gets up, the image of Earth catches his eye again: their lonely, vulnerable jewel, hanging there in blackness. Suddenly last night's dream jumps back, he sees again the monster penis groping toward the stars with *Centaur* at its tip. Pulsing with pressure, barely able to wait for the trigger that will release the human deluge—

He swats his forehead; the hallucination snaps out. Angry with himself he plods back to the Observation cubby.

The image of Bruce Jang is waiting on the screen; his compatriot, the young Chinese-American engineer on a ship where everyone is a token something. Only not "young" any more, Aaron admonishes himself.

"They have me in the coop, Bruce. I'm told you saw Tighe. Where and when?"

Bruce considers. Two years ago Bruce had still looked like Supersquirrel, all fast reflexes, buck teeth, and mocking see-it-all eyes. Cal Tech's answer to the universe.

"He came by my quarters about oh-seven-hundred. I was cleaning up, the door was open, I saw him looking in at me. Sort of, you know, fon-nee." Bruce shrugs, a joyless parody of his old jive manner.

"Funny? You mean his expression? Or was there anything peculiar about him, I mean visually different?"

A complex pause.

"Now that you mention it, yes. His refraction index was a shade off."

Aaron puzzles, finally gets it. "Do you mean Tighe appeared somewhat blurred or translucent?"

"Yeah. Both," Bruce says tightly. "But it was him."

"Bruce, Tighe never left Isolation. We've checked his tapes."

Very complex pause; Aaron winces, remembering the shadow waiting to enshroud Bruce. The near-suicide had been horrible. "I see," Bruce says too casually. "Where do I turn myself in?"

"You don't. Somebody else saw Tighe, too. I'm checking them out next."

"Somebody else?" The fast brain snaps, the shadow is gone. "Once is accident, twice is coincidence." Bruce grins, ghost of Supersquirrel. "Three times is enemy action."

"Check around for me, will you, Bruce? I'm stuck here." Aaron doesn't believe in enemy action but he believes in helping Bruce Jang.

"Right. Not exactly my game of course, but—right."

He goes out. The Man Without a Country. Over the years Bruce had attached himself to the Chinese scout team and in particular to Mei-Lin, their ecologist. He had confidently expected to be one of the two nonnationals Commander Kuh would, by agreement, take on the planet-seeking mission. It had nearly been a mortal blow when Kuh, being more deeply Chinese, had chosen Lory and the Aussie mineralogist.

The second Tighe-seer is now coming on Aaron's screen: Ahlstrom, their tall, blonde, more-or-less human computer chief. Before Aaron can greet her she says resentfully, "It is not right you should let him out."

"Where did you see him, Chief Ahlstrom?"

"In my Number Five unit."

"Did you speak to him? Did he touch anything?"

"Nah. He went. But he was there. He should not be."

"Tell me, please, did he look different in any way?"

"Different, yah," the tall woman says scornfully. "He has half no head."

"I mean, outside of his injury," says Aaron carefully, recalling that Ahlstrom's humor had once struck him as hearty.

"Nah."

"Chief Ahlstrom, Lieutenant Tighe was never out of this Isolation ward. We've verified his heartrate and respiration record. He was here the entire time."

"You let him out."

"No, we did not. He was here."

"Nah."

Aaron argues, expecting Ahlstrom's customary punchline: "Okay, I am stubborn Swede. You show me." Her stubbornness is a *Centaur* legend; during acceleration she had saved the mission by refusing to believe her own computers' ranging data until the hull sensors were rechecked for crystallization. But now she suddenly stands up as if gazing into a cold wind and says bleakly, "I could wish to go home. I am tired of this machine."

This is so unusual that Aaron can find nothing useful to say before she strides out. He worries briefly; if Ahlstrom needs help, he is going to have a job reaching that closed crag of a mind. But he is all the same relieved; both the people who "saw" Tighe seem to have been under some personal stress.

Hallucinating Tighe, he thinks; that's logical. Tighe stands for disaster. Appropriate anxiety symbol, surprising more people haven't cathected on him. Again he feels pride in *Centaur's* people, so steady after ten years' deprivation of Earth, ten years of cramped living with death lying a skin of metal away. And now something more, that spark of alien life, sealed in *China Flower's* hold, tethered out there. Lory's alien. It is now hanging, he feels, directly under the rear of his chair.

"Two more people waiting to see you, boss," says Coby's voice on the intercom. This also is mildly unusual, *Centaur* is a healthy ship. The Peruvian oceanographer comes in, shamefacedly confessing to insomnia. He is religiously opposed to drugs, but Aaron persuades him to try an alpha regulator. Next is Kawabata, the hydroponics chief. He is bothered by leg spasms. Aaron prescribes quinine, and Kawabata pauses to chat enthusiastically about the state of the embryo cultures he has been testing.

"Ninety percent viability after ten year cryostasis," he grins. "We are ready for that planet. By the way, Doctor, is Lieutenant Tighe recovering so well? I see you are allowing him freedom."

Aaron is too startled to do more than mumble. The farm chief cuts him off with an encomium on chickens, an animal Aaron loathes, and departs.

Shaken, Aaron goes to look at Tighe. The sensor lights outside his door indicate all pickups functioning: pulse regular,

EEG normal if a trifle flat. He watches the alphascope break into a weak REM, resume again. The printouts themselves are outside. Aaron opens the door.

Tighe is lying on his side, showing his poignant Nordic profile, deep in drugged sleep. He doesn't look over twenty: rose-petal flush on the high cheekbones, a pale gold cowlick falling over his closed eyes. The prototype Beautiful Boy who lives forever with his white aviator's silk blowing in the wind of morning. As Aaron watches, Tighe stirs, flings up an arm with the i.v. taped to it, and shows his whole face, the long blond lashes still on his cheek.

It is now visible that Tighe is a thirty-year-old boy with an obscene dent where his left parietal arch should be. Three years back, Tiger Tighe had been their first—and so far, only—serious, casualty. A stupid accident; he had returned safely from a difficult EVA and nearly been beheaded by a loose oxy tank while unsuiting in the freefall shaft.

As if sensing Aaron's presence Tighe smiles heartbreakingly, his long lips still promising joy. The undamaged Tighe had been the focus of several homosexual friendships, a development provided for in *Centaur's* program. Like so much else that has brought us through sane, Aaron reflects ruefully. He had never been one of Tighe's lovers. Too conscious of his own graceless, utilitarian body. Safer for him, the impersonal receptivity of Solange. Which was undoubtedly also in the program, Aaron thinks. Everything but Lory.

Tighe's mouth is working, trying to say something in his sleep.

"Hoo, huh." The speech circuits hunt across the wastelands of his ruined lobe. "Huhhh... Huh-home." His lashes lift, the sky-blue eyes find Aaron.

"It's all right, Tiger," Aaron lies, touches him comfortably. Tighe makes saliva noises and fades back into sleep, his elegant gymnast's body turning a slow arabesque in the low gee. Aaron checks the catheters and goes.

The closed door opposite is Lory's. Aaron gives it a brotherly thump and looks in, conscious of the ceiling scanner. Lory is on the bunk reading. A nice, normal scene.

"Tomorrow at oh-nine-hundred," he tells her. "The wrap-up. You okay?"

"You should know." She grimaces cheerfully at the biomonitor pickups.

Aaron squints at her, unable to imagine how he can voice some cosmic, lifelong suspicion with that scanner overhead. He goes out to talk to Coby.

"Is there any conceivable chance that Tiger could have got to where an intercom screen could have picked him up?"

"Absolute negative. See for yourself," Coby says, loading tape-spools into the Isolation pass-through. His eyes flick up at Aaron. "I didn't bugger them."

"Did I say that?" Aaron snaps. But he's guilty, they both know it; because it was Coby who was Frank Foy's other important case, five years back. Aaron had caught his fellow doctor making and dealing dream-drugs. Involuntarily now, Aaron sighs. A miserable business. There had been no question of "punishing" Coby, or anyone else on *Centaur* for that matter; no one could be spared. And Coby is their top pathologist. If and when they got back to Earth he will face—who knows what? Meanwhile he has simply gone on with his job; it was then he had started calling Aaron "boss."

Now Aaron sees a new animation flickering behind Coby's clever-ape face. Of course—the planet. Never to go back. Good, Aaron thinks. He likes Coby, he relishes the unquenchable primate ingenuity of the man.

Coby is telling him that the Drive chief Gomulka has come in with a broken knuckle, refusing to see Aaron. Coby pauses, waiting for Aaron to get the implication. Aaron gets it, unhappily; a physical fight, the first in years.

"Who did he hit?"

"One of the Russkies, if I had to guess."

Aaron nods wearily, pulling in the tapes he has to check. "Where's Solange?"

"Over with Xenobiology, checking out what you'll need to analyze that thing. Oh, by the way, boss—" Coby gestures at the service roster posted on their wall—"you missed your turn on the shit detail. Last night was Common Areas. I got Nan to swap you for a Kitchen shift next week, maybe you can talk Berryman into giving us some real coffee."

Aaron grunts and takes the tapes back to Interview to start the comparator runs. It is a struggle to keep awake while the spools speed through the discrepancy analyzer, eliciting no reaction. His own and Lory's are all nominal, nominal, nominal, nominal—all variation within normative limits. Aaron goes out to the food dispenser, hoping that Solange will show. She doesn't. Reluctantly he returns to run Tighe's.

Here, finally, the discrepancy indicator stirs. After two hours of input the analyzer has summed a deviation bordering on significance; it hovers there as Aaron continues the run. Aaron is not surprised; it's the same set of deviations Tighe has shown all week, since his problematical contact with the alien. A slight, progressive flattening of vital function, most marked in the EEG. Always a little less theta. Assuming theta correlates with memory, Tighe is losing capacity to learn.

Aren't we all, Aaron thinks, wondering again what actually happened in Gamma corridor. The scoutship *China Flower* has been berthed there with the ports sealed, attended by a single guard. Boring duty, after two weeks of nothing. The guard had been down by the stern end having a cup of brew. When he turned around Tighe was lying on the deck up by the scout's cargo hatch and the port was open. Tighe must have come out of the access ramp right by the port; he had been EVA team-leader before his accident, it was a natural place for him to wander to. Had he been opening or closing the lock when he collapsed? Had he gone inside and looked at the alien, had the thing given him some sort of shock? Nobody can know.

Aaron tells himself that in all likelihood Tighe had simply suffered a spontaneous cerebral seizure as he approached the lock. He hopes so. Whatever happened, Yellaston ordered the scoutship to be undocked and detached from *Centaur* on a tether. And Tighe's level of vitality is on the downward trend, day after day.

Unorthodox, unless there is unregistered midbrain deterioration. Aaron can think of nothing to do about it. Maybe better so.

Bone-weary now, he packs up and forces himself to go attend to Tighe's necessities. Better say good night to Lory, too.

She is still curled on her bunk like a kid, deep in a book. *Centaur* has real books in addition to the standard microfiches; an amenity.

"Finding some good stuff?"

She looks up, brightly, fondly. The scanner will show that wholesome sisterly grin.

"Listen to this, Arn." She starts reading something convoluted; Aaron's ears adjust only in time to catch the last of it *"...Grow upward, working out the beast, and let the ape and tiger die....* It's very old, Arn. Tennyson." Her smile is private.

Aaron nods warily, acknowledging the earnest Victorian. He has had enough tiger and ape and he will not get drawn into another dialog with Lory, not with that scanner going.

"Don't stay up all night."

"Oh, this rests me," she tells him happily. "It's an escape into truth. I used to read and read on the way back."

Aaron flinches at the thought of that solitary trip. Dear Lory, little madwoman.

"Night."

"Good night, dear Arn."

He gets himself into his bunk, grumbling old curses at *Centaur's* selection board. Pedestrian clots, no intuition. Lory the non-sex-object, sure. Barring the fact that Lory's prepubescent body is capable of unhinging the occasional male with the notion that she contains some kind of latent sexual lightning, some secret supersensuality lurking like hot lava in the marrow of her narrow bones. In their years on Earth, Aaron had watched a series of such idiots breaking their balls in the attempt to penetrate to Lory's mythical marrow. Luckily none on *Centaur*, so far.

But that wasn't the main item the selection board missed. Aaron sighs, lying in the dark. He knows the secret lightning in Lory's bones. Not sex, would that it were. Her implacable innocence — what was the old phrase, *a fanatic heart*. A too-clear vision of good, a too-sure hatred of evil. No love lost, in between. Not much use for living people. Aaron sighs again, hearing the frightening condemnation in her unguarded voice. Has she changed? Probably not. Probably doesn't matter, he tells himself; how could it matter that chance has put Lory's head between us and whatever's on that planet? It's all a technical problem, air and water and bugs and so on...

Effortfully he pushes the thoughts away. I've been cooped up here twenty days with her and Tighe, he tells himself; I'm getting deprivation fantasies. As sleep claims him his last thought is of Captain Yellaston. The old man must be getting low on his supplies.

II

... Immensely tall, eternally noble, the woman paces through gray streaming clouds. In rituals of grief she moves, her heavy hair bound with dark jewels; she gestures to her head, her heart, a mourning queen pacing beside a leaden sea. Chained beasts move slowly at her heels, the tiger stepping with sad majesty, the ape mimicking her despair.

She plucks the bindings from her hair in agony, it streams on the icy wind. She bends to loose the tiger, urging it to freedom. But the beast-form wavers and swells, thins out; the tiger floats to ghostly life among the stars. The ape is crouching at her feet; she lays her long fingers on its head. It has turned to stone. The woman begins a death chant, breaking her bracelets one by one beside the sea...

Aaron is awake now, his eyes streaming with grief. He hears his own throat gasping, *Uh – uhh-uhh,* a sound he hasn't made since – since his parents died, he remembers sharply. The pillow is soaked. What is it? What the hell is doing it? That was Lory's goddam ape and tiger, he thinks. Stop it! Quit.

He stumbles up, finds it's the middle of the night, not morning. As he douses his face he is acutely aware of a direction underfoot, an invisible line leading down through the hull to the sealed-up scouter, to the alien inside. Lory's alien in there.

All right. Face it.

He sits on his bunk in the dark. Do you believe in alien telepathic powers, Dr. Kaye? Is that vegetable in there broadcasting on a human wavelength, sending out despair?

Possible, I suppose, Doctor. Anything – almost anything – is *possible.*

But the tissue samples, the photos. They showed no differentiated structure, no neural organization. No brain. It's a sessile plant-thing. Like a cauliflower, like a big lichen; like a bunch of big grapes, she said. All it does is metabolize and put out a little bioluminescence. Discrete cellular potentials *cannot* generate anything complex enough to trigger human emotions. Or can they? No, he decides. We can't do it ourselves, for god's sake. And it's not anything physical like subsonics, not with the vacuum between. And besides, if it is doing this, Lory couldn't possibly have got back here sane. Nearly a year of living ten feet away from a thing sending out nightmares? Not even Lory. It has to be me. I'm projecting.

Okay; it's me.

He lies down again, reminding himself that it's time he ran another general checkup. He should expand the free-association session, too; other people may be getting stress phenomena. Those Tighe-sightings... Last time he caught two incipient depressions. And he'll do all that part himself, people won't take it from Coby he thinks, and catches himself in the fatuity. The fact is that people talk a lot more to Coby than they do to him. Maybe I have some of Lory's holy-holies. He grins, drifting off.

... *Tighe drifts in through the walls, curled in a foetal clasp, his genital sac enormous. But it's a different Tighe. He's green, for one thing, Aaron sees. And vastly puffy, like a huge cauliflower or a cumulus cloud. Not frightening. Not anything, really; Aaron watches neutrally as cumulus-cloud-green Tighe swells, thins out, floats to ghostly life among the stars. One bulbous baby hand waves slowly, Ta-ta...*

With a jolt Aaron discovers it really is morning. He lurches up, feeling vile. When he comes out Solange is sitting at the desk beyond the vitrex; Aaron feels instantly better.

"Soli! Where the hell were you?"

"There are so many problems, Aaron." She frowns, a severe flower. "When you come out you will see. I am giving you no more supplies."

"Maybe I'm not coming out." Aaron draws his hot cup.

"Oh?" The flower registers disbelief, dismay. "Captain Yellaston said three weeks, the period is over and you are perfectly healthy."

"I don't feel so healthy, Soli."

"Do you want to come out, Aaron?" Her dark eyes twinkle, her bosom radiates the shapes of holding and being held, she warms him through the vitrex. Aaron tries to radiate back. They have been lovers five years now, he loves her very much in his low-sex-drive way.

"You know I do, Soli." He watches Coby come in with Aaron's printouts. "How'm I doing, Bill? Any sign of alien plague?"

Solange's face empathizes again: tender alarm. She's like a play, Aaron thinks. If a brontosaurus stubbed its toe, Soli would go *Oooh* in sympathy. Probably do the same at the Crucifixion, but he doesn't hold that against her. Only so much band-width for anybody; Soli is set low.

"Don't pick up a thing on visual, boss, except you're not sleeping too good."

"I know. Bad dreams. Too much excitement, buried bogies stirring up. When I get out we're going to run another general checkup."

"When the doc gets symptoms he checks everybody else," Coby says cheerfully, the leer almost unnoticeable. He's happy, all right. "By the way, Tiger's awake. He just took a pee."

"Good. I'll see if I can bring him out to eat."

When Aaron goes in he finds Tighe trying to sit up.

"Want to come out and eat, Tiger?" Aaron releases him from the tubes and electrodes, assists him outside to the dispenser. As Tighe sees Solange his hand whips up in his old, jaunty greeting. Eerie to see the well-practiced movements so swift and deft; for minutes the deficit is hidden. Quite normally he takes the server, begins to eat. But after a few mouthfuls a harsh noise erupts from his throat and the server falls, he stares at it tragically as Aaron retrieves it.

"Let me, Aaron, I have to come in." Solange is getting into her decontamination suit.

She brings in the new batch of tapes. Aaron goes down the hall to run them. The interview room is normally their data-processing unit. *Centaur's* builders really did a job, he muses while the spools spin nominal-nominal, as before. Adequate provision for quarantine, provision for every damn thing. Imagine it, a starship. I sit here in a ship among the stars. *Centaur*, the second one ever... *Pioneer* was the first, Aaron had been in third grade when *Pioneer* headed out for Barnard's star. He was in high school when the signal came back red: Nothing.

What circles Barnard's star, a rock? A gasball? He will never know, because *Pioneer* didn't make it back to structured-signal range. Aaron was an intern when they declared her lost. Her regular identity code had quit and there was a new faint radio source in her direction. What happened? No telling... She was a much smaller, slower ship. *Centaur's* builders had redesigned on the basis of the reports from *Pioneer* while she was still in talking distance.

Aaron pulls his attention back to the tapes, automatically suppressing the thought of what will happen if *Centaur* too finds nothing after all. They have all trained themselves not to think about that, about the fact that Earth is in no shape to mount another mission if *Centaur* fails. Even if they could, where next? Nine light-years to Sirius? Hopeless. The energy and resources to build *Centaur* almost weren't there ten years ago. Maybe by now they've cannibalized the emigration hulls, Aaron's submind mutters. Even if we've found a planet, maybe it's too late, maybe nobody is waiting for our signal.

He snaps his subconscious to order, confirms that the tapes show nothing, barring his own nightmare-generated peaks. Lory's resting rates are a little up too, that's within bounds. Tighe's another fraction down since yesterday. Failing; why?

It's time to pack up. Lory and Solange are waiting to come in and hook up for the final debriefing, as Yellaston courteously calls it. Aaron goes around into the Observation cubicle and prepares to observe.

Frank Foy bustles first onto his screen to run his response-standardizing questions. He's still at it when Yellaston and the two scout commanders come in. Aaron is hating the scene again; he makes himself admit that Don and Tim are wearing decently neutral expressions. Space training, they must know all about bodily humiliation.

Foy finishes. Captain Yellaston starts the sealed recorder and logs in the event-date.

"Dr. Kaye," Foy leads off, "referring to your voyage back to this ship. The cargo module in which you transported the alien life-form had a viewing system linked to the command module in which you lived. It was found welded closed. Did you weld it?"

"Yes. I did."

"Why did you weld it? Please answer concisely."

"The shutter wasn't light-tight. It would have allowed my daily light cycle to affect the alien. I thought this might harm it, it seems to be very photosensitive. This is the most important biological specimen we've ever had. I had to take every precaution. The module was equipped to give it a twenty-two hour circadian cycle with rheostatic graded changes, just like the planet — it has beautiful long evenings, you know."

Foy coughs reprovingly.

"You went to the length of welding it shut. Were you afraid of the alien?"

"No!"

"I repeat, were you afraid of the alien?"

"No. I was not — well, yes, I guess I was, a little, in a sense. You see I was going to be alone all that time. I was sure the life-form is harmless, but I thought it might, oh, grow toward the light, or even become motile. There's a common myxomycetes — a fungus that has a motile phase, *Lycogala epidendron*, called Coral Beads. I just didn't know. And I was afraid its luminescent activity might keep me awake. I have a little difficulty sleeping."

"Then you do believe the alien may be dangerous?"

"No! I know now it didn't do a thing, you can check the records."

"May I remind you to control your verbalization, Dr. Kaye. Referring again to the fact that the cover was welded; were you afraid to look at the alien?"

"Of course not. No."

Young Frank really is an oddy, Aaron thinks; more imagination than I figured.

"Dr. Kaye, you state that the welding instrument was left on the planet. Why?"

"Commander Kuh needed it."

"And the scoutship's normal tool complement is also missing. Why?"

"They needed everything. If something went wrong I couldn't make repairs; it was no use to me."

"Please, Dr. Kaye."

"Sorry."

"Were you afraid to have a means of unsealing the alien on board?"

"No!"

"I repeat. Dr. Kaye, were you afraid to keep with you a tool by which you could unseal the port to the alien?"

"No."

"I repeat. Were you afraid to have a means of unsealing the alien?"

"No. That's silly."

Foy makes checks on his tapes; Aaron's liver doesn't need tapes, it has already registered that hyped-up candor. Oh god — what is she lying about?

"Dr. Kaye, I repeat—" Foy starts doggedly, but Yellaston has lifted one hand. Foy puffs out his cheeks, switches tack.

"Dr. Kaye, will you explain again why you collected no computerized data after the first day of your stay on the planet?"

"We did collect data. A great deal of data. It went to the computer but it didn't get stored because the dump cycle had cut in. Nobody thought of checking it, I mean that's not a normal malfunction. The material we lost, it's sickening. Mei-Lin and Liu did a whole eco-geologic stream bed profile, all the biota, everything—"

She bites her lips like a kid, a flush rising around her freckles. After ten years in outer space Lory still has freckles.

"Did you dump that data, Dr. Kaye?"

"*No!*"

"Please, Dr. Kaye. Now, I want to refresh your memory of the voice recording allegedly made by Commander Kuh." He flips switches; a voice says thinly: "Very... well, Dr. Ka-yee. You... will go."

It's Kuh's voice all right; Aaron knows the audiograms match. But the human ear doesn't like it.

"Do you claim that Commander Kuh was in good health when he spoke those words?"

"Yes. He was tired, of course. We all were."

"Please restrict your answers, Dr. Kaye. I repeat. Was Commander Kuh in normal physical health other than fatigue when he made that recording?"

"Yes."

Aaron closed his eyes. Lory, what have you done?

"I repeat. Was Commander Kuh in normal physical and mental—"

"Oh, *all right!*" Lory is shaking her head desperately. "Stop it! Please, I didn't want to say this, sir." She gazes blindly at the screen behind which Yellaston must be, takes a breath. "It's really very minor. There was—there was a difference of opinion. On the second day."

Yellaston lifts a warning finger at Foy. The two scout commanders are statues.

"Two members of the crew felt it was safe to remove their space suits," Lory swallows. "Commander Kuh—did not agree. But they did so anyway. And they didn't—they were reluctant to return to the scouter. They wanted to camp outside." She stares up in appeal. "You see, the planet is so pleasant and we'd been living in that ship so long."

Foy scents a rat, pounces.

"You mean that Commander Kuh removed his suit and became ill?"

"Oh no! There was a—an argument," Lory says painfully. "He was, he sustained a bruise in the laryngeal area. That's why—" She slumps down in the chair, almost crying.

Yellaston is up, brushing Foy away from the speaker.

"Very understandable, Doctor," he says calmly. "I realize what a strain this report has been for you after your heroic effort in returning to base alone. Now we have, I think, a very full account—"

Foy is staring bewilderedly. He has started a rat all right, but it is the wrong, wrong rat. Aaron understands now. The supersensitive Chinese, the undesirability of internal dissension on the official log. Implications, implications. There was a fracas among Kuh's crew and somebody wiped *China Flower's* memory.

So that is Lory's secret. Aaron breathes out hard, euphoric with relief. So that's all it was!

Captain Yellaston, an old hand at implications, is going on smoothly. "I take it, Doctor, that the situation was quickly resolved by Commander Kuh's decision to commence colonization, and his confidence that you would convey his report to us for transmission to Earth, as in fact you have done?"

"Yes, sir," says Lory gratefully. She is still trembling; everyone knows that violence of any sort upsets Lory. "You see, even if something serious happened to me, the scoutship was on automatic after midpoint. It would have come through. You picked it up."

She doesn't mention that she was unconscious from ulcerative hemorrhage when *China Flower's* signal came through the electronic hash from Centaurus's suns; it had taken Don and

Tim a day to grapple and bring her in. Aaron looks at her with love. My little sister, the superwoman. Could I have done it? Don't ask.

He listens happily while Yellaston winds it up with a few harmless questions about the planet's moons and throws the screen open two-way to record a formal commendation for Lory. Foy is still blinking; the two scout commanders look like tickled tigers. Oh, that planet! They nod benevolently at Lory, glance at Yellaston as if willing him to fire the green signal out of the top of his head.

Yellaston is asking Aaron to confirm the medical clearance. Aaron confirms no discrepancies, and the quarantine is officially terminated. Solange starts unwiring Lory. As the command party goes out, Yellaston's eye flicks over Aaron with the expressionlessness he recognizes; the old man will expect him in his quarters that evening with the usual.

Aaron draws himself a hot drink, takes it into his cubicle to savor his relief. Lory really did a job there, he thinks. Whatever kind of dust-up the Chinese had, it must have shocked her sick. She used to get hives when I played hockey, he remembers. But she's really grown up, she didn't spill the bloody details all over the log. Don't mess up the mission. That idiot Foy... You did that nicely, little sister, Aaron tells the image at the back of his mind. You're not usually so considerate of our imperfect undertakings.

The image remains unmoving, smiling enigmatically. Not usually so considerate of official sensibilities? Aaron frowns.

Correction: Lory has *never* been considerate of man's imperfection. Lory has *never* been diplomatic. If I hadn't sat on her head Lory would be in an Adjustment Center with a burn in her cortex instead of on this ship. And she's been as prickly as a bastard with poor old Jan. Has a year alone in that scouter worked a miracle?

Aaron ponders queasily; he doesn't believe in miracles. Lory conscientiously lying to preserve the fragile unity of man? He shakes his head. Very unlikely. A point occurs unwelcomely; that story did save something. It saved her own credibility. Say the Chinese wrangle happened. Was Lory using it, letting Foy pry it out of her to account for those blips on the tape? To get herself—and something—through Francis Xavier Foy's PKG readouts? She had time to figure it, ample time—

Aaron shudders from neck to bladder and strides out of his cubicle to collide with Lory coming out of hers.

"Hi!" She has a plain little bag in her hand. Aaron realizes the scanners are still on overhead.

"Glad to be getting out?" he asks lamely.

"Oh, I didn't mind." She wrinkles her nose. "It was a rational precaution for the ship."

"You seem to have become more, ah, tolerant."

"Yes." She looks at him with what the scanner will show as sisterly humor. "Do you know when Captain Yellaston plans to examine the specimen I brought back?"

"No. Soon, I guess."

"Good." The smiley look in her eye infuriates him. "I really brought it back for you, Arn. I wanted us to look at it together. Remember how we used to share our treasures, that summer on the island?"

Aaron mumbles something, walks numbly back to his room. His eyes are squeezed like a man kicked in the guts. Lory, little devil—how could you? Her thirteen-year-old body shimmers in his mind, sends helpless heat into his penile arteries. He is imprinted forever, he fears; the rose-tipped nipples on her child's chest, the naked mons, the flushed-pearl labia. The incredible sweetness, lost forever. He had been fifteen, he had ended both their virginities on a spruce island in the Fort Ogilvy Officers' Recreational Reserve the year before their parents died. He groans, wondering if he has lost both their souls, too, though he doesn't believe in souls. Oh, Lory... is it really his own lost youth he aches for?

He groans again, his cortex knowing she is up to some damn thing while his medulla croons that he loves her only and forever, and she him. Damn the selection board who had dismissed such incidents as insignificant, even healthy!

"Coming out, boss?" Coby's head comes in. "I'm opening up, right? This place needs a shake-out."

Aaron shakes himself out and goes out to check over Coby's office log. Lots of catching up to do. Later on when he is more composed he will visit Lory and shake some truth out of her.

He walks through the now-open vitrex, finds freedom invigorating. The office log reveals three more insomnia complaints, that's four in all. Alice Berryman, the Canadian nutrition chief, is constipated; Jan Ing, his Xenobiology colleague, has the trots. Quartermaster Miriamne Stein had a migraine. Van Wal, the Belgian chemist, has back spasm again. The Nigerian Photolab chief has sore eyes, his Russian assistant has cracked a toe-bone. And there's Gomulka's knuckle. No sign of whoever he hit, unless he broke Pavel's toe. Unlikely... For *Centaur*, it's a long list; understandable, with the excitement.

Solange bustles in carrying a mess of Isolation biomonitors. "We have much work to do on these, Aaron. Tighe will stay where he is, no? I have left his pickups on." She still pronounces it "peekups."

Warmed, Aaron watches her coiling input leads. Surprising, the forcefulness some small women show. Such a seductive little person. He knows he shouldn't find it mysterious and charming that she is so capable with any kind of faulty circuit.

"Tighe's not doing too well, Soli. Maybe you or Bill can lead him around a bit, stimulate him. But don't leave him alone at any time. Not even for a minute."

"I know, Aaron." Her face has been flashing through her tender repertory while her hands wham the sensor boxes around. "I know. People are saying he is out."

"Yeah... You aren't getting any, oh, anxiety symptoms yourself, are you? Bad dreams, maybe?"

"Only of you." She twinkles, closing a cabinet emphatically, and comes over to lay her hand on the faulty circuits in Aaron's head. His arms go gratefully around her hips.

"Oh, Soli, I missed you."

"Ah, poor Aaron. But now we have the big meeting downstairs. Fifteen hundred, that is twenty minutes. And you must help me with Tighe."

"Right." Reluctantly he lets sweet comfort go.

By fifteen hundred he is in a state of tentative stability, going down-ramp to the main Commons Ring where gravity is Earth-normal. Commons is *Centaur's* chief amenity, as her designers put it. It really is an amenity, too, Aaron thinks as he comes around a tubbed sweet-olive tree and looks out into the huge toroid space stretching all the way round the hull, fragrant with greenery from the Farm. Kawabata's people must have moved in a fresh lot.

The unaccustomed sounds of voices and music intimidate him slightly; he peers into the varied lights and shadows, finding people everywhere. He can see only a chord of the great ring, with its rising perspective at each end showing only leaning legs and feet beyond the farthest banks of plants. He hasn't seen so many people all here at once since Freefall Day, their annual holiday when *Centaur's* roll is stopped and the floor viewports opened. And even the last few viewing days people tended to slip in and look alone. Now they are all here together, talking animatedly. Moving around some sort of display. Aaron follows Miriamne Stein and finds himself looking at a bank of magnificent back-lighted photos.

Lory's planet.

He has been shown a few small frames from *China Flower's* cameras, but these blow-ups are overpowering. The planet seen from orbit—it looks like a flower-painted textile. Its terrain seems old, eroded to gentleness. The mountains or hills are capped with enormous gaudy rosettes, multi-ringed labyrinths ruffled in lemon-yellow, coral, emerald, gold, turquoise, bile-green, orange, lavender, scarlet—more colors than he can name. The alien vegetables or whatever. Beautiful! Aaron gapes, oblivious of shoulders touching him. Those "plants" must cover miles!

The next shots are from atmosphere, they show horizon and sky. The sky of Lory's planet is violet-blue, spangled with pearl-edged cirrus wisps. Another view shows alto-stratus over a clear silver-green expanse of sea or lake, reflecting cobalt veins—an enchanting effect. Everything exhales mildness; there is a view of an immense smooth white beach lapped by quiet water. Farther on, a misty mountain of flowers.

"Isn't it wonderful?" Alice Berryman murmurs in his general direction. She's flushed, breathing strongly; the medical fraction of Aaron's mind surmises that her constipation problem has passed.

They move on together, following the display which goes on and on across the Common's normal hobby bays and alcoves. Aaron cannot get his fill of looking at the great vegetable forms, their fantastic color and variety. It is hard to grasp their size; here and there Photolab has drawn in scales and arrows pointing out what appear to be fruits or huge seed-clusters. No wonder Akin's crew has sore eyes and stubbed toes, Aaron thinks; a tremendous job. He goes around an aviary cage and finds a spectacular array of night-shots showing the "plants'" bioluminescence. Weird auroral colors, apparently flickering or changing continuously. What the nights must be like! Aaron peers at the dark sky, identifies the two small moons of Lory's planet. He really must stop calling it Lory's planet, he tells himself. It's

Kuh's now if it's anybody's. Doubtless it will be given some dismal official name.

The mynah bird squawks, drawing his attention to another panel in the chess alcove: close-ups of the detached fruit-clusters or whatever they are, with infrared and high-frequency collations. It was one of these detached clusters that Lory brought back, along with samples of soil and water and so on. Aaron studies the display; the "fruits" are slightly warm and a trifle above background radiation level. They luminesce, too. Not dormant. A logical choice, Aaron decides, momentarily aware that the thing is out there on a line with his shoulder. Is it menacing? Are you giving me bad dreams, vegetable? He stares probingly at the pictures. They don't look menacing.

Beyond the aquariums he comes upon the ground pictures taken before the computer was dumped. The official first-landing photo, almost life-size, showing everybody in suits and helmets beside *China Flower's* port. Behind them is that enormous flat beach and a far-off sea. Faces are almost invisible; Aaron makes out Lory in her blue suit. Beside her is the Australian girl, her gloved hand very close to that of Kuh's navigator, whose name is also Kuh; "little" Kuh is identifiable by his two-meter height. In front of the group is a flagstaff flying the United Nations flag. Ridiculous. Aaron feels his throat tighten. Ludicrous, wondrous. And the flag, he sees, is blowing. The planet has winds. Moving air, imagine!

He has been too fascinated to read the texts by each display, but now the word "wind" catches his attention. "Ten to forty knots," he reads. "Continuous during the period. We speculate that the dominant life-forms, being sessile, obtain at least some nourishment from the air constantly moving through their fringed 'foliage.' (See atmospheric analyses.) A number of types of airborne cells resembling gametes or pollen have been examined. Although the dominant plantlike forms apparently reproduce by broadcast methods, they may represent the culmination of a long evolutionary history. Over two hundred less-differentiated forms ranging in size from meters to a single cell have been tentatively identified. No self-motile life of any kind has been found."

Looking more closely at the picture, Aaron sees that the foreground is covered with a tapestry of lichenlike small growths and soft-looking tufts. The smaller forms. He moves on through to a series of photos showing the crew deploying vehicles out of *China Flower's* cargo port, and bumps into a ring of people around the end of the display.

"Look at that," somebody sighs. "Would you look at that." The group makes way and Aaron sees what it is. The last photo, showing three suited figures—with their helmets off.

Aaron's eyes open wide, he feels his guts stir. There is Mei-Lin, her short hair blowing in the wind. Liu en-Do, his bare head turned away to look at a range of hills encrusted with the great flower-castles. And "little" Kuh, smiling broadly at the camera. Immediately behind them is a ridge which seems to be covered with vermilion lace-fronds bending to the breeze.

Air, free air! Aaron can almost feel that sweet wind, he longs to hurl himself into the viewer, to stride out across the meadows, up to the hills. A paradise. Was it just after this that the crew ripped off their foul space suits and refused to go back to the ship?

Who could blame them, Aaron thinks. Not he. God, they look happy! It's hard to remember when we lived, really lived. A corner of his mind remembers Bruce Jang, hopes he will not linger too long by that picture.

The crowd has carried him half around the toroid now; he is entering a wide section full of individual console seats that is normally the library. With the privacy partitions down it is used for their rare general assemblies. The rostrum is at the middle, where the speaker's whole figure will be most visible. It's empty. Beyond it is a screen projecting the star-field ahead; year by year Aaron and his shipmates have watched the suns of Centaurus growing on that screen, separating to doubles and doubledoubles. Now it shows only a single sun. The great blazing component of Alpha around which Lory's planet circles.

Several people are using the scanners while they wait. Aaron sits down beside a feminine back he recognizes as Lieutenant Pauli, Tim Bron's navigator. Her head is buried in the scanner hood. The title-panel on the console reads: GAMMA CENTAURUS MISSION. V, VERBAL REPORT BY DR. LORY KAYE, EXCERPTS FROM. That would be Lory's original narrative session, Aaron decides. Nothing about the "argument" there.

Pauli clicks off and folds down the scanner hood. When Aaron catches her eye she smiles dreamily, looking through him. Ahlstrom is sitting down just beyond; unbelievably, she's smiling too. Aaron looks around sharply at the rows of faces, thinking I've been shut away three weeks, I haven't realized what the planet is doing to them. Them? He finds his own risor muscle is tight.

Captain Yellaston is moving to the speaker's stand, being stopped by questions, Aaron hasn't heard so much chatter in years. The hall seems to be growing hot with so many bodies bouncing around. He isn't used to crowds any more, none of them are. And this is only sixty people. Dear god — *what if we have to go back to Earth?* The thought is horrible. He remembers their first year when there was another viewscreen showing the view astern: yellow Sol, shrinking, dwindling. That had been a rotten idea, soon abolished. What if the planet is somehow no good, is toxic or whatever — what if they have to turn around and spend ten years watching Sol expand again? Unbearable. It would finish him. Finish them all. Others must be thinking this too, he realizes. Doctor, you could have a problem. A big, big problem. But that planet *has* to be all right. It looks all right, it looks beautiful.

The hall is falling silent, ready for Yellaston. Aaron catches sight of Soli on the far side, Coby is by her with Tighe between them. And there's Lory by the other wall, sitting with Don and Tim. She's holding herself in a tight huddle, like a rape victim in court; probably agonized by her tapes being on the scanners.

Aaron curses himself routinely for his sensitivity to her, realizes he has missed Yellaston's opening words.

"... the hope which we may now entertain." Yellaston's voice is reticent but warm; it is also a rare sound on *Centaur*—the captain is no speechmaker. "I have a thought to share with you. Doubtless it has occurred to others, too. One of my occupations in the abundant leisure of our recent years—" pause for the ritual smiles —"has been the reading of the history of human exploration and migrations on our own planet. Most of the story is unrecorded, of course. But in the history of new colonies one fact appears again and again. That is that people have suffered appalling casualties when they attempted to move to a new habitation in even the more favorable areas of our own home world.

"For example, the attempts by Europeans to settle on the Northeast coast of America. The early Scandinavian colonies may have lasted a few generations before they vanished. The first English colony in fertile, temperate Virginia met disaster and the survivors were recalled. The Plymouth colony succeeded in the end, but only because they were continuously resupplied from Europe and helped by the original Indian inhabitants. The catastrophe that struck them interested me greatly.

"They came from northern Europe, from above fifty degrees north. Winters there are mild because the coast is warmed by the Gulf Stream, but this ocean current was not understood at that time. They sailed south by west, to what should have been a warmer land. Massachusetts was then covered by wild forests, like a park if we can imagine such a thing, and it was indeed warm summer when they landed. But when winter came it brought a fierce cold like nothing they had ever experienced, because that coast has no warming sea-current. A simple problem to us. But their technical knowledge had not foreseen it and their resources could not meet it. The effect of the bitter cold was compounded by disease and malnutrition. They suffered a fearful toll of lives. Consider: There were seventeen married women in that colony; of these, fifteen died the first winter."

Yellaston pauses, looking over their heads.

"Similar misfortunes befell numberless other colonies from unforeseen conditions of heat or drought or disease or predators. I am thinking also of the European settlers in my own New Zealand and in Australia and of the peoples who colonized the islands of the Pacific. The archeological records of Earth are filled with instance after instance of peoples who arrived in an area and seemingly vanished away. What impresses me here is that these disasters occurred in places that we now regard as eminently favorable to human life. The people were moving to an only slightly different terrain of our familiar Earth, the Earth on which we have evolved. They were under our familiar sun, in our atmosphere and gravity and other geophysical conditions. They met only very small differences. And yet these small differences killed them."

He was looking directly at them now, his fine light greenish eyes moving unhurriedly from face to face.

"I believe we should remind ourselves of this history as we look at the splendid photographs of this new planet which Commander Kuh has sent back to us. It is not another corner of Earth nor an airless desert like Mars. It is the first totally alien living world that man has touched. We may have no more concept of its true nature and conditions than the British migrants had of an American winter.

"Commander Kuh and his people have bravely volunteered themselves to test its viability. We see them in these photographs apparently at ease and unharmed. But I would remind you that a year has passed since these pictures were made, a year during which they have had only the meager resources of their camp. We hope and trust that they are alive and well today. But we must remember that unforeseeable hazards may have assailed them. They may be wounded, ill, in dire straits. I believe it is appropriate to hold this in mind. We here are safe and well, able to proceed with caution to the next step. They may not be."

Very nice, Aaron thinks. He has been watching faces, seeing here and there a lip quirked at the captain's little homily, but mostly expressions like his own. Moved and sobered. He's our pacemaker, as usual. And he's taken the edge off our envy of the *China* crew. Dire straits—wonderful old phrase. Are they really in dire straits, maybe? Yellaston is concluding a congratulatory remark for Lory. With a start Aaron recalls his own suspicion of her, his conviction that she is hiding something. And ten minutes ago I was ready to rush out onto that planet, he chides himself. I'm losing balance, I have to stop these mood swings. A thought has been percolating in him, something about Kuh. It surfaces. Yes. Bruised larynxes croak or wheeze. But Kuh's weak voice had been clear. Should check on that.

People are moving away. Aaron moves with them, sees Lory over by the ramp, surrounded by a group. She's come out of her huddle, she's answering their questions. No use trying to talk to her now. He wanders back through the displays. They still look tempting, but Yellaston has broken the spell, at least for him. Are those happy people now lying dead on the bright ground, perhaps devoured, only skeletons left? Aaron jumps; a voice is speaking in his ear.

"Dr. Kaye?"

It's Frank Foy, of all people.

"Doctor, I wanted to say—I hope you understand? My role, the distressing aspects. One sometimes has to perform duties that are most repugnant, as a medical man you too must have had similar—"

"No problem." Aaron collects himself. Why is Frank so embarrassing? "It was your job."

Foy looks at him emotionally. "I'm so glad you feel that way. Your sister—I mean, Dr. Lory Kaye—such an admirable person. It seems incredible a woman could make that trip all alone."

"Yeah... By the way, speaking of incredible, Frank, I know Lory's voice pretty well. I believe I was able to spot the points that were bothering you, in fact I'm inclined to share your—'"

"Oh, not at all, Aaron," Foy cuts him off. "You need say no more, I'm entirely satisfied. *Entirely*. Her explanation clears up every point." He ticks them off on his fingers. "The fate of the recording system, the absence of the welder and other tools, Commander Kuh's words, the question of injury—he *was* injured—the emotion about living on the planet. Dr. Kaye's revelation of the, ah, conflict dovetails perfectly."

Aaron has to admit that it does. Frank goes in for chess problems, he remembers; a weakness for elegant solutions.

"What about welding that alien in and being afraid to look at it? Between us, that thing gives me willies, too."

"Yes," Foy says soberly. "Yes, I fear I was giving in to my natural, well, is *xenophobia* the word? But we mustn't let it blind us. Undoubtedly Commander Kuh's people stripped that ship, Aaron. A dreadful experience for your sister, I felt no need to make her relive all that must have gone on. Among all those Chinese, poor girl."

When xenophobias collide... Aaron sees Foy isn't going to be much help, but he tries again.

"The business of the planet being ideal, a paradise and so on, that bothered me, too."

"Oh, I feel that Captain Yellaston put his finger on the answer there, Aaron. The excitement, the elation. I hadn't appreciated it. Now that I've seen these, I confess I feel it myself."

"Yeah." Aaron sighs. In addition to the elegant solution, Frank has received the Word. Captain Yellaston (who art in Heaven) has explained.

"Aaron, I confess I *hate* these things!" Foy says unexpectedly.

Aaron mumbles, thinking, possible, maybe he does. On the surface, anyway. With a peculiar smiling-through-tears look Foy goes on, "Your sister is such a wonderful person. Her strength is as the strength of ten, because her heart is pure."

"Yeah, well..." Suddenly the evening chow-call chimes out, saving him. Aaron bolts into the nearest passageway. Oh, no. Not Frank Foy. No ball-breaking here, though. Abelard and Héloise, so pure. A perfect match, really... What would Frank say if he told him about Lory and himself? Hey, Frank, when we were kids I humped my little sister all over the Sixth Army District, she screwed like a mink in those days. On second thought, forget it, Aaron tells himself. He knows how Frank would react. "Oh." Long grave pause. "I'm terribly sorry, Aaron. For you." Maybe even in priestly tones, "Would it help you to talk about it?" Etsanctimoniouscetera. A tough case, will the real Frank Foy ever stand up? No. Lucky it doesn't interfere with his being a damn good mathematician. Maybe it helps, for all I know. Humans!... A good food-smell is in his nose, lifting his mood. Chemoreceptors have pathways to the primitive brain. Ahead are voices, music, lights.

Maybe Foy's right, Aaron muses. How about that? Lory's story does dovetail. Am I getting weird? Sex-fantasies about Sis, I haven't had that trouble for years. It's being locked up with her, Tighe, that alien—a big armful of Soli, that's what I need. Solace, Soul-ass... Resolutely ignoring a sensation that the alien is now straight overhead outside the hull, Aaron fills a server and takes it over to a seat by Coby and Jan Ing, the Xenobiology chief with whom he will be working tomorrow. He's Lory's boss; Lory herself isn't here.

"Quite a crowd tonight."

"Yeah." In recent years more and more of *Centaur's* people have been eating alone at odd hours, taking their food to their rooms. Now there's a hubbub here. Aaron sees the Peruvian oceanographer has a chart propped by his server, he's talking to a circle of people with his mouth full, pointing. Miriamne Stein and her two girl friends — *women* friends, Aaron corrects himself — who usually eat together are sitting with Bruce Jang and two men from Don's crew. Ahlstrom is over there with Akin the Photo chief, for heaven's sake. The whole tranquillized ship is coming to life, tiger-eyes opening, ape-brains reaching. Even the neat sign which for so long has read, THE CENTRAL PROBLEMS OF OUR LIVES IS GARBAGE. PLEASE CLEAN YOUR SERVERS has been changed: someone has taped over GARBAGE and lettered BEAUTY.

"Notice the treat we're getting, boss," says Coby munching. "How did Alice get Kawabata to let loose some chicken? Oh, oh — look."

The room falls silent as Alice Berryman holds up dessert — a plate of real, whole peaches.

"One half for each person," she says severely. She is wearing a live flower over her ear.

"People are becoming excited," the XB chief observes. "How will it sustain itself for nearly two years?"

"*If* we go to that planet," Aaron mutters.

"I could make an amoral suggestion," Coby grins. "Tranks in the water supply."

Nobody laughs. "We've made out so far without, uh, chemical supplementation, as Frank would say," says Aaron. "I think we'll hold out."

"Oh, I know, I know. But don't say I didn't warn you it may come to that."

"About tomorrow," Jan Ing says. "The first thing we will get will be the biomonitor records from the command section of the scoutship, right? Before we proceed to open the cargo space?"

"That's the way I hear it."

"Immediately after opening the alien's module I plan to secure biopsy sections. Very minimal, of course. Dr. Kaye says she doesn't believe that will harm the alien. We're working on extension probes that can be manipulated from outside the hatch."

"The longer the better," Aaron says, imagining tentacles.

"Assuming the alien life-form is still alive..." The XB chief taps out a silent theme probably from Sibelius. "We'll know when we get our hands on the record."

"It should be." Aaron has been feeling the thing lying out beyond the buffet wall. "Tell me, Jan, do you ever have an impression that the thing is, well, *present*?"

"Oh, we're all conscious of that." Ing laughs. "Biggest event in scientific history, isn't that so? If only it is alive."

"You getting bad vibrations, boss? The dreams?" Coby inquires.

"Yeah." But Aaron can't go on, not with Coby's expression. "Yeah, I am. A xenophobe at heart."

They go into a discussion of the tissue-analyzing program and the type of bioscanners that will be placed inside the alien's module.

"What if that thing comes charging out into the corridor?" Coby interjects. "What if it's had kittens or split into a million little wigglers?"

"Well, we have the standard decontaminant aerosols," Jan frowns. "Captain Yellaston has emphasized the precautionary aspect. He will, I believe, be personally standing by the emergency vent control which could very quickly depressurize the corridor in case of real emergency. This means we will be wearing suits. Awkward working."

"Good." Aaron bites the delicious peach, delighted to hear that old Yellaston's hand will be on the button. "Jan, I want a clear understanding that no part of that thing is taken into the ship. Beyond the corridor, I mean."

"Oh, I entirely agree. We'll have a complete satellite system there. Including mice. It will be crowded." He swabs his server with cellulose granules from the dispenser, frowning harder. "It would be unthinkable to harm the specimen."

"Yeah." Lory has still not come in, Aaron sees. Probably eating in her room after that mob scene. He joins the recycle line, noticing that the usual glumness of the routine seems to have evaporated. Even Coby omits his scatological joke. What are Kuh's people eating now, Aaron wonders, telepathic vegetable steaks?

Lory is quartered — naturally — in the all-female dorm on the opposite side of the ship. Aaron hikes up a spiral cross-ship ramp, as usual not quite enjoying the sharp onset of weightlessness as he comes to *Centaur's* core. Her central core is a wide freefall service shaft from bow to stern, much patronized by the more athletic members of the crew. Aaron kicks awkwardly across it, savoring the rich air. It comes from a green-and-blue radiance far away at the stern end — the Hydroponics Farm and the Hull Pool, their other chief amenity. He shudders slightly, recalling the horrible months when the air even here was foul and the passageways dark. Five years ago an antibiotic from somebody's intestinal tract had mutated instead of being broken down by passage through the reactor coolant system. When it reached the plant beds it behaved as a chlorophyll-binding quasi-virus and Kawabata had had to destroy 75 percent of the oxygenating beds. A terrible time, waiting with all oxygen-consuming devices shut down for the new seedlings to grow and prove clean. Brr... He starts "down" the exit ramp to Lory's dorm, past the cargo stores and service areas. People aren't allowed to live in less than three-quarters gee. Corridors branch out every few meters leading to other dorms and living units. *Centaur* is a warren of corridors, that's part of the program, too.

He comes to the tiny foyer or commons room outside the dorm proper and sees red hair beyond a bank of ferns: Lory —

chewing on her supper, as he'd guessed. What he hadn't expected is the large form of Don Purcell, hunched opposite her deep in conversation.

Well, well! Mildly astounded, Aaron right flanks into another passage and takes himself off toward his office, blessing *Centaur's* design. The people of *Pioneer* had suffered severely from the stress of too much social contact in every waking moment; the answer found for *Centaur* was not larger spaces but an abundance of alternative routes that allow her people to enjoy privacy in their comings and goings about the ship, as they would in a village. Two persons in a two-meter corridor must confront each other but in two one-meter corridors each is alone and free to be his private self. It has worked well, Aaron thinks; he has noticed that over the years people have developed private "trails" through the ship. Kawabata, for instance, makes his long way from Farm to Messhall by a weird route through the cold sensor blister. He himself has a few. He grins, aware that his mind is demonstrating his total lack of irritation at finding Lory with another man.

In the clinic office Bruce Jang is chatting up Solange. When Aaron comes in Bruce holds up five spread fingers meaningfully. Aaron blinks, finally remembers.

"Five more people think they've seen Tighe?"

"Five and a half. I'm the half, I only heard him this time."

"You heard Tighe's voice? What did he say?"

"He said good-bye. That's all right with me, you know?" Bruce shows his teeth.

"Bruce, does your five include Ahlstrom or Kawabata?"

"Kawabata, yes. Ahlstrom, no. Six then."

Solange is registering discovery, puzzlement. "Do these people understand they have not really seen him?"

"Kidua and Morelli, definitely no. Legerski is suspicious, he said Tighe looked weird. Kawabata — who knows? The oriental physiognomy, very opaque." Supersquirrel lives.

"I think it is good I brought him to the meeting," Solange said. "I had the hunch, so people will see he is around and not worry."

"Yeah, good." Aaron takes a breath. "I've been having nightmares lately, if it's of any interest. The last one featured Tighe. He said good-bye to me, too."

Bruce's eyes snap. "Oh? You're in Beta section. That's bad."

"Bad?"

"My five sightings had a common factor before you blew it. Everyone was in Gamma section, fairly near the hull, too. That was nice."

"Nice." Aaron knows at once what Bruce means; *China Flower's* official name is *Gamma,* and the Gamma section is above her berth. But of course she isn't docked, now.

"Bruce, does that tether extend straight out? I'm no engineer. I mean, we're rotating; is she trailing?"

"Not much. A shallow tractrix. She already had our rotation when they ran her out."

"Then that alien is right under all the people who hallucinated Tighe."

"Yeah. All but you. We're in Beta here. And of course Ahlstrom is pretty far forward."

"But Tighe himself is here," says Solange. "In Beta with you."

"Yeah, but look," Aaron leans back. "Aren't we getting into witch-doctoring? There are other common factors. First, we've all been under stress for a long time and we're in a damn spooky place. Then along come two big jolts—the news about the planet and a genuine alien from outer space no one can look at. You've seen the ship, Bruce, people are lighted up like Christmas. Hope is a terrible thing, it brings fear that the hope won't be realized. Suppress the fear and it surfaces as symbol— and poor Tiger is our official disaster symbol, isn't he? Talk about common factors, it's a wonder we aren't all seeing green space-boogies."

Aaron is pleased to find he believes his own argument; it sounds very convincing. "Moreover, Tighe is linked with the alien now."

"If you say so, Doc," says Bruce lightly.

"Well, I do say so. I say there's sufficient cause to account for the phenomena. Occam's razor, the best explanation is that requiring fewer unsupported postulates, or whatever."

Bruce chuckles. "You're citing the law of parsimony, actually." He jumps up, turns to examine a telescoping metal rod on Solange's desk. "Don't forget, Aaron, old William ended up proving god loves us. I shall continue to count."

"Do that," Aaron grins.

Bruce comes close, says softly to Aaron alone, "What would you say if I told you I also saw... Mei-Lin?"

Aaron looks up wordlessly. Bruce lays the rod diagonally across Aaron's console. "I thought so," he says dryly and goes out.

Solange comes over to take the rod, her face automatically tuned to the pity on his. Bruce hallucinating Mei-Lin? That fits, too. It doesn't upset Aaron's theory. "What's this for, Soli?"

"The extension for the section cutter," she tells him, striking a fencing pose. "It needs many wires, it will be a mess."

"Oh Soli—" Aaron finally gets his arms around her, where they begin to feel alive at last. "Smart and beautiful, beautiful and smart. You're such a healthy person. What would I do without you?" He buries his unhealthy nose in her fragrant flesh.

"You would do your house calls," she tells him tenderly, her hips delicious in his hands.

"Oh god. Do I have to, now?"

"Yes, Aaron. Now. Think how it will be nice, afterward."

Ruefully Aaron extricates himself, confirming the board's estimate of his drives. Getting out his kit he recalls another duty and stuffs two liter flasks into the kit while Solange checks her file.

"Bustamente number one," she tells him. "I think he is very tense."

"I wish to god we could get him in here for an EKG."

"He will not come. You must do your best." She ticks off two more people Aaron would have visited during his weeks in quarantine. "And your sister, h'mm?"

"Yeah." Closing the kit, he wonders for the thousandth time if Solange knows about the flasks inside. And Coby? Christ, Coby has to know, he'd have been checking that distillation apparatus from Day One. Probably saving it for some blackmail scheme, who knows, Aaron thinks. Could I ever explain that I'm not doing what I damned him for? Or am I?

"Make the records nicely, please, Aaron."

"I will, Soli, I will. For you."

"Ha ha."

He wants poignantly to turn back, forces himself to trot up a ramp at random and discovers he is heading again toward Lory's dorm. Don must be long gone now, but still he reconnoiters the lounge area before going in. Lory's head—and good god, Don is still there! Aaron retreats, but not before he has seen that the shoulders actually belong to Timofaev Bron.

Feeling almost ludicrously dismayed, like a character in a bedroom farce, Aaron strides through the mixed-dorm commons, vaguely aware of the number of couples among the shadows. What the hell is Lory becoming, Miss Centaur? They have no right to bother Lory this way, he fumes, not with that ulcer still unhealed. Don't they know she needs rest? *I am the doctor...* The inner voice comments that more than Lory's ulcers are unhealed; he disregards it. If Tim is not out of there in thirty minutes he will break it up, and — what?

Sheepishly, he admits his intention to, well, question her, although he cannot for the moment recall the urgency of what he had to ask. Well, confession is good for ulcers, too.

The next turn-off leads to the quarters of his first patient, a member of Tim Bron's crew who came back to *Centaur* in full depressive retreat. Aaron has worked hard over him, prides himself on having involved the man in a set of correspondence chess games which he plays in solitary, never leaving his room. Now he finds the privacy-lock open, the room empty. Has Igor gone to Commons? His chess book is gone. Another point for the planet, Aaron decides, and goes cheerfully on to Andre Bachi's room.

Bachi is out of bed, his slender Latin face looking almost like its old self despite the ugly heaviness of glomerule dysfunction.

"To think I will live to see it," he tells Aaron. "Look, I have here the actual water, Jan sent it to me. Virgin water, Aaron. The water of a world, never passed through our bodies. Maybe it will cure me."

"Why not?" The man's intensity is heartbreaking; can he live two years, assuming they do go to Lory's world? Maybe... Bachi is the board's only failure so far. Merhan-Briggs syndrome, exceedingly rare, Coby's brilliant diagnosis.

"With this I can die happy, Aaron," Bachi says. "My god, for an organic chemist to experience this!"

"Is there life in it?" Aaron gestures at Bachi's scanning scope.

"Oh yes. Fantastic. So like, so unlike. Ten lifetimes' work. I have only two mounts made yet; I am slow."

"I'll leave you to it." Aaron puts Bachi's urine and saliva vials in his kit.

When he comes out he will not turn back toward Lory; instead he takes a midship passage toward the bridge. *Centaur's* bridge is in her big, shielded nose-module, which is theoretically capable of sustaining them all in an emergency. Theoretically; Aaron does not believe that most of his fellow crewmen could bear to pack themselves into it now, merely to survive. Up here is most of their important hardware, Ahlstrom's computers, astrogation gear, backup generators, and the gyros and laser system, which are their only link with Earth. Yellaston, Don, and Tim have quarters just aft of the bridge command room. Aaron turns off before Computers at a complex of panels giving access to *Centaur's* circuitry and stops under the door-eye of *Centaur's* Communications chief. There is no visible call-plate.

Nothing happens — and then the wall beside his knee utters a grating cough. Aaron jumps.

"Enter, Doc, enter," says Bustamente's bass voice.

The door slides open. Aaron goes warily into a maze of shifting light-forms in which six or seven big black men in various perspectives are watching him.

"I'm working on something in your field, Doc. Comparing startle stimuli. Nonlinear, low decibels give a bigger jump."

"Interesting." Aaron advances gingerly through unreal dimensions; visiting Ray Bustamente is always an experience. "Which one is you?"

"Over here." Aaron strikes some kind of mirrored surface and makes his way around it to comparative normality. Bustamente is on his lounger in a pose of slightly spurious relaxation.

"Roll up that sleeve, Ray. We have to do this, you know that."

Bustamente complies, grumbling. Aaron winds on the cuff, admiring the immense biceps. No fat on the triceps either; maybe the big man really does pay some heed to his advice. Aaron watches his digital read-out swing, relishing his feelings for Ray, what he thinks of as Ray's secret. The man is another rarity, a natural-born king. The real living original of which Yellaston is only the abstraction. Not a team-leader like Don or Tim. The archaic model, the Boss, Jefe, Honcho, whatever — the alpha human male who outfights you, outdrinks you, outroars you, outsmarts you, kills your enemies, begets his bastards on your woman, cares for you as his property, tells you what to do—and you do it. The primordial Big Man who organized the race and for whom the race has so little more use. Ten years ago it hadn't been visible; ten years ago there was a tall, quiet young Afro-American naval electronics officer with impeccable degrees and the ability to tune a Mannheim circuit in boxing gloves. That was before the shoulders thickened and the brow-ridges grew heavy over the watchful eyes.

"I really wish you'd come by the clinic, Ray." Aaron tells him, unwinding the cuff. "This thing isn't a precision instrument."

"What the hell can you do if you don't like my sound? Give me a stupid-pill?"

"Maybe."

"I'm making that planet, you know, Doc. Dead or alive."

"You will." Aaron puts his instruments away, admiring Bustamente's solution to his problem. What does a king do, born into a termite world, barred even from the thrones of termites? Ray had seen the scene, spotted his one crazy chance. And his decision has brought him twenty trillion miles from the termite heap, headed for a virgin planet. A planet with room, maybe, for kings.

A girl-shape is wavering among the mirrors, suddenly materializes into Melanie, the little white-mouse air-plant tech. She has an odd utensil in her hand. Aaron identifies it as a food-cooking device.

"We're working on a few primitive arts," Bustamente grins. "What's it going to be tonight, Mela?"

"A tuber," she says seriously, pushing back her ash-pale hair. "It's sweet but not much protein, it would have to be combined with fish or meat. You'll get fat." She nods impersonally at Aaron, goes back behind the screens.

"She's mine, you know." Bustamente stretches, one eye on Aaron. "Is that air as good as it looks? Ask your sister if it *smells* good, will you?"

"I'll ask her when I drop by tonight."

"Lot of dropping by recently." Bustamente suddenly flicks a switch and a screen Aaron hadn't noticed comes to life. It's an overhead shot of the communications office. The gyro chamber beyond is empty. Bustamente grunts, rolls his switch; the view flips to the bridge corridor, flip-flip-flips to others he can't identify. No people in sight. Aaron goggles; the extent of Bustamente's electronic surveillance network is one of *Centaur's* standing myths. Not so mythical, it seems; Ray really has been weaving in *Centaur's* walls. Oddly, Aaron doesn't resent it.

"Tim dropped by the ship today. Just looking to talk, he said." Bustamente flips back to the gyro chamber, zooms in on the locked laser-console. There is a definitely menacing flavor to the show; Aaron recalls with pleasure the time Frank Foy tried to set a scanner on Coby without clearing with the Commo chief.

As if reading his thought, Bustamente chuckles. "To quote the words of an ancient heavyweight boxing champion, George Foreman, *'Many a million has fall and stumble when he meet Big George in that ol' black jungle...'* Plans to make, you know, Aaron? Melanie, that's one. She's tougher than she looks but she's kind of puny. Need some muscle. That big old Daniela, she's my number two. Marine biology, she knows fish."

He flicks another image on the screen. Aaron gets a flash of a strong female back, apparently in the Commons game-bay.

"You're selecting your, your prospective family?" Aaron is charmed by the big man's grab at the guts of life. A king, all right.

"I don't plan to hang in too close, you know, Doc." His eye is on Aaron. "Should have medical capability. You'll be sticking with the others, right? So I figure number three is Solange?"

"Soli?" Aaron stares, forces himself to hold his own grin. "But have you, I mean what does she — Ray, we're nearly two years away, we may not even—"

"Don't worry about that, Doc. Just thought I'd warn you. You can use the time to teach Soli what to do when the babies come."

"Babies." Aaron reels mentally; the word hasn't been heard on *Centaur* for years.

"Maybe time you did a little planning yourself. Never too soon, you know."

"Good thought, Ray." Aaron makes his way out through the light-show jungle, hoping his smile expresses professional cheer rather than the sickly grin of one whose mate has just been appropriated by The Man. Soli! Oh, Soli, my only joy... but there's years yet, nearly two years, he tells himself. Surely he can think of something. Or can he?

A ridiculous vision of himself fighting Bustamente in a field of giant cauliflowers floats through his mind. But the woman they're fighting for isn't Solange, Aaron realizes. It's Lory.

Shaking his head at his subconscious, Aaron goes on up to the command corridor, taps the viewplate at Captain Yellaston's door. He feels a renewed appreciation for the more abstract forms of leadership.

"Come in, Aaron." Yellaston is at his console, filing his nails. His eyes don't flicker; Aaron has never been able to catch him checking on his loaded kit. The old bastard knows.

"That speech was a good idea, sir," Aaron says formally.

"For the time being." Yellaston smiles — a surprisingly warm, almost maternal smile on the worn Caucasian face. He puts the file away. "There's a point or two we should discuss, Aaron, if you're not too pressed."

Aaron sits, noting that Yellaston's faint maxillary tic has surfaced again. The only indicator he has ever given of the solitary self-combat locked in there; Yellaston has an inhuman ability to function despite what must be extensive CNS toxicity. Aaron will never forget the day *Centaur* officially passed beyond Pluto's orbit; that night Yellaston had summoned him and announced without preamble, "Doctor, I am accustomed to taking an average of six ounces of alcohol nightly. I have done so all my life. For this trip I shall reduce it to four. You will provide them." Staggered, Aaron had asked him how he had come through the selection year? "Without." Yellaston's face had sagged then, his eyes had frightened Aaron. "If you care for the mission, Doctor, you will do as I say." Against every tenet of his training, Aaron had. Why? He has wondered that many times, he knows all the conventional names for the demons the old man must poison nightly. Hidden ragings and cravings and panics, all to be exorcised thusly. His business the names—but the fact is that Aaron suspects the true name of Yellaston's demon is something different. Something inherent in life itself, time or evil maybe, for which he has no cure. He sees Yellaston as a complicated fortress surviving by strange rituals. Perhaps the demon is dead now, the fort empty. But he has never dared to risk inquiring.

"Your sister is a very brave girl." Yellaston's voice is extra warm.

"Yes, incredible."

"I want to be sure you know that I appreciate the full extent of Dr. Kaye's heroism. The record will so show. I am recommending her for the Legion of Space."

"Thank you, sir." Aaron acknowledges Yellaston's membership in the Love-Lory Club. Suddenly he wonders, Is this the start of one of Yellaston's breaks? It has only happened a few times, the giving-way of the iron man's defenses, but it has caused Aaron much grief. The first was when they were about two years out, with young Alice Berryman. Yellaston began chatting with her. The chats became increasingly intense. Alice was star-eyed. So far nothing wrong, only puzzling. Alice told

Miriamne that he spoke of strange strategic and philosophical principles that she found hard to grasp. The culmination came when Aaron found her weeping before breakfast and hauled her to his office to let the story out. He had been dismayed. Not sex—worse. A night of incoherent, unstoppable talk, ending in maudlin childhood. "How can he be so, so *silly*—?" All stars gone, traumatic disgust. Daddy is dead. Aaron had tried to explain to her the working of a very senior, idiosyncratic old primate; hopeless. He had given up and shamelessly narco-twisted her memory, made her believe it was she who had been drunk. For the good of the mission... After that he had kept watch. There were three more, periodicity about two years. The poor bastard, Aaron thinks; childhood must have been the last time he was free. Before the battle began. So far Yellaston has never used him for release. Perhaps he values his bootlegger; more likely, Aaron has decided, he is simply too old. Is that about to change?

"Her courage and her accomplishment will be an inspiration."

Aaron nods again, warily.

"I wanted to be sure you understand I have full confidence in your sister's report."

She snowed him, Aaron thinks dismally. Oh Lory. Then he catches the tension in the pause and looks up. Is this leading somewhere?

"There is too much at stake here, Aaron."

"That's right, sir," says Aaron with infinite relief. "That's what I feel, too."

"Without in any way subtracting from your sister's achievement, it is simply too much to risk on anyone's unsupported word. Anyone's. We have no objective data on the fate of the Gamma crew. Therefore I shall continue to send code yellow, not code green, until we arrive at the planet and confirm."

"Thank god," says Aaron the atheist.

Yellaston looks at him curiously. It's the moment for Aaron to speak about the Tighe-sightings, the dreams, to confess his fears of Lory and alien telepathic vegetables. But there's no need now, Yellaston wasn't snowed, it was just his weird courtesy.

"I mean I do agree... Does this mean we're going to the planet, that is, you've decided before we check out that specimen?"

"Yes. Regardless of what we find, there is no alternative. Which brings up this point." Yellaston pauses. "My decision with respect to the signal may not be entirely popular. Although two years is a very short time."

"Two years is an eternity, sir." Aaron thinks of the flushed faces, the voices; he thinks of Bustamente.

"I realize it may seem so to some. I wish it could be shortened. *Centaur* does not have the acceleration of the scouters. More pertinently, Aaron, some crew members may also feel that we owe it to the home world to let them know as soon as possible. The situation there must be increasingly acute."

They are both silent for a moment, in deference to the acuteness of Earth's "situation."

"If *Centaur* were to have an accident before we verify the planet, this could deprive Earth of knowledge of the planet's existence, perhaps forever. The fear of such a catastrophe will weigh heavily with some. On the other hand, we have had no major malfunctions and no reason to think we shall. We are proceeding as planned. The most abysmal error we could make would be to send the green code now and then discover, after the ships have been irreversibly launched, that the planet is uninhabitable. Those ships cannot return."

Aaron perceives that Yellaston is using him to try out pieces of his formal announcement; a bootlegger has many uses. But why not his logical advisors, his execs, Don and Tim? Oh, oh. Aaron begins to suspect who "some" people may include.

"We would doom all the people in the pipeline. Worse, we would end forever any hope of a new emigration effort. Our hastiness would be criminal. Earth has trusted us. We must not risk betraying her."

"Amen."

Yellaston broods a moment, suddenly gets up and goes over to his cabinet wall. Aaron hears a gurgle. The old man must have saved his last one until relief arrived.

"God damn it." Yellaston suddenly sets a flask down hard. "We never should have had women on this mission."

Aaron grins involuntarily, thinking, there speaks the dead dick. Thinking also of Soli, of Ahlstrom, of all the female competences on *Centaur*, of the debates on female command that had yielded finally to the policy of minimal innovation on a mission where so much else would be new. But he knows exactly what Yellaston means.

Yellaston turns around, letting Aaron see his glass; an unusual intimacy. "Going to be a bitch, Doctor. These two will be the toughest we've had to face. Two years. The fact that we're going to the planet ourselves will suffice for most, I think." He massages his knuckles again. "It might not be a bad idea for you to keep your eyes and ears rather carefully open, Aaron, during the time ahead."

Implications, implications. Doctors, like bootleggers, have their uses, too.

"I believe I see what you mean, sir."

Yellaston nods. "On a continuing basis," he says authoritatively. He and Aaron exchange regards in which is implicit their mutual views of the relevance of Francis Xavier Foy.

"I'll do my best," Aaron promises; he has recalled his general checkup plan, maybe he can use that projective-recall session to spot trouble.

"Good. Now, tomorrow we examine that specimen. I'd like to hear your plans." Yellaston comes back, glassless, to his console and Aaron gives him a rundown on his arrangements with the Xenobiology chief.

"All the initial work will take place in *situ,* right?" Aaron concludes, conscious that the alien's *situ* is now directly to his left. "Nothing goes into the ship?"

"Right."

"I'd like to have authority to enforce that. And guards on the corridor entrances, too."

"The authority is yours, Doctor. You'll have the guards."

"That's fine." Aaron rubs his neck, remembering his medikit. "There've been a couple of, oh, call them psychological reactions to the alien I'm looking into. Nothing serious, I think. For instance, have you experienced an impression of localization, about the alien, I mean? A sense of where the thing is, physically?"

Yellaston chuckles. "Why yes, as a matter of fact I do. Right north, over there." He points high toward Aaron's right. "Is that significant, Doctor?"

Aaron grins in relief. "Yeah, it is to me. It signifies that my personal orientation still isn't any good after ten years." He picks up his kit, moves over to Yellaston's cabinets. "I thought the thing was down under your bunk." Unobtrusively he substitutes the full flasks, noting that that drink was indeed the old man's last.

"Give your sister my personal regards, Aaron. And don't forget."

"I'll remember, Captain."

Obscurely moved, Aaron goes out. He knows he must do some serious thinking; if Don or Tim decide to kick up, what the hell can Dr. Aaron Kaye do about it? But he is euphoric. The old man isn't buying Lory's story blind, he isn't going to rush it. Daddy will save us from the giant cauliflowers. I better get some exercise, he thinks, and trots down-ramp to one of the long outer corridors on the hull. There are six of these bow-stern blisters; they form the berths that hold the three big scoutships. Gravity is strong down here, slightly above Earth-normal, and people use the long tubes for games and exercise — another good program-element, Aaron thinks approvingly. He comes out into Corridor Beta, named for Don Purcell's scouter. *Beta* has long been known as the *Beast*, as in beast-of-Fascist-imperialism, a joke of *Centaur's* early years when Tim's *Alpha* was likewise christened the *Atheist Bastard*. Kuh's *Gamma* became only *China Flower* — the flower which is now hanging on her stem with her cryptic freight.

This corridor is identical to Gamma where the alien will be examined tomorrow. Aaron strides along effortfully savoring the gee-loading, counting access portals which will need guards. There are fourteen, more than he had thought. Ramps lead down here from all over the ship — the scouters were designed as lifeboats, too. The corridor is so long the far end is hazy. He fancies he can feel a chill on his soles. Imagine, he is in a starship! A fly walking the wall of a rotating can in cosmic space; there are suns under his feet.

He remembers the scenes of ceremony that had taken place in these corridors three years back, when the scoutships were launched to reconnoiter the suns of Centaurus. And the sad returns four months ago when first Don and then Tim had come back bearing news of nothing but methane and rock. Will the *Beast* and the *Bastard* soon be ferrying us down to Lory's planet? — I mean in two years, and it's Kuh's planet, Aaron corrects himself, so preoccupied that he bumps blindly into the rear of Don Purcell, backing out of Beta's command lock.

"Getting ready to land us, Don?"

Don only grins, the all-purpose calm grin that Aaron believes he would wear if he were going down in flames. Tough to get behind a grin like that if Don really was, well, disaffected. He doesn't look mutinous, Aaron thinks. Hard to imagine him leading an assault on Ray's gyros. He looks like an order man, a

good jock. Like Tim. Kuh was the same breed, too. Transistor-
ized. The genotype that got us here, the heavy-duty transport of
the race.

Aaron ducks into the ramp that leads to Lory's quarters,
imagining Don and the scoutships and them all superimposed
on that planet, that mellow flowery world. Pouring out to make
a new Earth. Will they find Kuh's colony, or silent bones? But
the freedom, the building... and then, then will come the fleet
from Earth. Fifteen years, that's what we'll have, Aaron thinks,
assuming we send the green signal when we land. Fifteen years.
And then the emigration ships will start coming in, the—what
was it Yellaston called it—the pipeline. Typical anal imagery.
The pipeline spewing Earth's crap across the light-years. Technicians first, of course, basic machinery, agriculture. Pioneer-
type colonists. And then pretty soon people-type people, ad-
ministrators, families, politicians—whole industries and nations
all whirling down that pipeline onto the virgin world. Covering
it, spreading out. What of Bustamente, then? What of himself
and Lory?

He is by Lory's door now, the lounge is empty at last.

When she opens it Aaron is pleased to see she's doing nothing more enigmatic than brushing her hair; the same old hygi-
enic black bristles pulling through the coppery curls which are
now just frosted gray, nice effect, really. She beckons him in,
brushing steadily; counting, he guesses.

"Captain sends you his personal regards." As he sits it occurs
to him that Foy may have bugged her room. No visuals, though.
Not Foy.

"Thank you, Arn... seventy... Your personal regards, too?"

"Mine too. You must be tired, I notice you had company.
Tried to look in earlier."

"Seventy-five... Everybody wants to hear about it, it means so
much to them."

"Yeah. By the way, I admired your tactfulness about our battling Chinese. I didn't know you had it in you, Sis."

She brushes harder. "I didn't want to *spoil* it. They—they stopped all that, anyway. There." She lays the brush down, smiles. "It's such a peaceful place, Arn. I think we could really live a new way there. Without violence and hatred and greed. Oh, I know how you—but that's the feeling it gave me, anyway."

The light tone doesn't fool him. Lory, lost child of paradise striving ever to return. That look in her eye, you could cast her as the young Jeanne, reminding the Dauphin of the Holy Cause. Aaron has always had a guilty sympathy for the Dauphin.

"There'll always be some bad stuff as long as you have people, Lor. People aren't all that rotten. Look at us here."

"Here? You look, Arn. Sixty hand-picked indoctrinated specimens. Are we really good? Are we even gentle with each other? I can feel the—the *savagery* underneath, just waiting to break loose. Why, there was a *fight* yesterday. Here."

How does she hear these things?

"It's a hell of a strain, Lor. We're human beings."

"Human beings must change."

"Goddamnit, we don't have to change. Basically, I mean," he adds guiltily. Why does she do this to him? She makes me defend what I hate, too. She's right, really, but, but—"You might try caring a little for people as they are—it's been recommended," he says angrily and hates the unctuousness in his voice.

She sighs, straightens the few oddments on her stand. Her room looks like a cell. "Why do we use the word human for the animal part of us, Arn? Aggression—that's human. Cruelty, hatred, greed—that's human. That's just what *isn't* human, Arn. It's so sad. To be truly human we must leave all that behind. Why can't we try?"

"We do, Lor. We do."

"You'd make this new world into another hell like Earth."

He can only sigh, acknowledging her words, remembering too the horrible time after their parents died, when Lory was sixteen... Their father had been Lieutenant-General Kaye, they had grown up sheltered, achievement-oriented in the Army enclaves' excellent schools. Lory had been into her biology program when the accident orphaned them. Suddenly she had looked up and seen the world outside—and the next thing Aaron knew he was bailing her out of a Cleveland detention center in the middle of the night. The ghetto command post had recognized her Army ID plate.

"Oh, Arn," she had wept to him in the copter going home. "It isn't right! It isn't *right*." Her face was blotched and raw where the gas had caught her, he couldn't bear to look.

"Lor, this is too big for you. I know it isn't right. But this is not like setting up a dog shelter on Ogilvy Island. Don't you understand you can get your brains cut?"

"That's what I mean, they're doing obscene things to people. It isn't *right*."

"You can't fix it," he'd snapped at her in pain. "Politics is the art of the possible. This isn't possible, you'll only get killed."

"How do we know what's possible unless we try?"

Oh god, that next year. Their father's name had helped some, luck had helped more. In the end what probably saved her was her own implacable innocence. He had finally tracked her down in the back shed of a mortuary in the old barrio section of Dallas; emaciated, trembling, barely able to speak.

"Arn, oh—they—" she whimpered while he wiped vomit off her chin, "Dave refused to help Vicky, he—he wants him to get caught... So he can be leader... He won't let us help him."

"I think that happens, Lor." He held her thin shoulders, trying to stop the shaking. "That does happen, people are human."

"No!" She jerked away fiercely. "It's terrible. It's terrible. They —*we* were fighting among ourselves, Arn. Fighting over *power*. Dave even wants his woman, I think—they hit each other. She, she was just property."

She heaved up the rest of the soup he'd brought her.

"When I said that they threw me out."

Aaron held her helplessly, thinking, her new friends can't live up to her any more than I can. Thank god.

"Arn," she whispered. "Vicky ... *he took some money*. I know..."

"Lor, come on home now. I fixed it, you can still take your exams if you come back now."

"... All right."

Aaron shakes his head, sitting in *Centaur* twenty trillion miles from Dallas, looking at that same fierce vision on the face of his little sister now going gray. His little sister whom chance has made their sole link with that planet, that thing out there.

"All right, Lor." He gets up, turns her around to face him. "I know you. What the hell happened on that planet? What are you covering?"

"Why, nothing, Arn. Except what I told you. What's the *matter* with you?"

Is it too innocent? He distrusts everything, cannot tell.

"Please let *go* of me."

Conscious of Foy's problematical ears he lets go, steps back. This would sound crazy.

"Do you realize this isn't games, Lor? Our lives are depending on it. Real people's lives, much as you hate humanity. You better not be playing."

"I don't hate humanity, I just hate some of the things people do. I wouldn't *hurt* people, Arn."

"You'd liquidate ninety percent of the race to achieve your utopia."

"What a *terrible* thing to say!"

Her face is all soul, he aches for her. But Torquemada was trying to help people, too.

"Lor, give me your word that Kuh and his people are absolutely okay. Your faithful word."

"They *are*, Arn. I give you my word. They're beautiful."

"The hell with beauty. Are they physically okay?"

"Of course they are."

Her eyes still have that look, but he can't think of anything else to try. Praise be for Yellaston's caution.

She reaches out for him, thin electric hand burning his. "You'll see, Arn. Isn't it wonderful, we'll be together? That's what kept me going, all the way back. I'll be there tomorrow when we look at it."

"Oh, no!"

"Jan Ing wants me. You said I'm medically fit. I'm his chief botanist, remember?" She smiles mischievously.

"I don't think you should, Lor. Your ulcers."

"Waiting around would be much worse for them." She sobers, grips his arm. "Captain Yellaston—he's going to send the green, isn't he?"

"Ask him yourself. I'm only the doctor."

"How sad. Oh well, he'll see. You'll all see." She pats his arm, turns away.

"What'll we see?"

"How harmless it is, of course... Listen, Arn. This is from some ancient work, the martyr Robert Kennedy quoted it before he was killed. 'To tame the savage heart of man, to make gentle the life of this world'... Isn't that fine?"

"Yeah, that's fine, Lor."

He goes away less than comforted, thinking, the life of this world is not gentle, Lory. It wasn't gentleness that got you out here. It was the drives of ungentle, desperate, glory-hunting human apes. The fallible humanity you somehow can't see...

He finds he has taken a path through the main Commons. Under the displays the nightly bridge and poker games are in session as usual, but neither Don nor Tim are visible. As he goes out of earshot he hears the Israeli physicist ante what sounds like an island. An island? He climbs up toward the clinic, hoping he heard wrong.

Solange is waiting for him with the medical log. He recites Ray and Bachi's data with his head leaning against her warm front, remembering he has another problem. Forget it, he tells himself, I have two years to worry about Bustamente.

"Soli, tomorrow I want to rig up an array of decontaminant canisters over the examination area. With the release at my station. Say a good strong phytocide plus a fungicide with a mercury base. What should I get from Stores?"

"Decon Seven is the strongest, Aaron. But it cannot be mixed, we will have to place many tanks." Her face is mirroring pity for the hypothetically killed plants, concern for the crew.

"Okay, so we'll place many tanks. Everything the suits will take. I don't trust that thing."

Soli comes into his arms, holds him with her strong small hands. Peace, comfort. *To make gentle the life of mankind.* His body has missed her painfully, demonstrates it with a superior erection. Soli giggles. Fondly he caresses her, feeling like himself for the first time in weeks. Do I see you as property, Soli? Surely not... The thought of Bustamente's huge body covering her floats through his mind; his erection increases markedly. Maybe the big black brother will have to revise his planning, Aaron thinks genially, hobbling with her to his comfortable, comforting bunk. Two years is a long time...

Drifting asleep with Soli's warm buttocks is his lap Aaron has a neutral, almost comic hypnagogic vision: Tighe's face big as the wall, garlanded with fruits and flowers like an Italian bambino plaque. The pink and green flowers tinkle, chime elfland horns. *Tan tara!* Centripetal melodies. *Tan tara! Tara! TARA!*

—and fairy horns turn into his medical alarm signal, with Soli shaking him awake. The call is from the bridge.

He leaps out of bed, yanking shorts on, hits the doorway with one shoulder and runs "up" to the freefall shaft. His kit is somehow in his hand. He has no idea what time it is. The thought that Yellaston has had a heart attack is scaring him to death. Oh god, what will they do without Yellaston?

He kicks free, sails and grabs clumsily like a three-legged ape, clutching the kit, is so busy figuring alternative treatment spectrums that he almost misses the voices coming from the Commo corridor. He gets himself into the access, finds his feet and scurries "down" still so preoccupied that he does not at first identify the dark columns occupying the Communication step. They are Bustamente's legs.

Aaron pushes in past him and confronts a dreadful sight. Commander Timofaev Bron is sagging from Bustamente's grasp, bleeding briskly from his left eye.

"All right, all right," Tim mutters. Bustamente shakes him.

"What the hell was that power drain?" Don Purcell comes in behind Aaron.

"This booger was sending," Bustamente growls. "Shit-eater, I was too slow. He was sending *on my beam*." He shakes the Russian again.

"All right," Tim repeats unemotionally. "It is done."

The blood is coming from a supra-orbital split. Aaron disengages Tim from Bustamente, sits him down with his head back to clamp the wound. As he opens his kit a figure comes slowly through the side door from Astrogation: Captain Yellaston.

"Sir—" Aaron is still confusedly thinking of that coronary. Then Yellaston's peculiar rigidity gets through to him. Oh Jesus, no. The man is not sick but smashed to the gills.

Bustamente is yanking open the gyro housing. The room fills with a huge humming tone.

"I did not harm the beam," Tim says under Aaron's hands. "Certain equipment was installed when we built it; you did not look carefully enough."

"Son of a bitch," says Don Purcell.

"What do you mean, equipment?" Bustamente's voice rises, harmonic with the processing gyros. "What have you done, fly-boy?"

"I was not sent here to wait. The planet is there."

Aaron sees Captain Yellaston's lips moving effortfully, achieving a strange pursed look. "You indicated..." he says ee-rily, "you indicated... that is, you have preempted the green..."

The others stare at him, look away one by one. Aaron is stabbed with unbearable pity, he is suspecting that what has happened is so terrible it isn't real yet.

"Son of a bitch," Don Purcell repeats neutrally.

The green signal has been sent, Aaron realizes. To the Russians, anyway, but everybody will find out, everybody will start. It's all over, he's committed us whether that planet's any good or not. Oh god, Yellaston—he saw this coming, if he'd been younger, if he'd moved faster—if half his brains hadn't been scrambled in alcohol. I brought it to him.

Automatically his hands have completed their work. The Russian gets up. Don Purcell has left, Bustamente is probing the gyro-chamber with a resonator, not looking at Tim. Yellaston is still rigid in the shadows.

"It was in the hull shielding," Tim says to Bustamente. "The contact is under the toggles. Don't worry, it was one-time."

Aaron follows him out, unable to believe in any of this. Lieu-tenant Pauli is waiting outside; she must be in it, too.

"Tim, how could you be so goddam sure? You may have killed everybody."

The cosmonaut looks down at him calmly, one-eyed. "The records don't lie. They are enough, we will find nothing else. That old man would have waited forever." He chuckles, a dream-planet in his eye.

Aaron goes back in, leads Yellaston to his quarters. The cap-tain's arm is trembling faintly. Aaron is trembling too with pity and disgust. That old man, Tim had called him. That old man... Suddenly he realizes the full dimensions of this night's disaster.

Two years. The hell with the planet, maybe they won't even get there. Two years in this metal can with a captain who has failed, an old man mocked at in his drunkenness? No one to hold us together, as Yellaston had done during those unbearable weeks when the oxygen ran low, when panic had hung over all their heads. He had been so good then, so right. Now he's let Tim take it all away from him, he's lost it. We aren't together any more, not after this. It'll get worse. *Two years...*

"In the... fan," Yellaston whispers with tragic dignity, letting Aaron put him onto his bed. "In... the fan... my fault."

"In the morning," Aaron tells him gently, dreading the thought. "Maybe Ray can figure some way."

"...."

Aaron heads hopelessly for his bunk. He knows he won't sleep. *Two years...*

III

Silence... Bright, clinical emptiness, no clouds, no weeping. Horizon, infinity. Somewhere words rise, speaking silence: I AM THE SPOUSE. Cancel sound. Aaron, invisible and microbe-sized, sees on the floor of infinity a very beautifully veined silver membrane which he now recognizes as an adolescent's prepuce, the disjecta of his first operation...

Almost awake now, in foetal position; something terrible ahead if he wakes up. He tries to burrow back into dream but a hand is preventing him, jostling him back to consciousness.

He opens his eyes and sees Coby handing him a hot cup; a very bad sign.

"You know about Tim." Aaron nods, sipping clumsily.

"You haven't heard about Don Purcell, though. I didn't wake you. No medical aspects."

"What about Don Purcell? What happened?"

"Brace yourself, boss."

"For Christ's sake, don't piss around, Bill."

"Well, about oh-three-hundred we had this hull tremor. Blipped all Tighe's tapes. I called around, big flap, finally got the story. Seems Don fired his whole scouter off on automatic. It's loaded with a complete set of tapes, records, everything he could get his hands on. The planet, see? They say it can punch a signal through to Earth when it gets up speed."

"But Don, is Don in it?"

"Nobody's in it. It's set on autopilot. The *Beast* had some special goodies, too, our people must have a new ear up someplace. Mars, I heard."

"Jesus Christ..." So fast, it's happening, Aaron thinks. Where does Coby get his information, anything bad he knows it all.

Then he sees the faint appeal under Coby's grin; this is what he can do, his wretched offering.

"Thanks, Bill." Aaron gets up effortfully... First Tim and now Don—war games on *Centaur*. It's all wrecked, all gone.

"Things are moving too fast for the old man." Coby leans back familiarly on Aaron's bunk. "Good thing, too. We have to get a more realistic political organization. This great leader stuff, he's finished. Oh, we can keep him on as a figurehead... Don and Tim are out, too, for now anyway. First thing to start with, we elect a working committee."

"You're crazy, Bill. You can't run a ship with a committee. We'll kill ourselves if we start politics."

"Want to bet!" Coby grins. "Going to see some changes, boss."

Aaron sluices water over his head to shut off the voice. Elections, two years from nowhere? That'll mean the Russian faction, the U.S. faction, the Third and Fourth Worlders; scientists versus humanists versus techs versus ecologists versus theists versus Smithites—all the factions of Earth in one fragile ship. What shape will we be in when we reach the planet, if we live that long? And any colony we start—Oh, damn Yellaston, damn me—"General meeting at eleven hundred," Coby is saying. "And by the way, Tighe really did go wandering for about twenty minutes last night. My fault, I admit it, I forgot the isolation seal was off. No harm done. I got him right back in."

"Where was he?"

"Same place. By the port where *China* was."

"Take him with you to the meeting," Aaron says impulsively, punishing them all.

He goes out to get some breakfast, trying to shake out of the leaden feeling of oversleep, of doom impending. He dreads the meeting, dreads it. Poor old Yellaston trying futilely to cover his lapse, trying to save public face. A figurehead. He can't take that, he'll go into depression. Aaron makes himself set up Tighe's tapes to occupy his thoughts.

Tighe's tapes are worse than before, composite score down another five points, Aaron sees, even before the twenty-minute gap. His CNS functions are coming out of synch, too, an effect he hasn't seen in an ambulant patient, especially one as coordinated as Tighe. Curious... Have to study it, Aaron thinks apathetically. All our curves are coming out of synch, we're breaking up. Yellaston was our pacemaker. Can we make it without him?... Am I as dependent as Foy?

It is time for the meeting. He plods down to the Commons, sick with pity and dread; he is so reluctant to listen that he does not at first notice the miracle: There is nothing to pity. The Yellaston before his eyes is firm-voiced, erect, radiating leaderly charisma; is announcing, in fact the *Centaur's* official green code for the Alpha sun was beamed to Earth at oh-five-hundred this morning.

"What?"

"As some of you are aware," Yellaston says pleasantly, "our two scout commanders have also taken independent initiative to the same effect in messaging their respective Terrestrial governments. I want to emphasize that their actions were pursuant to specific orders from their superiors prior to embarkation. We all regret, we here who are joined in this mission have always regretted—that the United Nations of Earth who sponsored our mission were not more perfectly united when we left. We may hope they are now. But this is a past matter of no concern to us, arising from tensions on a world none of us may ever visit again. I want to say now that both Tim Bron and Don Purcell—" Yellaston makes a just-perceptible fatherly nod toward the two commanders, who are sitting quite normally on his left, despite Tim's taped eye "—faithfully carried out orders, however obsolete, just as I or any of us would have felt obligated to do in their places, had we been so burdened. Their duties have now been discharged. Their independent signals, if they arrive, will serve as confirmation to our official transmission to Earth as a whole.

"Now we must consider our immediate tasks."

Jesus god, Aaron thinks, the old bastard. The old fox, he's got it all back, he took the initiative right out from under them while I thought he was dead out. Fantastic. But how the hell? Running those lasers up is a job. Aaron looks around, catches a hooded gleam from Bustamente. Ol' Black George was cooking in his electronic jungle, he and Yellaston. Aaron grins to himself. He is happy, so happy that he ignores the inner murmur: *At a price.*

"The biologic examination of the planetary life-form returned to us by Commander Kuh will start at about sixteen hundred this afternoon. It will be conducted in Corridor Gamma One under decontaminant seal, but the entire operation will be displayed on your viewers." Yellaston smiles. "You will probably see it better than I will. Next, and concurrently, the Drive section will prepare to initiate change of course toward the Alpha planet. Each of you will secure your areas for acceleration and course-change as speedily as possible. The vector loadings will be posted tomorrow. Advise Don and Tim of any problems in their respective sections. First Engineer Singh will deal with Gamma section in the absence of Commander Kuh. And finally, we must commence the work of adapting and refining our general colonization plan to the planetary data now at hand. Our first objective is a planetary atlas incorporating every indicator that your specialties can extract from the *Gamma* tapes. On this we can build our plans. I remind you that this is a task requiring imagination and careful thought of every contingency and parameter. Gentlemen, ladies: The die is cast. We have only two years to prepare for the greatest adventure our race has known."

Aaron starts to smile at the archaism, finds he has a fullness in the throat. The hush around him holds for a minute; Yellaston nods to Don and Tim and they get up and exit with him. Perfect, Aaron thinks. We'll make it, we're okay. Screw Coby. Daddy lives. Everyone is jabbering now, Aaron makes his way through them past the great flowering wonder of Lory's — of the Alpha planet. Our future home. Yellaston will get us there, he's pulled it out.

But at a price, the gloomy corner of his forebrain repeats. The big green light is on its way to Earth. Not only we but all the people of Earth are committed, committed to that world. That planet *has* to be all right now.

He goes to assemble his equipment, irrationally resolved to double his emergency decontaminant array.

log 124 586 sd 4100 X 1200 notice to all personnel

corridor gamma one will be under space hazard seal starting 1545 this day for the purpose of bioanalysis of alien life specimen // attendance will be limited to: [1] centaur command cadre alpha [2] designated xenobiosurvey/medical personnel [3] eva team charlie [4] safety/survival staff assigned to corridor access locks // the foregoing personnel will be suited at all times until the unsealing of the corridor // because of the unknown risk-factor in this operation additional guards will also be stationed on the inboard side of all access ports: see special-duty roster attached // unauthorized personnel will not, repeat not, enter gamma one starting as of now // video cover of the entire operation from the closest feasible points will be available on all screens on ship channel one, starting approximately 1515 *hours*

yellaston, cmdg

In Corridor Gamma One, the major risk-factor is wires. Aaron leans on a bulkhead amid his tangle of equipment, holding his bulky suit and watching Jan Ing wrangle with Electronics. The Xenobiology chief wants a complete computer capability in the corridor; there is no way of passing the cable through the lock seals. The EVA team is appealed to but they refuse to give up any of their service terminals. Finally the issue is resolved by sacrificing an access-lock indicator panel. Engineer Gomulka, who will double as a guard, starts cutting it out to bring the computer leads in.

Wires are snaking all over the deck. XB has brought in half their laboratory, and he can see at least eight other waldo-type devices in addition to the biomonitor extension equipment. On top of it all the camera crew is setting up. One camera opposite the small hatch that will open into *China Flower's* command section, two by the big cargo hatch behind which the alien thing will be, plus a couple of overhead views. They are also mounting some ceiling slave screens for the corridor, Aaron is glad to find. He is too far back to see the hatches. The Safety team is trying to get the cables cleared into bundles along the wall, but the mess is bound to get worse when the suit umbilicals come into use. Mercifully, general suiting-up will not take place until the EVA team has winched *China Flower* up to her berth.

Aaron's station is the farthest one away at the stern end of the corridor. In front of him is an open space with the EVA floor lock, and then starts the long Xenobiology clutter. Beyond XB is the cargo hatch and then the small hatch, and finally in the distance is the corridor command station. Command Cadre Alpha means Yellaston and Tim Bron. Aaron can just make out Tim's eye-patch, he's talking with Don Purcell who will go back to man *Centaur's* bridge. In case of trouble... Aaron peers at his racks of decontaminant aerosols mounted opposite the hatches. They have wires, too, running to a switch beside his hand. He had trouble with XB about those cans; Jan Ing would rather be eaten alive than risk damaging their precious specimen of alien life.

A hand falls on his shoulder — Captain Yellaston, coming in the long way round, his observant face giving no hint of what must be the chemical conditions in his bloodstream.

"The die is cast," Aaron observes.

Yellaston nods. "A gamble," he says quietly. "The mission... I may have done a fearful thing, Aaron. They were bound to come, on the strength of the other two."

"The only thing you could have done, sir."

"No." Aaron looks up. Yellaston isn't talking to him; his eyes are on some cold cosmic scoreboard. "No. I should have sent code yellow and announced I had sent the green. Ray would have kept silent. That would have held back the U.N. ships at least. It was the correct move. I failed to think it through in time."

He moves on down the corridor, leaving Aaron stunned. Sent the yellow and lied to us for two years? *Captain Yellaston?* But yes, Aaron sees slowly, that would have saved something, in case the planet is no good. It would have been better. What he did was good but it wasn't the best. Because he was drunk... My fault. My stupid susceptibilities, my romanticism —

People are jostling past him, it's the EVA team, suited and ready to go out. The last man by punches Aaron's arm — Bruce Jang, giving him a mean wink through his gold-washed face-plate. Aaron watches them file down into the EVA blister lock, remembering the same thing three weeks ago when they had gone out to bring in *China Flower* with Lory unconscious inside. This time all they have to do is reel up the tether. Risky enough.

The rotational mechanics could send a man into space, Aaron thinks; he is always awed by skills he doesn't have.

A videoscreen comes to life, showing stars. A space suit occults them; when it passes, three small yellow stars are moving toward a blackness — the helmet lights of the team going down to *China Flower* far below. Aaron's gut jumps; an *alien* is out there, he is about to meet an *alien*. He blinks, begins to sort and assemble the extensor mounts on which his sensors will be intruded into the scouter's cargo hold. As he does so, he notices faces peering at him through the vitrex of the nearest access lock. He waves. The faces, perceiving that the scenario has not yet started, go away. It will be, Aaron realizes, a long afternoon.

By the time he and Ing have lined up their equipment all non-operational people except the suit team have left the corridor. The hull has been groaning softly; *China Flower* is rising to them on her winch. Suddenly the wall beside him clanks, grinds reverberatingly — the port probes engage, the grinding stops. Aaron shivers involuntarily: the alien is here.

As the EVA lock cycle begins flashing, Tim Bron's voice says on the audio, "All hands will now suit up."

The EVA team is coming back inside. The suit men work down the corridor, checking and paying out the umbilicals as neatly as they can. It's going to be cramped working. The suit team reach him last. As he seals in he sees more faces at the side lock. The videoscreens are all on now giving a much better view, but still the faces remain. Aaron chuckles to himself; the old ape impulse to see with the living eye.

"All non-operational personnel will now clear the area."

The EVA team is lined up along the wall opposite *China Flower's* command hatch. The plan is to open this first in order to retrieve the scoutship's automatic records of the alien's life-processes. Is it still alive in there? Aaron has no mystic intuitions now, only a great and growing tension in his gut. He makes himself breathe normally.

"Guards, secure the area."

The last corridor entrances are dogged tight. Aaron sees a faceplate turned toward him three stations up the XB line. The face belongs to Lory. He flinches slightly; he had forgotten she would be here. He lifts his gloved hand, wishing he was between her and that cargo port.

The area is secure, the guards stationed. Bruce Jang and two other EVA men move up to open the lock coupled to *China Flower's* command port. Aaron watches the close-up on the overhead screen. Metal clinks, the lock hatch slides sideways. The EVA men go in carrying vapor analyzers, the hatch rolls shut. Another wait. Aaron sees the XB people tuning their suit radios, realizes the EVA men are reporting. He gets the channel: "Nominal.... Atmosphere nominal (crackle, crackle)..." The hatch is sliding back again, the men come out accompanied by a barely perceptible fogginess. Lory looks back at him again; he understands. This is the air she had breathed for nearly a year.

The ship's tapes are being handed out. The alien is, it appears, alive.

"Metabolic trace regular to preliminary inspection, envelope unchanged," Jan Ing's voice comes on the audio. "Intermittent bioluminescence, two to eighty candlepower." Eighty candlepower, that's *bright* So Lory hadn't lied about that, anyway. "A strong peak coinciding with the original docking with *Centaur*... a second peak occurred, yes, about the time the scoutship was removed from its berth."

That would be about when Tighe did—or didn't—open its container, Aaron thinks. Or maybe it was stimulated by moving the ship.

"One of the fans which circulate its atmosphere is not operating," the XB chief goes on, "but the remaining fans seem to have provided sufficient movement for adequate gas exchange. Its surface atmosphere requires continuous renewal, since it is adapted to constant planetary wind. It also exhibits pulselike internal pressure changes—"

Aaron's mind is momentarily distracted by the vision of himself stepping out into planetary wind, a stream of wild unrecycled air. That creature in there dwells on wind. A podlike mass about four meters long, Lory had described it. Like a big bag of fruit. Squatting in there for a year, metabolizing, pulsing, luminescing—what else has it been doing? The functions of life: assimilation, excitation, reproduction. Has it been reproducing? Is the hold full of Coby's tiny monsters waiting to pounce out? Or ooze out, swallowing us all? Aaron notices he has drifted away from his decontaminant switches; he moves back.

"The mass is constant, activity vectors stable," Jan concludes.

So it hasn't been multiplying. Just squatting there. Thinking, maybe? Aaron wonders if those bioluminescence peaks would correlate with any phenomena on *Centaur*. What phenomena? Tighe sightings, maybe, or nightmares? Don't be an idiot, he tells himself; the imp in his ear replies that those New England colonists didn't correlate ocean currents and winter temperatures, either... Absently he has been following the EVA team's debate on whether to cut open the viewport to the alien that Lory welded shut. It is decided not to try this but to proceed directly to the main cargo lock.

The team comes out and the men assigned to the extension probes pick up their equipment, cables writhing in a slow snake dance. Bruce and the EVA chief undog the heavy cargo hatch. This is the port through which the scoutship's groundside equipment, their vehicles and flier and generator were loaded in. The hatch rolls silently aside, the two men go into the lock. Aaron can see them on the videoscreen, unsealing the scouter's port. It opens; no vapor comes out because the hold is unpressurized. Beyond the suited figures Aaron can see the shiny side of the cargo-module in which the alien is confined. The sensor men advance, angling their probes into the lock like long-necked beasts. Aaron glances up at another screen which shows the corridor as a whole and experiences an odd, oceanic awareness.

Here we are, he thinks, tiny blobs of life millions and millions of miles from the speck that spawned us, hanging out here in the dark wastes, preparing with such complex pains to encounter a different mode of life. All of us, peculiar, wretchedly imperfect—somehow we have done this thing. Incredible, really, the ludicrous tangle of equipment, the awkward suited men, the precautions, the labor, the solemnity—Jan, Bruce, Yellaston, Tim Bron, Bustamente, Alice Berryman, Coby, Kawabata, my saintly sister, poor Frank Foy, stupid Aaron Kaye—a stream of faces pours through his mind, hostile, suffering each in his separate flawed reality: all of us. Somehow we have brought ourselves to this amazement. Perhaps we really are saving our race, he thinks, perhaps there really is a new earth and heaven ahead...

The moment passes; he watches the backs of the men inside *China,* still struggling with the module port. The sensor men have closed in, blocked the view. Aaron glances up at the bow end of the corridor where Yellaston and Tim Bron stand. Yellaston's arm is extended stiffly to the top of his console. That must be the evacuation control; if he pulls it the air ducts will open, the corridor will depressurize in a couple of minutes. So will the alien's module if it's open. Good; Aaron feels reassured. He checks his own canister-release switch, finds he has again strayed forward and moves back.

Confused exclamations, grunts are coming over the suit channel; apparently there is a difficulty with the module port. One of the sensor men drops his probe, moves in. Another follows. What's the trouble?

The screen shows nothing but suit backs, the whole EVA team is in there—Oh! Sudden light, cracks of radiance between the men silhouetting them blue against a weird pink light—Is it fire? Aaron's heart jumps, he clambers onto a stanchion to see over heads. Not fire, there's no smoke. Oh, of course, he realizes—that light is the alien's own luminescence! They have opened the module.

But why are they all in there, why aren't they falling back to push the sensors in? Wide rosy light flashes, hidden by bodies. They must have opened the whole damn port instead of just cracking it. Is that thing trying to come out?

"Close it, get out!" Aaron calls into his suit mike. But the channel is a bedlam of static. Everybody is crowding forward toward that hatch, too. That's dangerous. "Captain!" Aaron shouts futilely. He can see Yellaston's hand still on the panel, but Tim Bron seems to be holding onto his arm. The EVA men are all inside *China Flower*, inside the module even, it's impossible to tell. A pink flare lights up the corridor, winks out again.

"Move back! Get back to your stations!" Yellaston's voice cuts in on the command channel override and the intercom babble goes dead. Aaron is suddenly aware of pressure around him, discovers that he is all the way up at the XB stations, being crowded by someone behind. It's Akin's face inside the safety guard visor. They disengage clumsily, move back.

"Go back to your stations! EVA team, report."

Aaron is finding movement oddly effortful. He wants very much to open his stifling helmet.

"George, can you hear me? Get your men out."

The screen is showing confused movement, more colored flashes. Is somebody hurt? There's a figure, coming slowly out of the hatch.

"What's going on in there, George? Why is your helmet open?"

Aaron stares incredulously as the EVA chief emerges into the corridor—his face-plate is open, tipped back on his head. What the hell is happening? Did the alien grab them? The chief's arm goes up, he is making the okay signal; the suit-to-suit channel is still out. The others are coming out behind him, the strange light shining on their backs, making a great peach-colored glow in the corridor. Their visors are open, too. But they seem to be all right, whatever happened in there.

The screen is showing the module port; all Aaron can make out is a big rectangle of warm-colored light. It seems to be softly bubbling or shifting, like a light show—globes of rose, yellow, lilac—it's beautiful, really. Hypnotic. They should close it, he thinks, hearing Yellaston ordering the men to seal their helmets. With an effort Aaron looks away, sees Yellaston still by his station, his arm rigid. Tim Bron seems to have moved away. It's all right, nothing has happened. It's all right.

"Get those suits closed before I depressurize!"

The EVA chief is slowly pulling his face-plate down, so are the others. Their movements seem vague, unfocussed. One of them stumbles over the biopsy equipment. Why doesn't he pick it up? Something *is* wrong with them. Aaron frowns. His brain feels gassy. Why aren't they carrying out the program, doing something about the bioluminescence? It's probably all right, though, Yellaston is there. He's watching.

At this moment he is jostled hard. He blinks, recovers balance, looks around. Jesus—he's in the wrong place—everybody is in the wrong place. The whole corridor is jamming forward of where it's supposed to be, staring at that marvelous glow. The guards—they're not by the ports! Something is not all right at all, Aaron realizes. It's that light, it's doing something to us! *Close the port,* he wills, trying to get back to his station. It's like moving in water. The emergency switch—he has to reach it, how did he ever get so far away? And the ports, he sees, the vitrex is crowded with faces, people are in the access ramps staring into the corridor. They've come from all over the ship. What's wrong? What's happening to us?

Cold fear bursts up in his gut. He catches the EVA lock and clings to it fighting an invisible slow tide. Part of him wants to push his helmet off and run forward to the radiance coming from that port. People ahead of him are opening their visors—he can see Jan Ing's sharp Danish nose.

"Stand away from that port!" Yellaston shouts. At that Jan Ing darts forward, pushing people aside. "Stop," Aaron yells into his useless mike, finds himself opening his own visor, moving after Jan. Voices, sounds fill his ears. He grabs another stanchion, pulls himself up to look for Yellaston. The captain is still there; he seems to be struggling slowly with Tim Bron. The light is gone now, hidden by a press of bodies around the port. That thing in there is doing this, Aaron tells himself; he is terrified in a curious unreal way, his head is singing thickly. He is also angry with those people down there—they are going in, blocking it. Lost! But is it they who are lost or the wonderful light?

Someone bumps breast-to-breast with him, pulling at his arm. He looks down into Lory's blazing face. Her helmet is gone.

"Come on, Arn! We'll go together."

Primal distrust sends an icicle into his mind; he grabs her suit, anchors himself to a console with his other arm. Lory! She's in league with that thing, he knows it, this is her crazy plot. He has to stop it. Kill it! Where is his emergency release? It's too far, too far—

"Captain!" he shouts with all his strength, fighting Lory, thinking, two minutes, we can get out. "Depressurize! Dump the air!"

"No, Arn! It's beautiful—don't be afraid!"

"Dump the air, kill it!" he yells again, but his voice can't override the confusion. Lory is yanking on his arm, her exultant face fills him with sharp fright. "What is it?" He shakes her by the belt. "What are you trying to do?"

"It's time, Arn! It's *time,* come on—there're so many people—"

He tries to get a better grip on her, hearing metal clang behind him and realizes too late he has let go his hold on the console. But her words are now making a kind of sense to him—there are too many people, it is important, quite important to get there before something is all used up. Why is he letting them hide that light? Lory has his hand now, drawing him toward the press of people ahead.

"You'll see, it will all be gone, the pain... Arn dear, we'll be together."

The beauty of it floods Aaron's soul, washes all fear away. Just beyond those bodies is the goal of man's desiring, the fountain—the Grail itself maybe, the living radiance! He sees an opening by the wall, pulls Lory through—and is suddenly squeezed by more bodies from the side, a wall of people flooding out of the access port. Aaron fights to hold his ground, hold Lory, only dimly aware that he is struggling against familiar faces—Ahlstrom is beside him, smiling orgasmically, he pushes past Kawabata, ducks under somebody's arm. As he does, a force slams their backs—he is clouted into something entangling and falls down under an XB analyzer still clutching Lory's wrist.

"Arn, Arn, come on!"

Legs are going by him. It was Bustamente who hit him, forging past followed by a forest of legs. They have all come here to claim the shining glory in the port! Wildly enraged, Aaron struggles up, falls again with his own leg deep in a web of cables.

"Arn, get up!" She jerks at him fiercely. But he is suddenly calmer, although he does not cease to wrench at his trapped leg. There is a small intercom screen by his head, he can see two tiny struggling figures—Yellaston and Tim Bron, their helmets gone. Dreamlike, tiny... Tim breaks away. Yellaston nods once, and fells Tim from behind with a blow of both locked fists. Then he slowly steps over the fallen man and goes off screen. Pink light flares out.

They have all gone in there, Aaron realizes, heartbroken. It has called us and we have come—I *must* go. But he frowns, blinks; a part of him has doubts about the pull, the sweet longing. It feels fainter down here. Maybe that pile of stuff is shielding me, he thinks confusedly. Lory is yanking at the cables around his legs. He pulls her up to him.

"Lor, what's happening to them? What happened to—" he cannot recall the Chinese commander's name " —what happened to your, your crew?"

"Changed," she is panting. Her face is incredibly beautiful. "Merged, healed. Made whole. Oh, you'll see, hurry—Can't you *feel* it, Arn?"

"But—" He can feel it all right, the pull, the promising urgency, but he feels something else too—the ghost of Dr. Aaron Kaye is screaming faintly in his head, threatening him. Lory is trying to lift him bodily now. He resists, fearing to be drawn from his shielded nook. The corridor around them is empty now but he can hear people in the distance, a thick babbling down by that hatch. No screams, nothing like panic. Disregarding Lory, he cranes to get a look at the big ceiling screen. They are all there, milling rather aimlessly, he has never seen so many people pressed so close. This is a medical emergency, he thinks. I am the doctor. He has a vision of Dr. Aaron Kaye getting to the levers that will seal that cargo hatch, standing firm against the crowd, saving them from whatever is in that hold. But he cannot; Dr. Aaron Kaye is only a thin froth of fear on a helpless, lunging desire to go there himself, to fling himself into that beautiful warm light. He is going to be very ashamed, he thinks vaguely, tied here like Ulysses against the siren call, huddling under an analyzer bench while the others—What? He studies the screen again, he can see no apparent trouble, no one has fallen. The EVA men came out all right, he tells himself. What I have to do is get out of here.

Lory laughs, pulling at his legs; she has freed him, he sees. He is sliding. Effortfully he reaches into his suit, finds the panic syringe.

"Arn dear—" Her slender neck muscles are exposed; he grabs her hair, seats the spray. She wails and struggles maniacally but he holds on, waiting for the shot to work. His head feels clearer. The aching pull is less; maybe all those people are blocking it somehow. The thought hurts him. He tries to disregard it, thinking, if I can get across the corridor, into that access ramp, I can seal it behind me. Maybe.

Suddenly there is movement to his left—a pair of legs, slowly stepping by his refuge. Pale gold legs he recognizes.

"Soli! Soli, stop!"

The legs pause, a small hand settles on the overturned stand beyond him. Just within reach—he can spring and grab her, letting go of Lory—to reach her he must let Lory go. He lunges, feels Lory pull away and clutches her again. He falls short. The hand is gone.

"Soli! Soli! Come back!" Her footsteps move on down the corridor, languidly. Dr. Aaron Kaye will be ashamed, ashamed; he knows it. "The EVA men were okay," he mutters. Lory is weakening now, her eyes vague. "No, Arn," she sighs, sighs deeply again. Aaron rolls her, gets a firm grip on her suit-belt and crawls out into the corridor.

As his head clears the shelter, the sweet pull grabs him again. There—down there is the goal! "I'm a doctor," he groans, willing his limbs. A thick cable is under his hand. From miles away he recognizes it—the XB computer lead, running toward the inboard lock. If he can follow that across the corridor he will be at the ramp.

He clasps it, starts to shuffle on his knees, dragging Lory. The thing down there is pulling at the atoms of his soul, his head is filled with urgent radiance calling to him to drop the foolish cable and run to join his mates. "I'm a *doctor*," he mumbles; it requires all his strength to slide his gloved hand along his lifeline, he is turning away from bliss beyond his dreams. Only meters to go. It is impossible. Why is he refusing, going the wrong way? He will turn. But something has changed... He is at the lock, he sees; he must let go the cable and drag Lory over the sill.

Sobbing, he does so; it is almost more than he can bear to nudge the heavy port with his heel and send it swinging closed behind them.

As it closes the longing lessens perceptibly. Metal, he thinks vacantly, it has blocked it a little, maybe it is some kind of EM field. He looks up. A figure is standing by the lock.

"Tiger! What are you doing here?" Aaron pulls himself upright with Lory huddled by his feet. Tighe looks at them uncertainly, says nothing.

"What's in that boat, Tiger? The alien, did you see it? What is it?"

Tighe's face wavers, crumples. "Mu... muh," his mouth jerks. "Mother."

No help here. Just in time, Aaron notices his own hands opening the port-lever. He takes Lory under the arms and drags her farther away up the ramp to the emergency intercom panel. Her eyes are still open, her hands are fumbling weakly at her suit-fastenings.

Aaron breaks out the caller. It's an all-ship channel.

"Don! Commander Purcell, can you hear me? This is Dr. Kaye, I'm in ramp six, there's been trouble down here."

No answer. Aaron calls again, calls Coby, calls the Commo and Safety COs, calls everybody he can think of, calls himself hoarse. No answer. Has everybody on *Centaur* gone into corridor Gamma One, is the whole damned ship out there with that—

Except Tighe. Aaron frowns at the damaged man. He was in here, he didn't join the stampede.

"Tiger, did you go out there?"

Tighe mouths, emits what could be a negative. He seems uninterested in the port. What does it take to stay sane near that thing, Aaron wonders, cortical suppressants? Or did one contact immunize him? Can we prepare drugs, can I lobotomize myself and still function? He notices he has drifted closer to the port, that Lory is crawling toward it, half out of her suit. He pulls her out of it, gets them both back up the ramp.

When he looks up there is a shadow on the port view-panel.

For a terrified instant Aaron is sure it is the alien coming for him. Then he sees a human hand, slowly tapping. Somebody trying to get in — but he dare not go down there.

"Tiger! Open the port, let the man in." He gestures wildly at Tighe. "The port, look! You remember, hit the latch, Tiger. Open up!"

Tighe hesitates, turns in place. Then an old reflex fires; he sidesteps and slaps double-handed at the latch with perfect coordination — and as quickly sags again. The port swings open. Captain Yellaston stands there. Deliberately he steps through.

"Captain, captain, are you all right?" Aaron starts to run forward, checks himself. "Tiger, close the port."

Yellaston is walking stiffly toward him, looking straight ahead. Face a little pale, Aaron thinks, no injuries visible. He's all right, whatever happened. It's all right.

"Captain, I—" But there are more figures at the port, Aaron sees, Tim Bron and Coby, coming in past Tighe. Others beyond. Aaron has never been so glad to see his assistant, he yells something at him and turns to catch up with Yellaston.

"Captain—" He wants to ask about sealing off the corridor, about examining them all. But Yellaston does not look around.

"The red," Yellaston says in a faint remote voice. "The red... is the correct... signal." He walks on, toward the bridge.

Some sort of shock, Aaron thinks, and sees movement by the wall ahead — it is Lory, up and staggering away from him. But she isn't going toward the corridor, she's going up a ramp into the ship. The clinic is where she belongs. Aaron starts after her, confident that the drug will slow her down. But his suit is awkward, he has not counted on that feral vitality. She stays ahead of him, she gains speed up the twisting tube as the gees let go. He pounds up after her, past the dormitory levels, past Stores; he is half-sailing now. Lory dives into the central freefall shaft— but not going straight, he sees her twist left, toward the bridge.

Cursing, Aaron follows her in. His feet miss the guides, he ricochets, has trouble regaining speed. Lory is a receding minnow-shape ahead of him, going like a streak. She shoots through the command-section sphincter, checks. Damn, she's closing it against him.

By the time he gets it open and goes through, the core shaft is empty. Aaron kicks on into the Astrogation dome. Nobody there. He climbs out of the freefall area and starts back around the computer corridor. Nobody here either. Ahlstrom's gleaming pets are untended. This has never happened before. It's like a ghost ship. Station after station is empty. The physics display-screen is running a calculation, unobserved.

A sound breaks the silence, coming from the next ring aft. Oh god, Bustamente's Commo room! Aaron can't find the inside door, he doubles back out into the corridor, races clumsily sternwards, terror in his guts as the sound rises to a scream.

The Commo room is open. Aaron plunges in, checks in horror. Lory is standing in the sacred gyro chamber. The scream is coming from the open gyro housings. Her arm jerks out sending a stream of objects—headsets, jacks, wrenches—into the flying wheels.

"Stop!" He lunges for her, but the sound has risen to a terrible yammering. A death cry—the great pure beings who have spun there faultlessly for a decade holding their lifeline to Earth are in mortal agony. They clash, collide horribly. A cam shoots past him, buries itself in the wall. She has killed them, his mad sister.

Gripping her he stands there stunned, scarcely able to take in other damage. The housing of the main laser crystals is wrecked; they have been hit with something. That hardly matters now, Aaron thinks numbly. Without the gyros to aim them the beam is only an idiot's finger flailing across the stars.

"We, we'll go together now, Arn." Lory hangs on him, weak now. "They can't—stop us any more."

Aaron's substrate takes over; he utters a howl and starts to shake her by the neck, squeezing, crushing—but is startled into stasis by a voice behind him, saying "Bustamente."

He wheels. It is Captain Yellaston.

"I will send... the red signal... now."

"You can't!" Aaron yells in rage. "You can't, it's broken! *She* broke it!" Preadolescent fury floods him, ebbs as he sees that remote, uncomprehending face.

"You will send... the red signal." The man is in shock, all right.

"Sir, we can't—we can't send anything right now." Aaron releases Lory, takes Yellaston's arm. Yellaston frowns down at him, purses his lips. A two-liter night. He lets himself be turned away, headed toward his quarters. Aaron is irrationally grateful: As long as Yellaston hasn't seen the enormity it isn't real. He pulls back the captain's glove, checks the pulse as they go. About sixty; slow but not arrhythmic.

"The technical capacity..." Yellaston mutters, going into his room. "If you have the efficiency... you'll wake up in the morning..."

"Please lie down awhile, Captain." Aaron closes the door, sees Lory wandering behind him. He takes her arm and starts back toward his office, resisting the faint urge to turn toward Gamma One. If he can only get to his office he can begin to function, decide what to do. What has hit *Centaur's* people, what did that alien do? A static discharge, maybe, like an electric eel? Better try his standard adrenergic stim-shot, if the heartrates are okay. That overwhelming attractant—he can feel it now, even here in Beta corridor on the far side of the ship. Like a phero-mone, Aaron decides. That thing is a sessile life-form, maybe it attracts food, maybe it gets itself fertilized that way. Just hap-pens that it works on man. A field, maybe, like gravity. Or some fantastically attenuated particle. The suits didn't stop it com-pletely. I should seal it off, that's the first thing, he tells himself, leading Lory, docile now. They are passing Don's scoutship berth. But the *Beast* isn't here, it's god knows how many thou-sand miles away now, blatting out its message.

Someone is here—Don Purcell is standing by an access ramp, staring at the deck. Aaron drags Lory faster.

"Don! Commander, are you okay?"

Don's head turns to him; the grin is there, the eyes have smile-wrinkles. But Aaron sees his pupils are unequally dilated, like a poleaxed steer. How severe was that shock? He takes the unresisting wrist.

"Can you recognize me, Don? It's Aaron. It's Doc. You've had a physical shock, you shouldn't be wandering around." Pulse slow, like Yellaston's; no irregularity Aaron can catch. "I want you to come with me to the clinic."

The strong body doesn't move. Aaron pulls at him, realizes he can't budge him alone. He needs his syringe-kit, too.

"That's a medical order, Don. Report for treatment."

The smile slowly focusses on him, puzzled.

"The power," Don says in the voice he uses at chapel. "The hand of the Almighty on the deep..."

"See, Arn?" Lory reaches out toward Don, pats him. "He's changed. He's gentle." She smiles tremulously.

Aaron leads her on, wondering how seriously people have been hit. *Centaur* can sustain itself for days, that part's all right. He will not think of the more fearful hurt, the murdered gyros;

Bustamente—Bustamente can do something, somehow. But how long are people going to remain in shock? How many of them got hit by that thing, who is functioning besides himself? Could it be permanent damage? Impossible, he tells himself firmly; a shock that severe would have finished poor Tighe. Impossible.

As he turns off to the clinic Lory suddenly pulls back.

"No, Arn, this way!"

"We're going to the office, Lor. I have work to do."

"Oh no, Arn. Don't you *understand?* We're going now, together." Her voice is plaintive, with a loose, slurred quality. Aaron's training wakes up. Chemical supplementation, as Foy said—this is the time to get some answers from the subject.

"I'm scared, Sis. Talk to me a minute, then we'll go. What happened to them, what happened to Mei-Lin and the others on the planet?"

"Mei-Lin?" she frowns.

"Yes, what did you see them do? You can tell me now, Lor. Did you see them out there?"

"Oh, yes..." She gives a vague little laugh. "I saw them. They left me in the ship, Arn. They, they didn't want me." Her lips quiver.

"What did they do, Lor?"

"Oh, they walked. Little Kuh had the video, I could see where they went. Up the hills, toward the, toward the beauty... It was hours, hours and hours. And then Mei-Lin and Liu went on ahead, I could see them running—Oh, Arn, I wanted to run too, you can't imagine how they look—"

"What happened then, Lor?"

"They took off their helmets and then the camera fell down, I guess the others were all running too. I could see their feet—it was like a mountain of jewels in the sun—" Tears are running down her face, she rubs her fist at them like a child.

"What did you see then? What did the jewel-thing do to them?"

"It didn't do anything." She smiles, sniffing. "They just touched it, you know, with their minds. You'll *see*, Arn. Please— let's go now."

"In a minute, Lor. Tell me, did they fight?"

"Oh, no!" Her eyes widen at him. "No! Oh, I made that up to protect it. No hurting any more, never. They came back so gentle, so happy. They were all changed, they shed all that. It's waiting for us, Arn, see? It wants to deliver us. We'll be truly human at last." She sighs. "Oh, I wanted so much to go, too, it was terrible. I had to tie myself, even in the suit. I *had* to bring it back to you. And I did, didn't I?"

"You got that thing in the scouter all by yourself, Lor?"

She nods, dream-eyed. "I found a little one, I poked it with the front-end loader." The contrast between her words and her face is weird.

"What were Kuh and his men doing all this time? Didn't they try to stop you?"

"Oh no, they watched. They were around. Please Arn, come on."

"How long did it take you!"

"Oh, days, Arn, it was so hard. I could only do a little at a time."

"You mean they didn't recover for days? What about that tape, Lor; you faked it, didn't you?"

"I, I edited it a little. He wasn't... interested." Her eyes shift evasively. Control returning. "Arn, don't be *afraid*. The bad things are over now. Can't you feel it, the goodness?"

He can—it's there, pulling at him faint and bliss-laden. He shudders awake, discovers he has let her lead him nearly to the core, toward Gamma One. Angrily he makes himself grab the handrail and start hauling her back toward the clinic. It is like moving through glue, his body doesn't want to.

"No, Arn, no!" She pulls back, sobbing. "You *have* to, I worked so hard—"

He concentrates grimly on his feet. The clinic door is ahead now, to his infinite relief he can see Coby inside at the desk.

"You aren't coming!" Lory wails and jerks violently out of his grasp. "You—Oh—"

He jumps for her, but she is running away again, running like a goddamned deer. Aaron checks himself. He cannot chase after her now, he has evaded his duty too long as it is. Days, she said. This is appalling. And they were walking around. Brain damage... Don't think of it.

He goes into the office. Coby is looking at him.

"My sister is in psychotic fugue," Aaron tells him. "She damaged our communication equipment. Sedation ineffective—" He perceives he is acting irrationally, he should tackle the major medical situation first.

"How many people got shocked by that thing, Bill?"

Coby's noncommittal gaze does not change. Finally he says dully, "Shock. Oh, yes. Shock." His lip twists in a ghostly sneer.

Oh, god no... Coby was in that corridor, too.

"Jesus, Bill, did it get you? I'm going to give you a shot of AD-twelve. Unless you have other ideas?"

Coby's eyes are following him. Maybe he isn't as severely affected, Aaron thinks.

"Post coitum tristum." Coby's voice is very low. "I am tristum."

"What did it do to you, Bill, can you tell me?"

The silent, sad stare continues. Just as Aaron opens the hypokit Coby says clearly, "I know a ripe corpus luteum when I see one." He gives a faint, nasty chuckle.

"What?" Obscene visions leap to life in Aaron's head as he bares Coby's elbow and sends the epidermal jet into the vein. "Did you, you didn't have some sort of intercourse with that thing, Bill?"

"In-ter-course?" Coby echoes in a whisper. "No... not ours, anyway. If somebody had... in-ter-course it was god, maybe... Or a planet... Not us... It had *us.*"

His pulse is slow, skin cold. "What do you mean, Bill?"

Coby's face quivers, he stares up into Aaron's eyes fighting to hang on to consciousness. "Say we were carrying it... carrying a load of jizzum in our heads, I guess... And the jizzum meets... the queen couzy, the queen couzy of all time... and it jumps... jumps across. It makes some kind of holy... zygote, out there... see? Only we're left... empty... What happens to a sperm's tail... afterwards?"

"Take it easy, Bill." Aaron will not listen, oh no, not to delirium. His best diagnostician raving.

Coby emits another ghastly snicker. "Good old Aaron," he whispers. "You didn't..." His eyes go blank.

"Bill, try to pull yourself together. Stay right there. People are in shock, they're wandering around disoriented. I have work to do, can you hear me? Stay here, I'll be back."

Visions of himself hustling through the ship, reviving people — more important, sealing off that corridor, too. He loads a kit of stim-hypos, adds cardiotropics, detoxicants. An hour too late, Dr. Aaron Kaye is on the job. He draws hot brew for them both. Coby doesn't look.

"Drink up, Bill. I'll be back."

He sets off to Stores, steering against the pull from Gamma One. It is weak here. He can make it quite easily. Is it in refractory phase maybe? Shot its bolt. How long to recovery? Better attend to that first, can't let it get them all over again.

Miriamne Stein is at her desk, her face absolutely quiet.

"It's Doc, Miri. You've had a shock, this will help you." He hopes, administering it to her passive arm. Her empty eyes slowly turn. "I'm checking out some EVA rope, see? I'll leave you a receipt right here, Miri, look. You stay there until you feel better."

Outside, he lets himself start across the ship, going with the pull. Joy opens in him, it is like a delicious sliding, like letting go sexually in his head... Am I acting rationally? He probes himself, scared. Yes—he can make himself turn, make himself go forward toward the first bow-ramp. His plan is to close all the ports the crowd left open on their way into the corridor. Fourteen. After that—after that he can, he knows, vent the air from the inboard side. Depressurizing will kill it, of course. The sensible thing to do. No, surely that isn't necessary? He will think about it later, something is hurting him right now.

At the bow-ramp his head still feels okay, the thing's... lure is weak. The port is open; Don probably came this way. Cautiously, Aaron risks going down to it without tying his rope. All right; he has it swinging shut. As it closes he peeks out down the corridor. A mess, no people he can see—but the rosy living radiance—his heart misses, jumps—and the port closes almost on his nose.

A near thing. He must take no chances on the next one—it will be nearer to that marvelous light, will be in fact behind the command console where Yellaston was. Aaron finds his feet hurrying, stops himself at the last turn in the ramp and ties one end of the tether to a wall-hold. The other end he knots around his waist. Multiple knottings, must not be able to untie these in a hurry.

It's well he did so, he finds; he is already stepping into the corridor itself, stumbling on helmets, gloves, cables. The great flare of warm light is about twenty meters ahead. He must go back, go back and close the port. He stops himself at the command console and looks up at the videoscreen, still focussed on *China Flower's* fiery heart. It *is* like jewels in there, he sees, awestruck—great softly glowing globes, dazzling, changing color as he looks... some are dark, like a heap of fiery embers burning out. *Dying?* Grief wells up in him, he puts his hand up to hide it, looks away. There are his useless, evil canisters... and the corridor a shambles. Aftermath of a stampede... What was Coby muttering about, sperm. They went through here, tails thrashing—

"Arn—you came!"

From nowhere Lory is hugging his arm.

"Oh, Arn dear, I waited—"

"Get out of here, Lor!" But she is working at his waist, trying to untie knots. Her face is ecstatic—a load of jizzum in the head, all right. "Go away, Lor. I'm going to depressurize."

"We'll be *together*, don't be afraid."

Angrily he pushes her behind him. "I'm going to vent the air, can't you hear me? The air is going out!"

He tries to head her back toward the ramp, but she twists away from him, gasping, "Oh, Arn, please Arn, I can't—" And she is running to the light, to *China's* hatch.

"Come back here!" He runs at her, is brought up by the rope. She wavers just beyond him outlined in pale fire, turning, turning, her fists at her mouth, sobbing, "I—I'm going—alone—"

"No! Lor, wait!"

His own hands are ripping at the knots but she is going, slipping away from him across the tangled floor. "No, no—" The warm light enwraps her, she has turned, is walking into it, is gone—

A harsh warble breaks into his ears, waking him. He staggers back, finally makes out that the flashings on the console are launch warnings. Somebody is in *China Flower*, taking off!

"Who's in there? Stop!" He flips channels at random. "You in the ship, answer me!"

"Good-bye, boy..." Bustamente's voice echoes from the speakers.

"Ray, are you in there? This is Aaron, Ray, come out, you don't know what you're doing—"

"I know to... set course. Keep your shit... world." The deep voice is flat, mechanical.

"Come out here! Ray, we need you. Please listen, Ray—the gyros are broken. The *gyros*."

"... Tough."

A heavy metal purring shivers the walls.

"Ray, wait!" Aaron screams. "My sister is in there, she'll be killed—your hatch is open! I'll be killed too, please, Ray, let her come out. I'll close it. Lory! Lory, get out!"

His eyes are seeking desperately for the hatch control, his hands tear at the knots.

"She can come, too." A deathlike chuckle—another lighter voice briefly there, too. Ray's women—is Soli in there? The knots are giving.

"I'm going to... that planet... boy."

"Ray, you'll wake up a million miles in space, for Christ's sake wait!" He jerks, pulls loose—he has to get there, get Lory out—he has to save that living beauty, that promise—

Other lights are flashing, there is a shudder in the walls. *The ship, Lory*, his brain cries faintly. He pulls the rope free and sees her shadow, her body wavering out blue against the radiance waiting there, waiting for him. With his last sanity he strikes the hatch lever, shoves it home.

The big hatch starts to slide shut across the radiant port.

"No, wait! No!" Aaron starts to run to it, his hand still grasping the rope, he is running toward all he has ever longed for— but the walls clang, scrape thunderously, and a wind buffets him sideways. He grips the rope in reflex, sees Lory stagger and start to slide in the howling air, everything is sliding toward the closing hatch. *China Flower* is going, falling away—taking it from him. They will all be blown out after her—but as Lory nears it the hatch slides home, the last ray vanishes.

The wind stops, the corridor is totally silent.

He stands there, a foolish man holding a rope, knowing that all sweetness is fading. Life itself is falling out to the dark beneath him, going away forever. Come back, he whispers, aching. Oh, come back.

Lory stirs. He lets fall the idiotic rope, goes to her bowed under a loss beyond bearing. What have I saved, what have I lost? Going away, fainter, fainter yet.

She looks up. Her face is clear, empty. Very young. All gone now, the load in her head... A feeling of dumb weight comes over him. It is *Centaur*, the whole wonderful ship he had been so proud of, hanging over him mute and flaccid in the dark. The life-spark gone away. Voiceless, unfindable in the icy wastes...

His gut knows it is forever now, nothing will ever be all right again.

Gently he helps Lory up and starts walking with her to noplace, she trustful to his hand; little sister as she had been long ago. As they move away from the corridor his eyes notice a body lying by the wall. It is Tighe.

IV

... Dr. Aaron Kaye recording. The ghosts, the new things I mean, they're starting to go. I see them quite well now awake. Yesterday — wait, was it yesterday? Yes, because Tim has only been here one night, I brought him in yesterday. His, his body, I mean. It was his ghost I saw — Christ, I keep calling them that — the *things*, the new things, I mean. The ghost is in Tim's bed. But I saw his go, it was still out in Beta corridor. Did I say they're fairly stationary? I forget what I said. Maybe I should go over it, I have the time. They're more or less transparent, of course, even at the end. They float. I think they're partly out of the ship. It's hard to tell their size, like a projection or afterimage. They seem big, say six or eight meters in diameter, but once or twice I've thought they may be very small. They're alive, you can tell that. They don't respond or communicate. They're not... rational. Not at all. They change, too, they take on colors or something from your mind. Did I say that? I'm not sure they're really visible at all, maybe the mind senses them and constructs an appearance. But recognizable. You can see... traces. I can identify most of them. Tim's was by ramp seven. It was partly Tim and partly something else, very alien. It seemed to swell up and float away out through the hull, as if it was getting closer and farther at the same time. The first one to go, so far as I know. Except Tighe's. I dreamed that. They do *not* dissipate. It throbbed—no, that isn't quite right. It swelled and floated. Away.

They're not ghosts, I should repeat that.

What I think they are—my subjective impression, I mean, a possible explanatory hypothesis—Oh, hell, I don't have to talk that way any more. What I think they are is, some kind of energy-thing, somewhat I think they are is blastomeres.

Holy zygotes, Coby said. I don't think they're holy. They're just there, growing. Definitely not spirits or ghosts or higher essences, they're not the *person* at all. They're a, a combined product. They develop. They stay at the site awhile and then... move on out.

Maybe I should record the order they go in, maybe it will correlate with the person's condition. That would be of scientific interest. The whole thing is of deep scientific interest, of course. Who will it be of scientific interest to? That's a good question. Maybe somebody will stumble on this ship in about a thousand years. Hello, friend. Are you human? If you are you won't be long. Kindly listen to Dr. Aaron Kaye before you—Oh, god, wait—

This is Dr. Aaron Kaye recording a message of deep scientific interest. Where was I? It doesn't matter. Tim—I mean Commander Timofaev Bron died today. I mean Tim himself. That's the first actual death except Tighe. Oh, and Bachi—I reported him, didn't I? Yes. The others are still functioning more or less. In a vegetable way. They feed themselves now and then. Since the meals stopped I carry rations around. We go over the ship every day or so. I'm pretty sure no one else has died. Some of them are still playing cards in Commons, they even say a word or two sometimes. Some cards have fallen down, the ten of spades has been by Don's foot for days. I made them drink water yesterday. I'm afraid they're badly dehydrated... Kawabata's the worst off, I think, he's sleeping in a soil bed. Earth to earth... He'll probably go soon. I have to learn to run all that, I suppose. If I go on.

... I know now I'll never be able to fix that laser. Christ, I spent a week in Ray's spookhouse. Funny thing, they gave us a big nondirectional Mayday transmitter. That means, "Come here and rescue us." But how can I send, "Stay the hell away?" Flaw in the program. That's all too short-range, anyway... I could blow up the ship, I guess I could work that out. What good would it do? It wouldn't stop them coming. They'd figure we had an accident. Too bad, hazards of space. Baby, you'll find out...

...Wonder where Ray is now, how long he lasted? His, his thing is here, of course. In Gamma One. The women too. I found Soli's, it's, no, I think we won't talk about that. They were with him, their bodies, I mean. *Them*... He was so strong, he did something, he acted, afterward. No use of course. The dead saving the dead. Help me make it through the night — quit that.

...Functioning, we were discussing functioning. The most intact is Yellaston. I mean, he isn't intact at all but we talk a little, sort of, when I go up there. Maybe a lifetime practice in carrying on with half of his cortex shot. I think he understands. It's not a highly technical concept, after all. He knows he's dying. He saw it as death, the whole thing. Intuition in his locked-up guts, the fear — Sex equals death. How right you are, old man. Funny, I used to treat patients for thinking that. Therapy — Of course it was a different, let's say order of sex. He's quit drinking. The thing he was holding in, the load, it's gone... I think of what's left as him, damn it, it *is* him, the human part. I've seen his, his product, it's by the bow-port. It's very strange. I wonder, has he seen it? Does a spent sperm recognize the blastomere? I think he must have. I found him crying, once. Maybe it was joy, I don't think so...

... Hello, friend. This is Dr. Aaron Kaye, your friendly scientific reporter. Dr. Aaron Kaye is also getting the tiniest bit ethanolized, maybe you'll forgive it. It has occurred to me as a matter of scientific justice that Coby deserves credit for the, the formulation of the hypothesis. Superb diagnostician, Coby, to the end. That's Dr. William F. Coby, late of Johns Hopkins/M.I.T. Originator of Coby's final solution—hypothesis, I mean. Remember his name, friend. While you can. I tried to get him to record this but he doesn't talk any more. I think he's right; I know he's right. He still functions, though, in a dying way. Goes to the narcotics locker quite openly. I let him. Maybe he's trying something. Why is he so intact? Didn't he have much of whatever it is they lost, not much jizzum there? No—that's not fair. Not even true... Funny thing, I find myself liking him now, really liking him. Dangerous stuff all gone, I guess. Comment on me. Call me Lory—no, we aren't going to talk about Lory, either. We were talking about, I was talking about Coby. His hypothesis. Listen, friend. You on your way with a load in your head.

Coby's right, I know he's right. We're gametes.

Nothing but gametes. The dimorphic set—call it sperm. Two types, little boy sperms, little girl sperms—half of the germplasm of... something. Not complete beings at all. Half of the gametes of some... creatures, some race. Maybe they live in space, I think so. The, their zygotes do. Maybe they aren't even intelligent. Say they use planets to breed on, like amphibians going to the water. And they sowed their primordial seed-stuff around here, their milt and roe among the stars. On suitable planets. And the stuff germinated. And after the usual interval—say three billion years, that's what it took us, didn't it?—

the milt, the sperm evolved to *motility*, see? And we made it to the stars. To the roe-planet. To fertilize them. And that's all we are, the whole damn thing—the evolving, the achieving and fighting and hoping—all the pain and effort, just to get us there with the loads of jizzum in our heads. Nothing but sperms' tails. Human beings—does a sperm think it's somebody, too? Those beautiful egg-things, the creatures on that planet, evolving in their own way for millions of years... maybe they think and dream, too, maybe they think they're people. All the whole thing, just to make something else, all for nothing—

... Excuse me. This is Dr. Aaron Kaye, recording two more deaths. They are Dr. James Kawabata and Quartermaster Miriamne Stein. I found her when I was taking Kawabata's body to cold Stores. They'll all be there, you'll find them, friend. Fifty-nine icicles and one dust pile... maybe. Cause of death—have I been reporting cause of death? Cause of death, acute—Oh, hell, what does a sperm's tail die of? Acute loss of ability to live any more. Acute post-functional irrelevance... Symptoms; maybe you'd like to know the symptoms. You should be interested. The symptoms start after brief contact with a certain life-form from the Alpha planet—did I mention that there does seem to have been momentary physical contact, apparently through the forehead? The gross symptoms are disorientation, apathy, some aphasia, anorexia. All responses depressed; aprosexia, speech echolalic. Reflexes weakly present, no typical catatonia. Cardiac functions subnormal, nonacute. Clinically—I've been able to test six of them—clinically the EEG shows generalized flattening, asynchrony. Early theta and alpha deficits. It is unlike, repeat totally unlike, post-ECS syndrome. Symptoms cannot be interpreted as due to a physical shock, electric or otherwise. Adrenergic systems most affected, cholinergic relatively less so. Adrenal insufficiency is not, repeat not, confirmed by hormonal bioassay. Oh hell—they've been drained, that's what it is. Drained of something... something vital. Prognosis... yes.

The prognosis is death.

This is of great scientific interest, friend. But you won't believe it, of course. You're on your way there, aren't you? Nothing will stop you, you have reasons. All kinds of reasons—saving the race, building a new world, national honor, personal glory, scientific truth, dreams, hopes, plans—does every little sperm have its reasons, thrashing up the pipe?

It calls, you see. The roe calls us across the light-years, don't ask me how. It's even calling Dr. Aaron Kaye, the sperm who said no—Oh, Christ, I can feel it, the sweet pull. *Why did I let it go?* ... Excuse me. Dr. Aaron Kaye is having another drink now. Quite a few, actually. Yellaston was right, it helps... The infinite variety of us, all for nothing. Where was I? ... We make our rounds, I check them all. They don't move much any more. I look at the new things, too... Lory comes with me, she helps me carry things. Like she used to, little sister—we're particularly not going to talk about Lory. The things, the zygotes—three more of them went away today, Kawabata's and the two Danes. Don's is still in Commons, I think it's going soon. Do they leave when the, the *person* dies? I think that's just coincidence. We're totally... *irrelevant*, afterward. The zygote remains near the site of impregnation for a variable period before moving on to implant. Where do they implant, in space, maybe? Where do they get born?—Oh, god, what are they like, the creatures that generated us, that we die to form? Can a gamete look at a king? Are they brutes or angels? Ah, Christ, it isn't fair, *it isn't fair!*

...Sorry, friend. I'm all right now. Don Purcell collapsed today, I left him in Commons. I visit my patients daily. Most of them are still sitting. Sitting at their stations, in their graves. We do what we can, Lory and I. *Making gentle the life of this world ...* It may be of great scientific interest that they all saw it different, the egg-things I mean. Don said it was god, Coby ova. Ahlstrom was whispering about the tree Yggdrasil. Bruce Jang saw Mei-Lin there. Yellaston saw death. Tighe saw Mother, I think. All

Dr. Aaron Kaye saw was colored lights. Why didn't I go, too? Who knows. Statistical phenomenon. Defective tail. My foot got caught... Lory saw utopia, heaven on earth, I guess. We will not talk about Lory... She goes round with me, looking at the dying sperms, our friends. All the things in their rooms, the personal life, all this ship we were so proud of. *Mono no aware*, that's the pathos of things, Kawabata told me. The wristwatch after the wearer has died, the eyeglasses... the pathos of all our things now.

... Yes, Dr. Aaron Kaye is getting fairly well pissed, friend. Dr. Aaron Kaye, you see, is avoiding contemplating what he'll do, afterward... after they are all gone. Coby broke his leg today. I found him, I think he was pleased when I put him to bed. He didn't seem to be in much pain. His, the thing he made, it went away quite a while ago, I guess I haven't been recording too well. A lot of them have gone. Not Yellaston's last time I looked. He's up in Astrogation, I mean Yellaston himself. Gazing out the dome. I know he wants to end there. Ah Christ, the poor old tiger, the poor ape, everything Lory hated—all gone now. Who cares about a sperm's personality? Answer: Another sperm... Dr. Kaye grows maudlin. Dr. Kaye weeps, in fact. Remember that, friend. It has scientific interest. What will Dr. Kaye do, afterward? It will be quiet around here on the good ship *Centaur*, which will probably last forever, unless it falls into a star... Will Dr. Kaye live out the rest of his life here, twenty-six trillion miles from his home testis? Reading, listening to music, tending his garden, writing notes of great scientific interest? Fifty-nine frozen bodies and one skeleton. Keep your eye on the skeleton, friend... or check on that last scoutship, *Alpha*. Will Dr. Kaye one day take off in little old *Alpha*, trying to head for somewhere?

Where? You guess... Tail-end Charlie, last man in the oviduct. Over the viaduct, via the oviduct. Excuse me.

... Not the last. Not at all, let's not forget all those fleets of ships, they'll start from Earth when the green signal gets there.

And they'll keep on coming for a while anyway... The green got sent, didn't it, no matter how we tried? The goal of man's desiring. No way to stop it. No hope at all, really.

But of course it's only a handful, the ones that will ever make it to the planet, compared to the total population of Earth. About the proportion of one ejaculandum to total sperm production, wouldn't you say? Should compute sometime, great scientific interest there. So most of the egg-creatures will die unfertilized, too. Nature's notorious wastefulness. Fifty million eggs, a billion sperm — one salmon...

... What happens to the people who don't go, the ones who stay on Earth, all the rest of the race? Let us speculate, Dr. Kaye. What happens to unused sperm? Stuck in testes, die of overheating. Reabsorbed. Remind you of anything? Calcutta, say. Rio de Janeiro, Los Angeles... Previews. Born too soon or too late — too bad. Rot away unused. Function fulfilled, organs atrophy... End of it all, just rot away. *Not even knowing* — thinking they were people, thinking they had a chance...

Dr. Kaye is getting rather conclusively intoxicated, friend. Dr. Kaye is also getting tired of talking to you. What good will it do you on your way up the pipe? Can you stop, man? Can you? Ha ha. As — someone used to say... God damn it, why can't you try? Can't you stop, can't you stay human even if we're — Oh Lord, can a half of something, can a gamete build a culture? I don't think so... You poor doomed bastard with a load in your head, you'll get there or die trying —

Excuse me. Lory stumbled a lot today... Little sister, you were a good sperm, you swam hard. You made the connection. She wasn't crazy, you know. Ever, really. She knew something was wrong with us... Healed, made whole? All those months... a wall away from heaven, the golden breasts of god. The end of pain, the queen couzy... fighting it all the way... Oh, Lory, stay with me, don't die — *Christ, the pull, the terrible sweet pull —*

... This is Dr. Aaron Kaye signing off. Maybe my condition is of deep scientific interest... I don't dream any more.

ABOUT THE EDITOR

SFWA Grandmaster Robert Silverberg is the multi-award-winning author of dozens of novels and countless short stories, including Lord Valentine's Castle and the rest of the Majipoor series, Dying Inside, and Sailing to Byzantium. Born in New York City, he now lives in California in the Bay area.

More books from Robert Silverberg are available at: www.ReAnimus.com/authors/robertsilverberg

ReAnimus Press

Breathing Life into Great Books

If you enjoyed this book we hope you'll tell others or write a review! We also invite you to subscribe to our newsletter to learn about our new releases and join our affiliate program (where you earn 12% of sales you recommend) at www.ReAnimus.com.

Here are more ebooks you'll enjoy from ReAnimus Press, available from ReAnimus Press's web site, Amazon.com, bn.com, etc.:

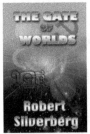

The Gate of Worlds, by Robert Silverberg
Info/buy:

An Alternate History adventure in the modern day Turkish and Aztec Empires.

Conquerors from the Darkness, by Robert Silverberg
Info/buy:

Long after the earth has been conquered by aliens and flooded, Dovirr Stargan longs to become one of the pirate-like Sea Lords.

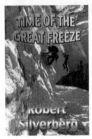

Time of the Great Freeze, by Robert Silverberg
Info/buy:

ICE AGE--NEW YORK CITY 2650 A.D. UNDERGROUND!

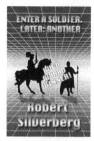

Enter a Soldier. Later: Another, by Robert Silverberg

Info/buy:

Hugo Award Winner, from an SF Grandmaster!

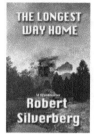

The Longest Way Home, by Robert Silverberg

Info/buy:

The planet's locals have risen up, trapping young Joseph thousands of miles from home.

The Alien Years, by Robert Silverberg

Info/buy:

"The ultimate alien invasion novel"

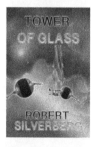

Tower of Glass, by Robert Silverberg

Info/buy:

Aliens have sent a mysterious signal, which Simeon Krug is determined to answer.

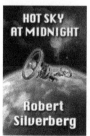

Hot Sky at Midnight, by Robert Silverberg

Info/buy:

Greed comes home to roost in a future Earth and her colonies, and the renegades look to take over. One of Silverberg's finest.

The New Springtime, by Robert Silverberg

Info/buy:

Humans emerge to reclaim Earth after the Long Winter, but never anticipated what awaits...

Shadrach in the Furnace, by Robert Silverberg

Info/buy:

Meet the new Khan! Soon to be immortal... A Hugo and Nebula Award Finalist novel from a Grand Master of science fiction.

The Stochastic Man, by Robert Silverberg

Info/buy:

Lew Nichols uses statistical methods to guess trends--then meets a man who can actually see the future.

Thorns, by Robert Silverberg

Info/buy:

Beauty and the Beast in the solar colonies

Kingdoms of the Wall, by Robert Silverberg

Info/buy:

Not all is at it seems on pilgrimages up the gigantic mountain called The Wall

Challenge for a Throne, by Robert Silverberg

Info/buy:

The real life Game of Thrones, and basis George R.R. Martin used for the GoT series.

Scientists and Scoundrels, by Robert Silverberg

Info/buy:

A good-humored tour through scientific frauds and how they were exposed.

1066, by Robert Silverberg

Info/buy:

The great battle had begun to make England into a world power...

The Crusades, by Robert Silverberg

Info/buy:

The story of the world history-changing wars between Christianity and Islam from a master writer.

The Pueblo Revolt, by Robert Silverberg

Info/buy:

The amazing story of the only time Native Americans overthrew colonialization

The Day the Sun Stood Still, by Robert Silverberg, Poul Anderson, Gordon R. Dickson
Info/buy:

What if the sun stood still? Three short novels by science fiction legends

Triax, by Robert Silverberg, James Gunn, Keith Roberts, Jack Vance
Info/buy:

Three original short science fiction novels by legends in the genre

Three for Tomorrow, by Robert Silverberg, James Blish, Roger Zelazny
Info/buy:

Three short novels by some of SF's greatest writers

Three Trips in Time and Space, by Robert Silverberg, John Brunner, Larry Niven, Jack Vance
Info/buy:

Three short novels of disruption by some of science fiction's greatest writers

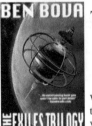

The Exiles Trilogy, by Ben Bova
Info/buy:

When all the best of Earth's scientists are exiled to a space station, they decide to embark on an even grander adventure to the stars. An epic trilogy in one volume.

The Star Conquerors (Collectors' Edition), by Ben Bova

Info/buy:

Special Collectors' Edition! Six time Hugo winner Ben Bova's most sought-after novel is now an ebook with the original Mel Hunter cover and an essay from Ben on the history of the book!

The Star Conquerors (Standard Edition), by Ben Bova

Info/buy:

Six time Hugo winner Ben Bova's most sought-after novel is back in print!

Colony, by Ben Bova

Info/buy:

Island One is a celestial utopia, and David Adams is its most perfect creation. But David is a prisoner, destined to spend his life in an island-sized cylinder orbiting a doomed home planet. David has a plan—one that will ultimately save humanity... or destroy it.

The Kinsman Saga, by Ben Bova

Info/buy:

Chet Kinsman is an astronaut ace who has done everything in space—including committing the first murder. Kinsman has to confront his hidden past and decide Earth's destiny, in a desperate countdown to nuclear annihilation.

Star Watchmen, by Ben Bova

Info/buy:

Mankind rules a giant galactic empire, but not all the worlds are pleased. Can the Star Watch prevent a revolt?

As on a Darkling Plain, by Ben Bova

Info/buy:

Dr. Sidney Lee races against time to prevent the huge alien machines on Titan from destroying mankind.

The Winds of Altair, by Ben Bova

Info/buy:

Altair VI isn't making it easy to Terraform!

Test of Fire, by Ben Bova

Info/buy:

A small group of survivors fight to rebuild civilization after the Earth is devastated by a huge solar flare.

The Weathermakers, by Ben Bova

Info/buy:

After conquering everything else, the last frontier was... controlling Mother Nature! By the award-winning hard SF author of the Grand Tour series.

The Dueling Machine, by Ben Bova

Info/buy:

Civilized, harmless virtual reality dueling has replaced all physical conflict — everything from punching someone over a personal insult to interstellar warfare... until a madman dictator of a small empire finds a way to cheat, and use the dueling machine to take over the galaxy!

The Multiple Man, by Ben Bova

Info/buy:

As the President is speaking inside an auditorium in Boston, the President's Press Secretary discovers a body in an alley outside: The body of the President.

Escape!, by Ben Bova

Info/buy:

No end to Danny's sentence, watched by a sentient computer, and no way out of the escape-proof prison, there was only one thing to do...

Forward in Time, by Ben Bova

Info/buy:

Get ready for a series of future shocks from the award-winning Ben Bova!

Maxwell's Demons, by Ben Bova

Info/buy:

Science fiction and science fact, humor and adventure, all await when you enter the unpredictable world of... MAXWELL'S DEMONS

Twice Seven, by Ben Bova

Info/buy:

Ben Bova's universe is always more than the sum of its parts...

The Astral Mirror, by Ben Bova

Info/buy:

Here are a dozen and a half views of the world, past present and future, as seen through the Astral Mirror....

The Story of Light, by Ben Bova

Info/buy:

In this all-encompassing work, Ben Bova explores the subject of light and shows how it has shaped every aspect of our existence.

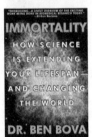

Immortality, by Ben Bova

Info/buy:

Dr. Bova explores the future effects of science and technology on the human life span. Death will no longer be the inevitable end of life.

Space Travel - A Science Fiction Writer's Guide, by Ben Bova

Info/buy:

An indispensible tool for all science fiction writers, Space Travel explains the science you need to help you make your fiction plausible.

The Craft of Writing Science Fiction that Sells, by Ben Bova

Info/buy:

Learn how to write SF from the master! Ben Bova, best-selling author and six-time Hugo Award winner for Best Editor explains step by step all the elements you need to write professionally selling science fiction.

Walls and Wonders, by S. R. Algernon

Info/buy:

Hugo finalist... If Hemingway wrote P.K.Dick-ian science fiction short stories...

The Unborn, by Brian Herbert

Info/buy:

In the summer of 2097, Riggio wakes up with amnesia--and his lover dead in their bed.

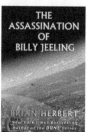

The Assassination of Billy Jeeling, by Brian Herbert

Info/buy:

From the New York Times Bestselling author of the DUNE series comes a spectacular science fiction novel.

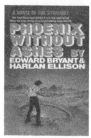

Phoenix Without Ashes, by Harlan Ellison and Edward Bryant

Info/buy:

Co-written with Harlan Ellison and based on the award-winning script, the story of mankind's last salvation gone awry.

Bloom, by Wil McCarthy

Info/buy:

In 2106, microscopic machine/creatures escape their creators to populate the inner solar system with a wild, deadly ecology all their own, pushing the tattered remnants of humanity out into the cold and dark of the outer planets. Seven astronauts must embark on mankind's boldest venture yet—the perilous journey home to infected Earth!

Aggressor Six, by Wil McCarthy

Info/buy:

An alien armada from the center of Orion makes its deadly way through the galaxy, destroying all human life in the process, and only Marine Corporal Kenneth Jonson and the Aggressor Six team can stop the onslaught.

Murder in the Solid State, by Wil McCarthy

Info/buy:

David Sanger, an ambitious young physicist, attends a party at which a pompous older scientist, who just happens to have thwarted the younger man's innovative ideas, is murdered. Suddenly it is not just David's career, but his life that is at stake. Are his ideas that important? Who's out to stop David from changing the world?

Flies from the Amber, by Wil McCarthy

Info/buy:

Forty light years from earth, the colonists on the world of Unua have somehow managed to keep civilization struggling on, despite twice daily earthquakes...

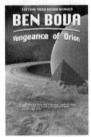

Vengeance of Orion, by Ben Bova

Info/buy:

Orion must travel back in time to change history and save Troy from the Greek army, or lose the only woman he has ever loved.

Orion in the Dying Time, by Ben Bova

Info/buy:

Time-traveling into the era of the dinosaurs, Orion must save the very fabric of spacetime from the satanic reptilian leader of the saurians.

Orion and the Conqueror, by Ben Bova

Info/buy:

Orion travels to the time of Alexander the Great, battling to save the future of mankind, and his own soul.

Orion Among the Stars, by Ben Bova

Info/buy:

The superhuman, time-traveling Orion leads interstellar warriors in a galactic war among the gods themselves.

The Starcrossed, by Ben Bova

Info/buy:

A stinging SFnal, futuristic satire on the TV industry, based a bit on reality.

To Save The Sun, by Ben Bova and A. J. Austin

Info/buy:

Earth's sun will soon explode, unless a massive engineering effort can save it.

Deep Quarry, by John E. Stith

Info/buy:

A private eye uncovers a long-buried starship...that's still occupied.

Manhattan Transfer, by John E. Stith

Info/buy:

Aliens kidnap Manhattan; read all about it!

Reunion on Neverend, by John E. Stith

Info/buy:

A man returning for a high school reunion on a distant colony finds an old flame in trouble—trouble that he's uniquely qualified to deal with.

Redshift Rendezvous, by John E. Stith

Info/buy:

One man must stop starship hijackers from using an unusual starship to plunder a wealthy colony.

Memory Blank, by John E. Stith

Info/buy:

Cal Donley regains consciousness on the beautiful orbital colony Daedalus—but Cal doesn't remember leaving Earth, or his name or the past dozen years!

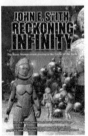

Reckoning Infinity, by John E. Stith

Info/buy:

A riveting exploration of what it means to be an alien... Explorers inside a moon-sized alien ship must find its secrets before it kills them.

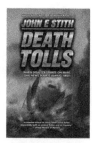

Death Tolls, by John E. Stith

Info/buy:

A great science fiction mystery: Dan sees the telecast from Mars where his brother dies—and it's not an accident. Why is a certain reporter uncannily at each disaster so quickly?

Scapescope, by John E. Stith

Info/buy:

Brother Sammy Wants YOU! In prison. For something you haven't done yet.

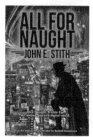

All for Naught, by John E. Stith

Info/buy:

Nick Naught, private eye, walks down some strange mean streets, in an action-packed comedy set in the future.

In Search of the Big Bang, by John Gribbin

Info/buy:

For Big Bang Theory fans, don't miss this indispensable guide! :) `A remarkably readable guide to the mysteries of cosmic creation' —Nature

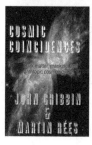

Cosmic Coincidences, by John Gribbin and Martin Rees

Info/buy:

A provocative search through space and time for a cosmic blueprint—and the source of life in the universe.

Q is for Quantum, by John Gribbin

Info/buy:

A comprehensive encyclopedia of quantum physics.

Ice Age, by John and Mary Gribbin

Info/buy:

The theory that came in from the cold...

In Search of the Double Helix, by John Gribbin

Info/buy:

Unraveling the mystery of life on earth...

The Living Labyrinth, by Ian Stewart and Tim Poston

Info/buy:

Sam, Jane, Felix, Elzabet, Tinka & Marco go quantum jumping on their path to galactic citizenship, only to end up in a very strange place indeed!

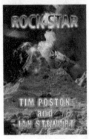

Rock Star, by Tim Poston and Ian Stewart

Info/buy:

The awesome sequel to The Living Labyrinth. It's all fun and games with syntei until they fall into the wrong hands...

Wheelers, by Ian Stewart and Jack Cohen
Info/buy:

Alien artifacts found on Callisto...

The Egg of the Glak, by Harvey Jacobs
Info/buy:

Some of Harvey's best, believably fantastical short stories.

A Guide to Barsoom, by John Flint Roy
Info/buy:

THE OFFICIAL, DEFINITIVE GUIDE TO EDGAR RICE BURROUGH'S BARSOOM. Everything there is to know about John Carter of Mars and his world — the people, places and things, with maps and fully illustrated.

Jewels of the Dragon, by Allen L. Wold
Info/buy:

The greatest of treasures awaits... on the deadliest of planets.

Crown of the Serpent, by Allen L. Wold
Info/buy:

In farthest space lie hidden fortunes... and unknown enemies.

Lair of the Cyclops, by Allen L. Wold

Info/buy:

Rickard Braeth and friends must find the galaxy's secret—before it's used to destroy everything!

The Planet Masters, by Allen L. Wold

Info/buy:

Troubleshooter Larson McCade searches for the alien Book of Aradka on the planet Seltique, and may find more than he bargained for.

Star God, by Allen L. Wold

Info/buy:

There is a strange force at work in the universe. It must be stopped. But first, it must be understood.

Anthopology 101: Reflections, Inspections and Dissections of SF Anthologies, by Bud Webster

Info/buy:

Bud expertly dissects the great SF anthologies. A must for writers and SF fans.

Woman Without a Shadow, by Karen Haber

Info/buy:

War Minstrels #1. Kayla, an extraordinarily gifted young telepath, is on the run after challenging the most powerful families on her home planet, who've tried to take everything from her.

The War Minstrels, by Karen Haber
Info/buy:

War Minstrels #2. With powerful forces trying to stop the Free Traders, the starship Falstaff is no longer a safe refuge for renegade empath Kayla John Reed. Now her survival and all the War Minstrels' hinges upon her finding a legendary weapon.

Sister Blood, by Karen Haber
Info/buy:

War Minstrels #3. Empath Kayla and her War Minstrels must rescue her friends from the evil Yates, and prevent the destruction of all they've fought for.

The Sweet Taste of Regret, by Karen Haber
Info/buy:

Live anywhere you want... in any time... A collection of Karen Haber's best short fiction.

The Science of Middle-earth, by Henry Gee
Info/buy:

How did Frodo's mithril coat ward off the fatal blow of an orc? Can Balrogs fly? Nature editor Dr. Henry Gee explains how. A must-read for Tolkien fans.

Commencement, by Roby James
Info/buy:

The Sting was what made Ronica McBride special—now she was crashed on an unknown planet without it.

Xenostorm: Rising, by Brian Clegg

Info/buy:

14 year old Davy finds himself facing a powerful underground group who have lived for hundreds of years—and want to see him dead. The future of human existence is in the balance...

The Cure for Everything, by Severna Park

Info/buy:

Finding the cure for all diseases comes with a heavy price. Nebula Award winner!

Ghosts of Engines Past, by Sean McMullen

Info/buy:

Award winning steampunk from a master!

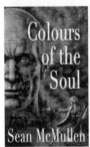

Colours of the Soul, by Sean McMullen

Info/buy:

Why are cheetahs the most perfect of creatures? Besides because they're cats, that is... Cool, mind-blowing stories from a master.

The Gilded Basilisk, by Chet Gottfried

Info/buy:

Add a basilisk, a dragon, and weirdragons to the mix-up of a theft going from bad to worse: Friends become enemies and enemies friends, wars loom, and the intrigues threaten the fate of two kingdoms.

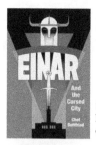

Einar and the Cursed City, by Chet Gottfried

Info/buy:

Sixteen-year-old Einar enters Jorghaven for dueling and desserts, but a curse has changed everyone except Barbara Bloodbath, who needs his help to free the city!

Neon Twilight, by Edward Bryant

Info/buy:

Neon Twilight by Edward Bryant : Three wonderful space opera stories, including Ed's Berserker story!

Particle Theory, by Edward Bryant

Info/buy:

Particle Theory by Edward Bryant : A collection of many of Ed's best works, including two Nebula Award winning short stories.

Trilobyte, by Edward Bryant

Info/buy:

A trio of twisted little tales from the master of twistedness.

Cinnabar, by Edward Bryant

Info/buy:

In the city at the center of time, paradox is just another urban renewal project.

Predators and Other Stories, by Edward Bryant

Info/buy:

Troubling tales as only Ed Bryant can tell. Don't miss the author introductions!

Timeshare, by Joshua Dann

Info/buy:

Have you ever wished you could go back to the good old days? At Timeshare Unlimited, you can.

Bug Jack Barron, by Norman Spinrad

Info/buy:

GET SET FOR THE BEST THING THAT EVER HAPPENED TO YOU! The banned book is back! You've heard of it, now you can read it! Lover and hero, Jack Barron, troubleshooter and media god of the Bug Jack Barron Show, has one last chance to hit it big when he meets Benedict Howards, the power-mad man with the secret to immortality. A Hugo and Nebula Award finalist!

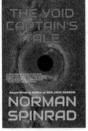

The Void Captain's Tale, by Norman Spinrad

Info/buy:

Symbiotically linked to her ship, Void Pilot Dominique Alia Wu senses something transcendent in the void...

The Last Hurrah of the Golden Horde, by Norman Spinrad

Info/buy:

"One of the greatest collections of science fiction short stories ever" — Goodreads.com

Costigan s Needle, by Jerry Sohl

Info/buy:

What really was Dr. Costigan's tool for medical research? Where did the eye of the needle actually lead to?

The Mars Monopoly, by Jerry Sohl

Info/buy:

One of the famous Ace Doubles, with the wonderful original cover, The Mars Monopoly still stands today as a great, fun story in the classic style.

One Against Herculum, by Jerry Sohl

Info/buy:

One of the famous Ace Doubles, with the wonderful original cover, One Against Herculum remains a fast-paced, fun story that you'll really enjoy.

The Time Dissolver, by Jerry Sohl

Info/buy:

How could they lose 11 years of their life—at the same time!? By a master of episodes from The Twilight Zone and Star Trek.

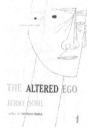

The Altered Ego, by Jerry Sohl

Info/buy:

Why would anyone murder a man marked for full body and brain restoration?

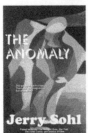

The Anomaly, by Jerry Sohl

Info/buy:

She couldn't have a baby... Then she got pregnant—but with what? By a master of episodes from The Twilight Zone and Star Trek.

The Haploids, by Jerry Sohl

Info/buy:

What is a Haploid? Are YOU a Haploid? A new take on an age-old battle! By a master of episodes from The Twilight Zone and Star Trek.

Underhanded Chess, by Jerry Sohl

Info/buy:

A hilarious handbook of devious diversions and stratagems for winning at chess.

Underhanded Bridge, by Jerry Sohl

Info/buy:

A hilarious handbook of devious diversions and stratagems for winning at bridge.

Local Knowledge (A Kieran Lenahan Mystery), by Conor Daly

Info/buy:

Lawyer-turned-golf pro Kieran Lenahan must solve the murder of millionaire country-club owner Sylvester Miles. "A FAST-PACED MYSTERY"—THE NEW YORK TIMES